Ab

Claire Boston fell in love with romance and romantic suspense at eleven when she discovered her mother's stash of Nora Roberts novels. Like Nora, she writes series set around families or groups of friends with a guaranteed happy ending.

She loves travelling and learning about new cultures and interesting vocations which she then weaves into her writing.

When Claire's not at the computer typing her stories she can be found creating her own handmade journals, swinging on a sidecar, or in the garden attempting to grow something other than weeds.

Claire lives in Western Australia with her husband, who loves even her most annoying quirks and is currently learning how to knit. You can find her complete book list on her website www.claireboston.com/books. You can connect with Claire through Facebook and Twitter, or join her reader group

(http://www.claireboston.com/reader-group/).

Also by Claire Boston

Trapped in Retribution Bay

Aussie Heroes: Retribution Bay

Claire Boston

BANTILLY
PUBLISHING

First published by Bantilly Publishing in 2021

Trapped in Retribution Bay: Aussie Heroes: Retribution Bay

EPUB format: 9781925696820
Print: 9781925696837
Large Print: 9781925696844

Cover design by Mayhem Cover Creations
Edited by Ann Harth
Proofread by Teena Raffa-Mulligan

Chapter 1

The sun beat relentlessly on Darcy Stokes' red-checked shirt, and a trickle of sweat ran down his back. He lifted his Akubra and wiped the sweat from his brow. Stifling heat was a constant in his life, one he embraced or ignored. His bigger concern was the trough float, which wouldn't shut off, wasting precious water. He swore he'd fixed it last week, so why was it broken again?

Maybe he was losing it. The past two and a half weeks had been hit after hit, starting with his parents' sudden deaths. Perhaps his brain couldn't take any more bad shit happening. He couldn't afford to lose it. He'd already cost the sheep station far more than it could sustain. It was his fault they were on the brink of bankruptcy. If only he hadn't pushed his father so hard... He squashed down the guilt and, with a final twist of his spanner, tightened the nut and tested the float. The water squeaked through the pipe before gushing out in a warm stream. As it reached the level, it cut off like it was supposed to.

Relief filled him. If it hadn't worked, he would have had to replace the whole mechanism, and that was an extra expense they couldn't afford. He shoved his tools in the toolkit and splashed the warm water on his face.

Mid-afternoon was always the most viciously hot. Getting to his feet, he scanned the land that had been in his family for over a century. Many would view the rich red dirt and scraggly low shrubs as ugly, but to him it held a harsh beauty. It was home.

For as long as they kept the debtors at bay.

He prayed he and his siblings could come up with a solution so it would stay in their family for another century.

The occasional baa of the sheep soothed him. Most of the sheep in this paddock would give birth in the next couple of weeks. He'd move them closer to the farmhouse on Monday to further protect them from wild dogs and dingoes.

His toolkit clanked as he tossed it into the tray of his ute, then he climbed into the cab and radioed Matt. "All done here. Heading back now."

Matt's response came back a moment later. "Roger. I'm almost done at the windmill. I swear you gave me the hardest job."

Darcy chuckled at the gripe. "Knew you'd be able to handle it, mate." He could picture Matt grumbling to himself.

"Flatterer," Matt answered. "See you back at the house."

Darcy started the engine, cranking the aircon to high. The radio crackled.

"Darce, are you still at the station?" It was Amy, their campground guest liaison and his brother, Brandon's fiancée.

"Yeah." Where else was he supposed to be? The answer hit him the moment Amy spoke.

"You need to pick up Lara from pony club."

Shit. He shoved the ute into gear as he calculated the quickest way to get into town. How could he have forgotten his daughter? "On my way now," he told

Amy. It would take him over an hour, but if he pushed it, he'd only be a few minutes late—ten at the most.

The ute bumped over the rough red track as his heart raced and he cursed his forgetfulness. He hated letting down his daughter, especially with her still grieving over his parents. Normally Amy drove into town with Lara's horse and picked up Lara from school to take her to the pony club, but today camp guests were coming in late and Amy had asked Darcy to do it.

It was one small thing. Amy had even taken Lara to school, dropped the horse at the pony club this morning, and arranged for Lara to get a lift from school with a friend so Darcy could work as late as possible before having to leave.

He was an idiot.

The idea of Lara waiting by herself while the other parents picked up their children made his chest squeeze.

It had been just the two of them almost since the moment Lara was born. Darcy's ex, Sofia, had taken less than a month to decide that having a baby at eighteen and living on a sheep station in the middle of nowhere was not the life she wanted. So she'd left them both.

Ripped his heart right out of his chest.

And if Sofia couldn't bear to stay in a place she'd grown up in, what chance did he have of finding a woman who loved this land as much as he did?

She'd left him with a tiny bundle of joy he'd no idea how to care for. Sofia's parents had wanted custody of Lara, but even as young as he was, he'd never seriously considered it. Lara had snuggled her head into his chest the first time he'd held her in his arms, and the moment he'd brushed her fine, dark hair, he was a goner. He would die to protect her.

But he would have been completely lost without his

mother. The sharp pang of loss had him rubbing his chest. She'd taught him to make formula, how to test the heat on the crook of his elbow, and refused to change dirty nappies if he was there to do it.

She'd been adamant he take responsibility for his actions, even on those early nights when Lara wouldn't sleep. He'd spent hours walking Lara around the yard, so as not to disturb his family, and yet his mother was always there when he came back inside, to offer support. She'd take care of Lara in the mornings, so Darcy could get a couple of extra hours of sleep.

He shook his head. Always there for him—until now.

Lara had lost another mother-figure in her life.

He blinked to clear the tears from his vision.

He reached the gate which led onto the main road and jumped out to open it. He frowned. The chain dangled rather than being wrapped around the post. A strong wind would blow it open. Maybe one of the camp guests had been this way.

Darcy drove through and latched the gate behind him before hitting the bitumen. He pressed his foot a little closer to the floor than he should, scanning the roadside for kangaroos, emus or feral goats that might want to mess with him.

Nothing moved.

He accelerated. He couldn't disappoint his girl.

***

Lara's father was late. Faith Arnold crossed her arms and tried not to let her agitation show to the young girl next to her. Lara had been the first to finish unsaddling her horse and brushing it down. She'd watched the other parents collect their children.

But instead of doing nothing, Lara had grabbed one of the shovels, and started cleaning up the piles of manure left in the arena after the lesson. Such a considerate kid.

Faith checked the time again. Her own father would be home soon, and if she wasn't there, he would be furious.

"Where's your favourite place to ride?" Lara tucked a stray chocolate brown hair behind her ear. "Mine is along the beach." She normally eagerly waited for Faith's response to questions, but now her gaze constantly flicked to the road into the pony club.

"I've never done it," Faith said.

That got Lara's attention. "You've never been riding on the beach?" Eyes wide, she stared at Faith as if she was an alien.

Faith chuckled. "Not many places in Perth where I can." Plus, work took up all her daylight hours. She shovelled the last pile of manure into the wheelbarrow and wheeled it out of the arena, Lara falling into step beside her.

"Well, Retribution Bay is better than Perth," Lara said. "Perth is noisy and smelly." She turned to glance back to the road.

"You don't think manure is smelly?"

Lara waved her argument aside. "That's normal. The city has all the dirty car smells."

Faith couldn't argue with her logic. On those two accounts, the small town of Retribution Bay was better. Lara was silent again, which was unusual for the normally chatty girl.

Faith dumped the manure in the composting pile, and when she turned, Lara's bottom lip trembled, and her worn boots scuffed the red dirt.

"Do you think he's had an accident?" Lara whispered.

Nuts. Lara's grandparents had died in a car accident less than a month ago. Faith placed her hand on Lara's back and rubbed it. "I'm sure he's fine. He might have been caught up with something at Retribution Ridge."

"But he never forgets me." The conviction was as sweet as it was worrying. If Lara was right, then something might have happened to Darcy.

Faith got her phone out of her pocket. She'd call Amy and check Darcy had left. As she dialled the number, a white ute sped down the road.

"There he is!" Lara yelled.

Faith hung up and waited for the ute to pull up next to the horse float. The man who climbed out was more good-looking than Faith remembered, and her memory put him at pretty darn hot.

He was tall and tanned, with his dark brown hair peeking out below the Akubra, but it was the rangy body of a man who worked with his hands that captured her attention. And his smile sent a shot of lust straight through her body.

"Hey, pumpkin…"

Lara burst into tears and flung herself into his arms. The smile vanished, and he scowled at Faith over his daughter's back as if she'd mortally wounded his child.

"What's wrong? Did something happen at pony club? Was Natasha mean to you again?"

Lara was sobbing too hard to answer him. Faith walked closer. Quietly she said, "Lara was worried you might have had an accident."

The devastation in his blue-grey eyes pierced her soul, and Faith pressed her lips together and turned away. They needed a minute.

Darcy lifted Lara under the arms, and she wrapped her limbs around him, hugging him like a koala. Not a mean feat because the ten-year-old already reached Faith's shoulder. "I'm sorry, pumpkin. I should have called Miss Arnold, but I didn't have her number in my phone. A trough out near the sheep was broken."

Lara's voice was muffled, but Faith still made out the words. "But you fixed it last week."

"I thought I did too," he said. "It broke again." He wandered away from Faith, rubbing circles on Lara's back and murmuring to her. Lara relaxed her death grip around his neck, and she rubbed his back in return as if soothing him. When he finally placed her back on the ground, his words carried. "Let's hitch up the float and get you and Starlight home. Amy mentioned something about a barbecue for dinner tonight."

Lara wiped her eyes and nose on her shirt and sniffed. "OK."

As they worked together to hitch the horse float, Faith's phone rang. One look at the caller made Faith suppress a groan. She walked away from them before answering. "Hi, Dad."

"Where the hell are you?" he demanded.

"I'm at the pony club," she said. "We ran a little late."

"You left your mother alone for that long!"

She shifted the phone away from her ear, the volume far too loud. She prayed for patience. "I asked if she wanted to come, but she wasn't interested."

"That's beside the point. I said you can't leave her alone. What if she had another stroke? No one would be here to help her. She'd die and her death would be on your conscience."

Fear put those words in his mouth, but she still rallied against them. At her mother's last check up, the doctor had assured Faith she was at little risk of another stroke. But her father refused to believe it. "I'll be home shortly. I need to talk to a father."

Darcy was leading the bay mare inside the float. He was efficient, she'd give him that.

"We'll discuss this more then." Her father hung up.

Faith sighed and strolled back to the father and

daughter team who were closing the float door.

Darcy turned. "I'm sorry about being late. I hope I haven't caused you any trouble."

How much of the conversation had he heard? "Nothing I can't handle."

Darcy retrieved his phone, one arm around Lara. "Can I have your number? I shouldn't be late again, but just in case…"

She told him and he saved it. "Thanks."

"Dad, Faith said she's never been horse-riding along the beach," Lara said. "Can she come out to our place and ride along the gulf?"

Faith's face heated. She hadn't expected an invitation. "Thank you, Lara, but it's not necessary."

Darcy smiled. "You're more than welcome," he said. "Think of it as an apology. I hope your husband won't be too cross at you."

She frowned. "My husb– " The penny dropped. She held up her phone. "Oh. No, that was my father. He doesn't like Mum being left alone for too long since her stroke."

Darcy shifted. "I'm sorry for putting you into that position. I'll set an alarm next time."

"We could all go on a picnic together!" Lara suggested, warming to the topic, her enthusiasm returned now her father was there. "On the weekend 'cos it takes a couple of hours to ride to the ocean from our place."

The urge to accept was strong. When was the last time she'd been on a decent trail ride? At least eight months ago when she'd been in Perth, probably longer. She glanced at Darcy to see if he was sincere.

He nodded. "I can take some time on Sunday. It's better if you have a guide, so you don't get lost. You can borrow one of our horses."

"I have my own horse," she said. "But I'll need to

find someone to look after Mum."

"There's always someone at the farmhouse if you want to bring her out too."

Such a kind offer and so tempting, but her father was already cross. "Can I let you know?"

"Sure. Probably best if we get an early start, say seven or eight so it's not too hot," Darcy continued. He pressed some buttons on his phone and her mobile beeped. "That's my number."

A thrill went through her and she ignored the flutter in her chest.

Lara jumped up and down. "You've got to come, Faith. Amy and I will put together an awesome picnic."

Faith smiled at the girl's enthusiasm. "I'll do my best."

Darcy dipped his hat as he climbed into the car. "I hope to see you Sunday."

She waved goodbye as they drove off, resisting the urge to fan her face. The man stirred all her insides. His strong hands, the way he dipped his hat in greeting and his sweet encouragement of Lara… She sighed as she broke off a hay biscuit and fed Spirit. It wouldn't be long before her mother wouldn't need a regular carer and Faith would go back to Perth, back to her corporate law job and her townhouse.

Faith retrieved a curry comb from the box of equipment, and brushed long strokes down Spirit's dappled grey coat.

Returning to Perth didn't hold as much appeal as it should. Lara's words *noisy and smelly* echoed in her head. She'd become accustomed to the small town, being able to walk to the shops, or down to the beach. If she was feeling energetic, she could even walk to the pony club and ride. She'd also made friends with people who worked on her father's tour boat and caught up with them at least once a week for a drink.

Life was less hectic, more enjoyable here. She barely had time to catch up with friends in Perth. There, seventy-hour work weeks were the norm.

"You get neglected in Perth, don't you, Spirit?" she murmured, moving behind her horse to brush its other side.

Spirit nickered at her voice. She had lost the roundness from her belly caused by a lack of exercise and her coat now shone from being brushed regularly.

Faith's tanned hands and unpolished nails made her chuckle. Spirit's appearance had improved, while she had let go of all the professional gloss that was part of her law job. She'd loved not needing makeup, and having to look the perfect part every moment of the day.

But she had enjoyed the challenge of a well-written contract, and the money that came with the job. Her townhouse was in a trendy part of the city, close to restaurants, so she never needed to cook, and she could walk when she went out occasionally with friends.

She shook her head. It was pointless comparing the two. The differences were too great. Faith returned the comb to the equipment box and gave Spirit one last hug. "See you tomorrow."

She couldn't delay her departure further. It was time to head home to face her father.

***

Faith's father was at the front door of his modest brick house before she closed her car door. The sun edged its way towards the horizon, casting him in shadow, but his entire posture was tense, and his grey hair was its normal dishevelled mess. Her father used to let nothing get to him, but Faith had discovered over the past eight months anything to do with his wife's health really riled him.

She sighed. "Hi, Dad. How was your day?" Sometimes she could distract him by asking about the boat.

"It would have been a lot better if I hadn't got home to find your mother alone."

Faith brushed past him, pecked a kiss on his cheek and continued to the kitchen to pour herself a glass of water. Her mother sat on the couch in the open plan living area, her walking stick beside her, her dark hair belying her age and as always, impeccably done. She shrugged apologetically at Faith.

"Now Rob, I told you I insisted Faith go to her class. She has a commitment to those children."

"The agreement was she would come to Retribution Bay to nurse you," her father argued. "Not to reinvigorate an abandoned pony club."

Faith would have lost her mind if she hadn't had something else to do after the first few difficult months of helping her mother with constant physiotherapy. "It was the only way I could agist Spirit there. *You* helped me arrange it."

"I didn't know it would take so much time."

A typical example of how her father never thought ideas through. Before he could bring up his other gripe, she said, "*And* you were the one who told your friends to bring their legal questions to me." She appreciated the chance to use her law skills, but it hadn't been enough. Four months after her stroke, Milly had improved to the stage where she was more independent, and had encouraged Faith to find a hobby.

"At least you can do that at home, with your mother here."

Her father would never admit his part in this. Time to defuse him. "Did you have a good group today?" Faith asked.

His posture relaxed. "We went a fair way to find a whale shark," he said. "I couldn't disappoint them." He rolled his shoulders a few times.

But he expected her to disappoint the children who came to her classes. Her father only ever considered what he wanted. Faith didn't know how her mother put up with him.

He scowled, turning to his wife. "You should have gone with Faith rather than stay here by yourself."

"It was far too hot outside," she said. "And a little alone time was pleasant."

"No." He slammed his fist on the kitchen table. "I won't have you here by yourself and that's final." He strode out of the room and a few seconds later the bathroom door banged, and the shower switched on.

Her mother sighed. "It will take some time for him to understand I'm all right."

Faith understood why her father was so protective— her mother had had her stroke while he'd been working, and it had been pure luck that a friend popping around to visit found her. His actions came from a place of love and fear, not of control. "I guess I won't be going on Sunday," she murmured. She sighed and opened the fridge, staring without seeing the items inside. A trail ride with her favourite student and a sexy farmer would have given her something to look forward to, but she didn't dare suggest it with her father already in a mood.

"What was that, Faith?"

Faith shook off the disappointment and retrieved the stir fry ingredients for dinner. "One of my students invited me on a trail ride to the beach on Sunday."

Her mother stood, a little unsteady on her feet, and then leaning on her walking stick, she tottered over to the kitchen bench. She'd put a little weight on during her recovery, and had more of a roundness to her ever-smiling face, when previously she'd been wiry. "You should go."

"Dad has a tour on Sunday."

Milly glanced behind as if to check her husband hadn't come back in. "Staying at home is driving me crazy," she said. "I want to join him on the boat and this is the perfect opportunity. We need to figure out how to convince him."

Faith studied her mother. She hadn't complained once of cabin fever, though she had been insistent about their little outings each day as she'd grown stronger. A walk down the street, a coffee at the local café, or going to visit a friend for an hour or more.

Before Faith could speak, Milly continued, "What excuse can we give?" She shuffled around and opened the soy sauce to add to the dish.

Faith hated seeing her mother so frail, but this was far better than she'd been a few months ago. It reminded her her parents were getting older, already in their seventies, definitely retirement age. She'd been the surprise child. Both her brothers were much older with families of their own.

"How about we say a friend of yours is in Coral Bay and you're meeting them?"

"Why don't we tell him the truth?" Faith asked. "Say you want to go on the boat with him, and I have plans."

Milly shook her head. "No, that won't work. He's cross with you anyway." She perked up. "You could say you're helping someone with a contract and the only day they have free is Sunday. Your dad's so proud of you being a lawyer and likes to brag. He couldn't refuse."

It seemed like a lot of work. "Mum, just tell him you're bored at home and want to go out."

"He doesn't think I'm ready yet."

"That's not his decision to make." She hated how

her mother always gave in to her father. Not once had she stopped one of his harebrained schemes which had seen them move every couple of years after the next shiny get rich scheme, even though as a child, Faith had begged her to.

The bathroom door slammed open and her father marched in. "Is dinner ready?"

Faith finished slicing the capsicum. "Just waiting for you to finish your shower." She turned on the gas stove and added oil to the wok. "Mum was saying how she misses going on the boat with you."

Her mother glared at her, but Rob didn't catch it. "The boat's no place for her. She's too unsteady."

Faith thought fast. "Inside the reef it's pretty calm most days. She could sit next to you on the captain's chair."

"She'd be bored."

Faith raised her eyebrows at her mother, hoping she would chime in.

"It might be nice to chat to some new people," Milly said. "I miss hearing everyone's travel stories."

Rob hesitated. For all of his bluster, he liked to keep his wife happy. "Let me check the forecast."

Faith added the garlic, ginger and chilli to the wok and hoped Sunday's forecast was for light winds and sunny weather.

Her father grunted. "The boat's going to sway a lot."

"I know. I'll stay seated. Perhaps when you stop to snorkel, I can jump in for a swim too."

"I don't know about that. You might have difficulty getting back on the boat."

"Oh, but you'll help me, won't you?" Milly said.

"Of course."

"Then how about we play it by ear?"

"All right."

Faith blinked. Just like that, her mother had got her

own way. Faith added the meat to her pan and it hissed, sending up a delightful aroma of spices.

"Faith, you'll have a day to yourself on Sunday," her mother continued. "Maybe you can take your horse for a long ride."

"We haven't agreed you're coming on the boat," Rob protested.

"Oh, but of course we did," Milly said. "Our Faith deserves a day off, don't you think?"

"So do I," her father grumbled, as he brushed a kiss on her cheek and then set out bowls for the stir-fry.

"Yes, but you chose to be a tourist boat operator, dear. They don't get days off during the season."

Faith added the vegetables, smiling to herself. She was surprised her father had stuck it out as long as he had on the tour boat. They'd been in Retribution Bay for almost three years. Perhaps her mother's condition had delayed the decision.

"You'll have fun together," Faith said as she switched off the stove and dished up the stir-fry. The excitement she hadn't allowed herself to feel bubbled up.

Already she could hear the pounding of hooves against the sand, and feel the salt air on her skin. Maybe she could even take Spirit for a swim.

She couldn't wait.

Chapter 2

"One more sleep," Lara declared at the dinner table on Saturday night. Darcy's gut clenched. Lara hadn't stopped talking about Faith coming out all week, and over the four days, he'd obsessed about his decision to invite her. He couldn't afford to take half a day away from the station. He didn't deserve it.

But Lara did. And her excitement soothed some of his guilt. "Amy, do you want to come?" he asked his soon to be sister-in-law.

"No, I'll slow you all down," she said.

"Scared of being alone with the sexy instructor?" Matt asked, his voice too low for Lara to hear.

Darcy elbowed his best friend and didn't bother responding. But damned if that wasn't another part of his anxiety. Faith was sexy and single, and it had been close to six months since he'd last been in town for a night out. And his pick-up skills had been pretty rusty.

Not that he expected Faith to be interested in him. Most of the women he dated weren't interested in a man with a ten-year-old daughter. OK, so dated was pushing it. Most women his age in town were married or tourists only interested in hooking up while in town.

The full Retribution Bay experience.

Darcy had long ago given up on the idea of remarrying. No one wanted to be trapped at the Ridge. Sofia had told him that in no uncertain terms when she'd left. But he acknowledged his jealousy that Brandon had found a woman who loved the Ridge as much as he did. He'd probably found the only one around.

Darcy blew out a breath. Stupid to get so worked up about it. All he was doing was making his girl happy. He could spend the day being friendly and ignoring the way Faith's jodhpurs clung to her curves, and forget how she had comforted Lara when he'd been late.

Since then, he'd set an alarm on his watch to make sure he was back at the farmhouse not long after she got home from school every day. Amy would be there, but he wanted to be as well, especially so close to his parents' deaths. Both Matt and Brandon understood his need and picked up his slack. And if Brandon got the early release from the army he'd requested, things would only get easier.

"Do you want me to pack a picnic for tomorrow?" Amy asked.

"No. Faith is bringing it," Darcy said. She'd insisted when she'd called him back to accept his offer. And she'd earned extra points by asking if Lara was allergic to anything.

"We should make a cake for her," Lara declared.

"A cake won't travel well in the backpack," Darcy said.

"Then we'll make biscuits."

They might have time after dinner. "Have we got the ingredients for choc chip biscuits?" he asked Amy.

She grinned. "We do."

Lara cheered, and the sound filled him with joy. "All right, pumpkin. We'll make biscuits and then it's

17

straight in bed with you. We're getting up early tomorrow."

"OK."

"When you're done, I want to have a word with you and Matt," Brandon said, getting to his feet to clear the table.

"Sure." It wouldn't be good news. Nothing to do with the station was these days. But he pushed the thought to the back of his mind as he made biscuits with his daughter and then walked her to the bathroom to ensure she cleaned her teeth.

"Wehgngrananbook?" Lara asked, mouth full of toothpaste and toothbrush held at the ready.

He raised his eyebrows. "You want to spit before you repeat that?"

She grinned and toothpaste squirted out her mouth onto the floor. She laughed, spitting the rest into the sink and rinsing her mouth, while Darcy plucked a tissue to clean up her mess.

"Are we still going to read a chapter?" Her hopeful expression was impossible to resist, but he made a fuss of checking his watch.

"Pleeease."

"All right. But *one* chapter only." They were nearing the end of the story, and she would want to keep reading. He appreciated she still enjoyed their nightly ritual and didn't yet think it was stupid. While she headed for her bedroom and began to say goodnight to every stuffed toy Sofia had ever sent her, he poured her a glass of water which she'd inevitably ask for before turning out the light.

He navigated through the maze of stuffed toys now lying on the floor, and shuffled onto the bed beside her. Bennet eyed him warily from his spot on the end of the bed. Lara had begged to let the dog sleep with her after his parents' accident, and he hadn't been able to say no.

Darcy was now resigned to Bennet sleeping on his daughter's bed forever.

Lara handed him the book. "We're up to here."

He cleared his throat, and prepared for all the voices he had to do. Lara snuggled into him, her head almost obscuring the pages. Her hair smelled like strawberries and tickled his nose.

All of the tension in him melted away. This was his favourite time of day, his favourite place to be. With a smile, he began to read.

When he returned to the kitchen Matt, Amy and Brandon were already seated at the table. Outside thunder rumbled and the occasional bolt of lightning lit up the sky. No rain yet. He hoped the lightning didn't start a bush fire. That was one headache he didn't need right now.

"Cuppa?" Brandon asked gesturing to the tea pot.

Darcy nodded and sat next to Matt. "What's up?"

"We need to discuss our finances."

He braced himself. He'd put them close to bankruptcy when his father had been conned by the company from which Darcy had recommended they buy cattle. "How bad is it?"

"We're limping along," Brandon said. "As long as we have no major unforeseen expenses before lambing we should be right, but Amy's put together ideas of how we can raise more money."

Darcy sent thanks to his sister, Georgie who had told Amy about the job. Amy had been a massive help since she'd arrived, and she would officially be part of the family when she married Brandon next month. "What have you got, Ames?"

She opened the folder in front of her and handed them each a proposal. "These are ideas, and we wouldn't do everything at once. Some of them have a cost involved."

And they had little money to spend as it was.

Brandon gave her an encouraging nod. "The past three months has seen the half dozen camp sites full eighty percent of the time," she said. "Even taking into account the long-stay discount we offer, it's brought in over ten grand."

Darcy blinked. He'd left managing the camp sites to Amy and had paid little attention to it aside from noting new caravans and tents on the property from time to time. "That's brilliant."

She smiled at him. "The key problem is we only have the single bathroom at the shearers' quarters for all those guests. We need more."

He flicked through the proposal and saw the figures. "These aren't too bad."

"Most of the cost is labour and Georgie knows a plumber who owes her a favour."

"Of course she does," Matt muttered, scowling at the document.

"I looked around the sheds and we have a lot of the materials lying around the place." She showed them a photo of a rustic-looking shower. "It's called a donkey shower. The water is heated by fire and then gravity fed to the shower. People love them." She handed around a map. "If we clear a little more land, we could expand to two dozen camp sites. It would be ideal if we offered powered and unpowered sites, but that might have to wait until we're a little more flush."

"Do you think there's the market for it?" Darcy asked.

"Absolutely. I've had to turn people away. The social media pages have been successful and we're getting a lot of hits on the website. If we expand, I'll invite a few influencers to stay for free so they can get the word out."

It was all a foreign language to him, but he trusted her instincts.

"We could also offer events," she continued. "Maybe a damper night, or coffee and scones for guests again. Perhaps even find an astronomer to show guests the stars, or offer horse rides." Amy glanced at Matt. "Could your parents run bush tucker tours for us? Teach people about traditional foods and medicines."

Matt nodded. "I can ask them. If they aren't interested, I could do it once a week, or maybe one of the elders will want to do it. We'd have to work out costs."

"Ed could recommend an astronomer," Brandon said. "He's into that isn't he?"

"Yeah." Their youngest brother volunteered at the Perth Observatory. Darcy read through the remaining suggestions and costings. "This is a lot of work for one person, Ames. Can you handle it?"

"We won't do it all at once. And if it gets too much, I can look at hiring someone else."

Her projections were very appealing, but the tourists dried up in summer when it became too hot. He looked at Brandon. "Think we can afford it?"

"We can't afford not to," he said. "The money will tide us over until we shear."

The pang of guilt settled in his gut. They wouldn't be in this situation if it weren't for him insisting they move to cattle. "All right. What do we need to do next?"

***

A high-pitched screech woke Darcy out of a dead sleep. He leapt out of bed, heart racing, searching for the source of the noise. His alarm. He swore and switched it off, noting the light coming through his window. Normally he didn't need an alarm to wake, his body clock in sync with the sun, but he'd set it because discussing the family finances had taken them way past his usual bedtime.

Now he was glad he'd done so.

He grabbed his clothes and went down the hall to shower. On his way back to his bedroom, he stopped in Lara's room. One arm lay across her face and her sheets were pooled around her ankles. Her Wonder Woman singlet rode up, exposing her white belly. His heart swelled as he looked at her. He couldn't ever regret getting Sofia pregnant. Not when it had brought him Lara. He walked closer and sat on the edge of the bed. She didn't stir.

"Pumpkin. It's time to wake up." Gently, he touched her arm.

She opened one eye, grumbled something indistinguishable, and turned over away from him.

He chuckled. "I thought you wanted to go riding with Miss Arnold. I'll have to call her and tell her not to come out."

That got her attention. Instantly Lara sat up, pushing her hair out of her face and blinking to clear her vision. "No more sleeps?"

He grinned. "No more sleeps. I'll make you breakfast, then we can get the horses ready. Miss Arnold said she'd be here by seven."

Lara brushed him aside as she clambered out of bed. "What time is it now?"

"Quarter past six."

"OK."

While she got dressed, Darcy made breakfast. The coffee was ready as Matt strolled in dressed for the day. Darcy handed him a mug.

"Morning, Uncle Matt," Lara chirped as she walked in, dressed in jodhpurs and a T-shirt with a horse on it.

"Morning, La La. What time is Faith getting here?"

"Soon," she said, getting the milk out of the fridge.

"Maybe I'll stick around and say hi." Matt grinned at Darcy.

Darcy didn't comment, though he wanted to tell his friend to bugger off.

"She's so nice, and she knows so much about horses. She says Starlight is a good racer."

A twinge of concern swept through him. Lara had latched on to Faith quickly. She'd been like that with Amy too. Was she after a mother figure? Sofia had sent her presents on her birthday and at Christmas, but otherwise had nothing to do with Lara. Not that Darcy minded any more. The last he'd heard she'd remarried and was living in Melbourne, which had hurt a little, but he hoped she was happy.

He made Lara a hot chocolate and then checked the bench for the backpacks his mother would have prepared. He stilled and closed his eyes. Not any longer. He was so used to her being one step ahead, always so organised. He sighed and fetched the backpacks from the laundry, packing beach towels and water into each one as well as throwing in the choc chip biscuits they'd made the night before. "You got bathers underneath your clothes, pumpkin?" The battery in the long-range radio was charged, and he placed it in his bag.

"Yep. Can we take goggles too? I think Faith would like to go snorkelling around the mangroves."

Or Lara would. He smiled and added three pairs of goggles.

After they'd eaten, they went out to the horses. Lara slipped her hand into his as they walked across the hard red dirt to the horse yard. She inhaled deeply. "It's going to be a beautiful day."

It was what his mother had always said. His heart squeezed, the pang of loss still sharp. He couldn't believe she was gone. "It sure is."

Lara took her halter from him and rounded up Starlight as he fetched Fezzik, and brought the bay gelding over to the fence, tying him up and then feeding them both. The layer of red dust on the horse's coat came away in puffs as he brushed. Lara's two pet sheep entered the yard, looking for food.

"I don't have anything for you today." Lara rubbed their wool.

The sound of a car engine made him glance towards the road. A white four-wheel drive slowly rolled down the road, towing a very rickety horse float. He waved and gestured for Faith to park nearby.

"Faith!" Before Lara could run over, Darcy grabbed her arm.

"Wait until the car has stopped."

She pouted but did as he asked, and then ran to greet Faith. Darcy followed more slowly, though his heart thumped when she climbed out of the car and smiled at him. Her short, brown hair had been brushed into a side parting and she wore a loose long-sleeved shirt which she had tucked neatly into her jodhpurs. Her calf high riding boots made him smile. He and Matt used to call people wearing that at the gymkhanas show ponies because they didn't know what actual work was like, but damned if it wasn't a good look for her.

"Morning." He unlatched the back of the horse float and frowned at the loose bolt. He examined the rest of the trailer. "Where'd you get this from?"

She winced. "I'm borrowing it from the pony club. I'm not sure when it was last used."

There was a reason for that. It was a miracle it hadn't fallen apart on the way here. "You can take our float home. This isn't fit for the road. I'll do some welding and return it at the next pony club meet." No way was he letting her take it back.

She opened her mouth as if to argue and then closed it. "Thank you. I appreciate it. It rattled far more than I'm comfortable with driving out here."

Concern filled him. "You should have called. I would have fetched you and your horse, or you could have borrowed one of our horses."

She smiled. "I didn't want to be a bother."

"Dad says it's better to be a bother and be safe than to risk an accident," Lara said.

"That's good advice."

Darcy flushed. He sounded boring. "Come on, Lara, you need to finish saddling Starlight."

She looked between Faith and Starlight as if she didn't want to miss a thing.

"Do you need help with your horse?" he asked Faith.

"Her name's Spirit," Lara interrupted. "Dad's horse is Fezzik. Georgie named him, because she said Dad reminds her of the character from *The Princess Bride*. I'm not sure she meant it as a compliment, but I think Fezzik is a teddy-bear." With a satisfied toss of her ponytail, she bounced away to saddle her horse.

Faith chuckled. "That's one of my favourite movies." She glanced at Darcy. "I've got her. Thank you."

He left her to get Spirit out of the float and saddled Fezzik before checking Lara had remembered to re-cinch Starlight's saddle.

"Da-ad. I'm not a baby."

"You're my baby," he said, pleased she had done everything correctly.

"Should I leave the car and float here?" Faith asked as they joined her.

"Yeah, it's out of the way. Did you want a drink before we go?"

"I've got a thermos in my backpack along with

food," she said. "I'm itching to get going."

He smiled. "Then let's go." He gave Lara a leg up and led them out of the yard. Faith's dappled grey horse was a standardbred and in excellent condition. It shouldn't have trouble with the trail.

As they rode across the main road to the gate to the gulf, Faith asked, "Is this all your land?"

"Yeah. We've got quarter of a million acres in total."

She shook her head. "I can't fathom that much land."

"It keeps us busy."

"We farm sheep," Lara told her. "But we were going to farm cattle too. Something happened to the cows Granddad bought and we can't get them now."

Darcy winced. It wasn't something he wanted people to know about.

Faith glanced at him. "Will you get them from someone else?"

He shook his head.

"We lost the money," Lara said.

Darcy looked at his daughter as heat crept to his cheeks. How did she know that? He'd been careful to keep discussions about the station's finances to when she wasn't around.

"I'm sure there must be a clause in the contract which deals with an inability to fulfil the goods," Faith assured her, giving him a sympathetic look.

Hope wriggled its head above Darcy's self-loathing. Did it matter if the company was fake? Though it could be traced back to a real company. "Do you know much about contracts?"

"I'm a contracts lawyer," she said. "Or at least I was when I was in Perth." She hesitated. "I could review your contract when we get back if you'd like."

He'd be a fool to refuse professional help, even if he was embarrassed by the situation. "That would be great."

The trail narrowed, and he dropped back so Lara and Faith could ride side-by-side, Lara giving her the entire history of Retribution Ridge as they rode.

"So my family arrived here when the Retribution smashed against the reef just off shore from where we're going," Lara began. "There was a cyclone, and they'd come into the gulf to take cover, but—" she lowered her voice. "It was their downfall."

Darcy smothered his smile.

"There's a plaque on the shore which lists the names of all those on board, but we don't know who died in the shipwreck and who died in the mutiny."

"Mutiny?" Faith asked.

"Yeah. Some of the sailors mutinied, but no one knows why. I think it was because there was secret treasure on board and they wanted their share."

Faith gasped. "What kind of treasure?"

"Gold," Lara said with certainty. Then she tilted her head to the side. "Or maybe jewels."

"So what happened?"

"No one knows for sure, but I have my ideas."

He almost interrupted Lara, but Faith leaned closer. "Tell me more." Her eagerness matched Lara's, so Darcy settled in, tuning out their conversation. He'd enjoy the slow pace and not having to be anywhere.

The past few weeks had been hectic. Brandon had finally returned home after over a decade of self-ostracism. He'd never admit how much he'd missed his older brother. They'd been best friends growing up and Darcy had suddenly been thrust into the older brother role when Brandon left, looking after Edward and Georgie, taking over more work on the farm and feeling like he was missing part of himself. But now Brandon was back, and was staying for good.

He sighed. Then there'd been the sabotage by

Stonefish, a consortium who wanted to buy the station. Thankfully it had stopped when a couple of men had been arrested, but Darcy still got the feeling they were out there, circling like sharks, waiting for the station to fail so they could buy it up and rip it apart, or whatever they wanted to do with it.

He sighed and stared up at the blue sky. Today wasn't a day for such worries. He should enjoy this time with Lara and Faith. It wasn't every day he spent a full day with Lara, and with a single, attractive woman his own age. He'd make the most of it.

"Dad, can we canter?" Lara called.

The trail was relatively flat. "Yes, but keep an eye on the road."

With a whoop, Lara kicked Starlight into a canter and Faith followed, the two of them leaving a trail of dust behind them. Fezzik pulled at the reins, wanting to follow, but he held him back a little longer. Anticipation thrummed in his veins. When was the last time he'd ridden for the pure joy of it?

Finally he gave Fezzik the freedom to gallop. The horse took off and the air and ground thundered by him. Darcy laughed, and exhilaration brushed his worries aside.

They would be back, but he would enjoy this moment. He urged his horse faster and grinned.

This was freedom.

Chapter 3

It was hard to believe they'd been riding for almost two hours and still hadn't left Retribution Ridge. Faith had heard about how big sheep and cattle stations were, but she'd never comprehended it. The land was dry, the dirt the colour of rusty nails and the bushes straggly, but around her insects buzzed and footprints marked the sand to reveal animals were everywhere. The sun's rays warmed the land despite the early hour, and she suspected the ride home would be edging into uncomfortably hot. She didn't care. She inhaled, raising her face to the sun, embracing the serenity of the isolation and the stark beauty of the land. It was stunning.

"We're almost there," Lara declared as they approached a small hill. "Are you ready?"

Faith smiled. "I'm ready." The girl was such a sweetheart. Darcy had obviously raised Lara well for the child to be so comfortable around people to talk almost non-stop about her family's history for two hours. Faith had been fascinated by her stories of mutinies and buried treasure and wanted to ask Darcy how much of it was true.

They crested the hill and Faith gasped. She'd lied. She hadn't been ready at all. The turquoise of the ocean was so clear, so blue it looked fake. It stretched towards the horizon, only broken by an island in the middle of the bay, which had to be the island Lara had spoken about. The vivid white sand blended to pink and then turned rusty red as it merged with the surrounding soil. It was like a watercolour painting where the colour had slowly faded into the canvas. To her left, green clumps of mangroves grew out of the water, adding another shade to the painting and to the right, the beach stretched into infinity.

Lara had already ridden down to a hitching post, dismounted and tied her horse to the post. Darcy stopped his horse next to Faith's. "It's something, isn't it?"

She nodded, still unable to form words.

"It's high tide, so it might be better to leave the ride along the shore for a couple of hours when there's more beach," he continued. "Lara wanted to go swimming, if that's all right with you."

"Sure." Her gaze didn't leave the beauty of her surroundings.

He chuckled. "Come down when you're ready." He clicked his tongue and joined Lara at the post where they unsaddled the horses, leaving a halter on. Nearby was a water trough, so they must regularly ride to the beach.

The two of them worked well together, Darcy helping Lara with the saddle and then spreading towels on the sand while Lara stripped off to her bathers. The easy relationship was enviable, especially since her own father still hadn't forgiven her for leaving her mum at home.

Faith nudged Spirit forward and after unsaddling her, she joined them at the towels where Darcy rubbed sun cream into Lara's back.

"You want to come snorkelling with me, Faith?" Lara asked, hope shining on her face.

Faith hesitated. "I don't have any goggles and I've never been snorkelling."

Lara's mouth dropped open. "You've *never* been snorkelling?"

She muffled a laugh at Lara's incredulity. "No."

Lara shook her head. "Dad will teach you. We brought spare goggles, and he's the best teacher."

"Pumpkin, not everyone loves the water as much as you and Georgie."

The girl bit her lip. "Can you swim?"

"Yes, I've just never learnt to snorkel. I'd love to try it." She glanced at Darcy. "If you can give me some tips?"

"Of course." His smile made her pulse flutter, and as he bent over the backpack, his jeans pulled nicely over his butt. "Don't your parents own a tour boat?" he asked.

"Yeah, but I've not been out on it yet." She'd been so busy with work when they'd first bought the boat, and since she'd been here, she'd been caring for her mother full time.

He handed her a pair of goggles with a snorkel attached. "Do you have bathers?"

She blinked. "Give me a second." By the time she'd stripped down to her bathers, Darcy stood in only a tight black pair of lycra bathers. Her mouth went dry. Hard abs, lean muscle and oh so fine tanned skin. Maybe she could rub sun cream into his chest or back.

His gaze roamed over her body, and she shifted, conscious of her crop top blue bikini. The approval in his eyes warmed her.

"Are you two coming?" Lara shouted.

The shout tore through Faith's attention and she

glanced over to where Lara was already waist deep in the water.

Darcy grinned. "Ready?"

Her body definitely needed a cool down. To distract herself from his sexy body, she called, "Race you," and dashed for the water.

Lara yelled, "Go Dad!" and her delight made Faith grin as she raced into the water. Her foot hit a hole and Faith shrieked as she tripped and plunged into the cool, clear ocean.

When Faith surfaced, Lara was laughing. "She beat you, Dad."

Darcy grinned. "She cheated."

Faith brushed her wet hair from her face. "I didn't. You were just too slow." She winked at Lara.

"She's right, Dad." Lara fitted her goggles and submerged.

While Lara swam circles around them, Darcy helped Faith fit her goggles. His gentle fingers brushed the side of her head to tighten the goggles a smidgen.

Faith cleared her throat. "Thanks for letting me win."

"I didn't," he said. "You caught me by surprise."

The goggles made her feel ridiculous and helped to smother her rampant attraction. "What do I do?"

"The snorkel rests inside your mouth like a mouth guard, but don't bite down on it." He showed her and breathed through his mouth, puffing through the snorkel.

Faith followed his instruction, and though the rubber felt weird, it wasn't uncomfortable.

"Lower your head under the water and keep breathing," he said.

She bobbed down to her knees and the underwater life came alive below the water. Such incredible clarity, she could see the whale shark pattern on Lara's bathers as the girl circled her and waved. She waved back.

Darcy tapped her shoulder, and she surfaced, taking the snorkel from her mouth.

"If you want to dive under the water, you need to hold your breath as you would normally and then when you surface, blow it out in a big puff," he said.

He demonstrated, and the water flew out the end of his snorkel.

She tried it, blowing hard when she surfaced but not hard enough, and she swallowed seawater on her next breath. She coughed, surfacing and spitting the snorkel out. Darcy hurried over and rubbed her back in firm circles and her coughing subsided.

"You all right?"

"Yeah, let me try again." The next time she blew harder and took a small experimental breath in to make sure she'd cleared her snorkel. It worked. She surfaced, smiling.

"Ready to explore the mangroves?" Darcy asked. "It's not deep over there so you can stand if you run into any problems."

"OK." She couldn't wait. The water was a perfect temperature and fish darted in and out of the trees' roots. Another world to explore.

Lara squawked and pointed to a sting ray which swam lazily along the bottom of the ocean.

Magical.

They swam around the mangroves in less than two metres of water, but the array of fish life was incredible. Lara kept grabbing her arm and pointing out things in case Faith had missed them. Faith glanced back to see how far they'd come and froze. Sleek grey fish, tiny eyes, sharp fin, and far, far bigger than the other fish around them.

Shark!

Her immediate thought was of the great white

sharks which lived in the waters around Perth.

Faith screamed—or did her best attempt with a tube of plastic in her mouth. The shark's tail continued a slow back and forth movement as it grew closer. She took her eyes off it momentarily to search for safety. The mangroves were too dense to escape the water through them. Her heart pounded. Darcy's hand on her arm made her jump and whirl towards him, arms raised in defence. He stood, taking the snorkel out of his mouth. "It's all right. It's just a baby reef shark."

Her entire body trembled as the shark changed direction, avoiding them, and glided past.

"Hey, it won't hurt you." He slid his arm around her waist and held her, his hand stroking her side.

Slowly the trembling subsided. Lara, seeing her father had things under control, paddled after the shark, not a care in the world.

Nuts. Way to make a fool of herself.

"Most of the sharks in Ningaloo are well fed and not interested in us," Darcy said, his tone low and calm. "The only time they get aggressive is if people are spear-fishing and then they're only after your catch." His hand continued its slow rhythm along her side. "That little reef shark is likely more scared of you then you are of it," he continued.

"I doubt it." Her heart rate slowed, and a warmth replaced the cold heart of fear as she became more aware of Darcy's touch. She swallowed and shifted away. "Do you see many sharks here?"

"Usually just the black tips," he said, motioning in the direction the shark had disappeared. "The tigers don't tend to come this way."

"Tiger sharks?" Her voice squeaked at the end.

"Yeah. They stick more to the reef further north."

The sandy shore was a hundred metres back the way they'd come.

Darcy chuckled. "I can take you back to shore if you'd like. Let me tell Lara."

The girl had stopped her shark chase and floated nearby, watching something under the water near the mangroves. Faith felt like a real wuss. "You're not worried about being attacked?"

He shook his head. "I wouldn't let my girl swim anywhere unsafe." He pointed to a point further west. "There's coral this way that's worth a look. I promise if a shark comes, I'll jump in front of it."

The chivalry made her smile and his words about Lara reassured her. "I hope it's not necessary." She put her snorkel back in her mouth and Darcy held out his hand. She couldn't resist, and she slipped her hand into his firm grip, feeling a blanket of safety settle over her. Together they swam hand in hand towards Lara with Darcy on the ocean side protecting her.

Her heart beat heavily for an entirely different reason.

After viewing the beautiful colours of the coral, Faith had had enough of swimming. Her whole body felt waterlogged, but Lara was still happily exploring. Faith squeezed Darcy's hand, and they both surfaced. "I'm going to head in."

"Let me get Lara and we'll join you."

Faith shook her head and let go of his hand. "No, you two keep swimming. I'll prepare morning tea for when you're finished."

Darcy frowned. "Are you comfortable going back alone?"

"Yeah." She'd seen two more sharks in their travels, and they hadn't been at all interested in her.

"All right. There's a spot up ahead Lara likes to visit, and then we'll turn back."

"Take your time." The journey back was a little less

relaxing as she kept her eye out for bigger fish in the sea, but she made it to the shore in one piece. On her way to their towels, she spotted a metal plaque not far from the mangroves. She wandered over.

Memorial to the Retribution.

As Lara had said, it included a list of names of passengers, and she spotted two Stokes on the list. Reginald and Lilian. They must be Darcy's ancestors. Several had 'dec' written next to them and she assumed it was because they had died during the shipwreck, or in the mutiny. A tough way to start life in a harsh land without any towns or support nearby. Even close to a hundred and fifty years on, this location was isolated. She couldn't imagine what it would have been like before roads or cars or telegraph communication.

At the towels, she dried herself then opened the backpack to pull out food. She couldn't wait to ride along the shore and maybe even take her horse for a swim.

It reminded her of her childish dream to open her own horse-riding company. She'd been living with her parents on a farm in Queensland, and decided her ideal job was to take people riding each day. She'd even briefly considered it after she graduated from high school before choosing the stable option of studying law. Now though, she was certain trail rides out here would be something other people would enjoy.

The tide was going out, revealing more of the shoreline and the perfect ground to gallop along. She dug her thermos into the sand so it would stand upright and reached for the fruit she'd brought.

She hadn't considered moving to Retribution Bay permanently, but she enjoyed running the pony club twice a week—one day for kids and another for adults. She'd wanted to explore the surrounding area on horseback but hadn't had the chance to investigate roads or permissions. Horses might be banned from the national park, and it was probably safer if she didn't go out on her own. It was land she could easily get lost in.

Faith glanced out at the ocean and spotted Lara and Darcy returning. She cut the fruit and arranged it in a container, then withdrew the caramel slice she'd made.

Spirit snorted and flicked her tail to remove the flies buzzing around.

Offering trail rides would require a proper commitment and investment. She'd need to buy horses, a float large enough for them, and all the other equipment. And she'd need somewhere to stable them too.

A pipe dream, similar to her father's ones, which had dragged her from place to place. The difference between them was, Faith was too sensible to think it would actually work.

Plus, she had a job waiting for her in Perth. Her boss had called on Friday, asking for an update, hinting she needed to be back soon, that they couldn't keep her job available forever.

Faith's muscles tightened. She'd been reluctant to promise anything, but now, with her mother ready for more independence, Faith had to consider what to do next. She hadn't missed living in the city. Life was slower in the country, or maybe it was simply because she wasn't working seventy-hour weeks. She'd had nothing to do for the first few months except nurse her mother back to health.

It had been rewarding as well as frustrating, but she felt closer to her mother than she had before. They'd got to know each other as adults, as people rather than mother and daughter, and Faith liked her mother. She'd also gone for drinks with a couple of the women who worked on her father's tour boat, and met Darcy's sister, Georgie, who worked on another of the boats.

She'd enjoyed the casual atmosphere and their discussions hadn't been full of legal talk, which used to frustrate Faith when she went out with friends in Perth. Instead, they spoke of movies, books and people.

Darcy stood, the water glistening off his chest. She swallowed to get moisture back in her dry throat. No one deserved to be that good looking. She wanted to spend more time with him, find out about this kind, considerate man who was a loyal father.

Perhaps he and Lara would be interested in dinner next week.

Without bothering to dry herself Lara flopped down on her towel and dumped her goggles in her backpack. "I'm starving." She reached for a caramel slice.

"Hey, pumpkin, where are your manners?" Darcy called.

Lara paused, arm outstretched, and asked, "Can I have a piece?"

"Help yourself to anything here," Faith told her.

"But make sure you have some fruit and not just sweets," Darcy added. He towelled himself dry and slipped his shirt on.

Nuts.

"I saw the Retribution memorial." Faith offered Darcy the slice and fruit and he took something from both containers.

Lara nodded as she chewed. "It's pretty cool, right?"

"Very cool," Faith assured her.

"Granny was going to get the old trunks from the shed and go through them with me, to see if we could find a treasure map." Lara's face fell and she glanced at Darcy for support.

"We can still do that, pumpkin." He squeezed her hand.

Faith hated seeing her sad. "Do you think X will mark the spot?"

"Yep. I reckon it's in the cave by the ridge." Lara continued to explain her theory and Faith listened with rapt attention. There was something about the idea of buried treasure that spoke to the child in her. She'd always loved pirate adventures.

"Do you think the memorial could hold a clue?" Faith asked.

Lara's eyes lit up. "I never thought of that!" She scrambled to her feet. "We should check."

Faith stood and had taken a step after Lara before she remembered Darcy. She turned to him, her cheeks hot.

"Go." He grinned. "I'll pack up here."

"Come on, Faith!" Lara yelled.

Faith smiled back at him. "Thanks." She raised her voice. "I'm coming!" And she ran after Lara, feeling like a kid again.

***

Darcy's spirits were high as he saddled his horse. It had been a perfect morning, one he would remember for a long time to come. He'd tuck it in his good memories box, to be retrieved when he needed cheering up. Faith genuinely seemed to enjoy Lara's company, and he'd enjoyed teaching her to snorkel. Perhaps he'd used the shark as an excuse to hold her in his arms, but she hadn't minded and her hand had fit so perfectly in his when they swam side by side. Then she'd been undemanding and understanding when she'd wanted to return to the shore. Sofia would have made them all turn back.

After Lara and Faith had discovered nothing of note on the memorial, they'd ridden the horses bareback along the sand, taking them swimming when the day grew hot. Then they'd eaten the gourmet rolls Faith had made for lunch.

He tightened the cinch on his saddle and mounted. Time to head home. He'd promised Matt he'd stop and check the sheep they had put in a nearby paddock, but it wasn't much of a detour. "Ready?" he called.

"Ready," Faith and Lara echoed, both grinning at him. "Jinx!" They called at the same time and their giggles made warmth spread through him.

They were a beautiful picture. His heart ached, and he kicked his horse to get him moving. "We'll swing by the sheep on the way back," he called. "Won't take too long."

The sun was directly overhead, but it wasn't the hottest part of the day yet. They should be back at the farmhouse before then. He led them down the road and then turned at a barely there path to where a gate stood. He opened it, letting the others through before closing it behind him.

They were due to move the sheep to closer paddocks tomorrow, ready for lambing.

They rode for about ten minutes without seeing any animals. Darcy frowned. He should at least hear the occasional bleat by now. Unease brushed his skin. He kicked his horse to a trot to get up a small slope and his stomach dropped. Sheep carcasses lay all over the ground, some red with blood, all unmoving. His pulse raced, and he scanned the area for the cause—a dingo or wild dog snacking on the bodies.

Nothing.

In the distance sheep gathered away from the massacre, some of his flock still alive and unwilling to be near the death. But what lay dead in front of him was about a third of his sheep.

Nausea burst into his stomach and he fought the urge to be sick, as his eyes watered. He inhaled, trying to get control before Lara saw him.

The station would be ruined. They'd been relying on

the money the lambs would fetch them.

"Dad? What happened?" The shock in Lara's voice snapped him out of his despair.

"I don't know, pumpkin," he said, injecting some calm into his tone. He swung the backpack from his back and retrieved the radio he always carried. The wind shifted and carried the stench of rotting meat with it. Lara gagged. "Faith, can you take Lara back down to the road? I'll join you in a minute." He was pleased with how normal he sounded when inside he wailed.

Faith nodded, her eyes full of concern. "Come on, Lara."

Lara glanced at him. "No. What if the dingoes attack Dad?"

"They're long gone, pumpkin, and even if they returned, they'd feast on the sheep rather than me," Darcy told her. "I'm going to radio Matt and Brandon. You'd be a big help if you meet them at the gate and tell them where I am."

She narrowed her eyes as she examined him for lies and then slowly nodded. "OK. Yell if you need help."

"Will do." He waited until they were at the base of the slope before he headed down to the carcasses. Fezzik stepped warily as they neared, so he dismounted, tied him to a nearby tree, and continued on foot. He pulled his bandanna over his nose when the smell turned his stomach.

It had been only a couple of days since he'd been here, distributing extra feed. The sheep had been in excellent condition and he'd had hope for the future of the station. At the first dead sheep he crouched, brushing away the flies swarming around him, and examined the wound. Definitely teeth marks.

The next one was the same, and the next.

It made no sense. The dingoes and wild dogs did attack the flock, but they always ate what they killed.

These sheep had been attacked and then left.

He switched on the radio. "Matt. Bran. You there?"

"Darcy? Something go wrong?" His brother's concern was clear.

"Yeah, but not with Lara or Faith. I'm at the northern flock."

A pause. "What's happened?" Brandon's tone was flat.

"Something's been in, killed about a third. Doesn't look like dingoes."

"Do I need to call Dot?"

Every instinct told him this wasn't natural. "Yeah, the police need to check this."

Matt's voice came over. "I'm on my way. Where's Lara?"

"I sent her back to the road with Faith. She'll be able to direct you."

"Be there soon."

"We both will be," Brandon echoed.

Darcy clipped the radio onto his belt and examined the next sheep. He should have moved them when he'd come to fix the water trough. His gaze lifted to its location, but he couldn't see it from here. He'd been sure he'd fixed the trough when he'd first moved the sheep into this area. He no longer doubted his skills.

Someone had tampered with it.

Stonefish were back.

Chapter 4

At the bottom of the rise, Faith looked back. Darcy sat on his horse, shoulders slumped, staring down at the death scene before him. He'd gone from someone with an easy grin and bright smile to a person who appeared as if a gentle breeze would knock him down. As she watched, he straightened his shoulders and nudged his horse forward to face reality. Faith's heart went out to him. A farmer's life wasn't easy. The devastation on his face when he'd seen all those dead sheep had ripped through her. She'd wanted to protect him, comfort him, and the intensity of her emotion scared her.

She sighed and continued towards the gate. Next to her, Lara was silent for the first time all day. "You OK, Lara?"

The girl pressed her lips together, then shook her head. "Something's wrong."

"Want to talk about it?"

Lara was silent.

"Seeing the dead sheep is upsetting, but dingoes have to eat too."

The girl glanced at her. "Dingoes didn't kill those sheep."

The certainty with which she spoke made goosebumps rise on Faith's skin. "What makes you say that?"

"Dad says dingoes kill the sheep so they can eat, but those sheep hadn't been eaten." Her eyes full of concern, she asked, "What else would kill sheep and not eat them?"

"Wild dogs?"

Lara shook her head. "They'd eat them too."

The only predator which killed for sport was man. Suddenly the surrounding land seemed too still, too silent, too isolated. Faith hunched her shoulders and nudged her horse into a trot. "Come on. We need to get back to the gate to show Matt and Brandon the way."

Lara kept up, but her expression was dark.

Faith hoped Lara was wrong, that she hadn't understood what Darcy had taught her, but she made sense. Dingoes and wild dogs didn't kill for fun, but who would want to harm the sheep, hurt the Ridge's livelihood?

She'd heard nothing but positive things about the Stokes family, and the entire town mourned when Bill and Beth had died. Her own interactions with the family had been positive, and she considered Georgie a friend. But if what Lara suggested was true, and someone was trying to hurt them, maybe she could help them.

Because they didn't deserve this.

Less than half an hour later, both Matt and Brandon arrived in a white ute. Faith and Lara had found a patch of shade under a less straggly tree, but the day was hot. She only had a few mouthfuls of water left in her water bottle.

Faith stood and brushed the red dirt from her jodhpurs while Lara ran to hug both men. "Something's wrong," she said. "Dingoes don't leave dead sheep."

While Brandon hugged her, Matt handed Faith a cold bottle of water from the esky in the tray.

"Thanks," she said.

"You both holding up all right?" he asked.

"Yeah. Darcy's still over there." She nodded in the direction and spotted Darcy riding back. He sat comfortably in his saddle, though his shoulders slumped as if he carried the weight of the world on them. The desire to help him was so strong it surprised her. It wasn't as if she didn't help people—she'd done pro bono work back in the city, but this was more than a need to help, more of a deep longing.

She pushed it aside and took a long drink of water. Lara had also been given a bottle and told to drink. When Darcy arrived, Brandon said, "I made the call. They'll be here in an hour."

"Who'd you call?" Lara asked.

"Someone who can help us with the sheep," Darcy said. "You and Faith should head back to the house. I'm going to be here a while." He smiled at Faith. "Sorry to ruin your trail ride. When you get back, tell Amy I said you should take our horse float. She'll be able to help you with it."

"Why don't you go with them?" Matt suggested. "You'll need to ride your horse back anyway."

Darcy hesitated.

"I can lead your horse if you need to stay," Faith offered.

"That would be great. The track is pretty straight the rest of the way."

She hadn't considered the risk of getting lost.

"I want to stay with Dad," Lara said.

"Not this time, pumpkin. We've got a lot of work, and I need you to show Faith the way home."

Lara scowled. "Will you tell me what Sergeant Dot

says?"

Darcy's eyes widened. "Sergeant Dot isn't here."

"But she's who Uncle Brandon called, isn't she? Something killed those sheep, and it wasn't dingoes."

Darcy sighed. "You're too smart for me, pumpkin." He hugged her. "I'll tell you what Dot says if you take Faith home and help her with the horses."

"Deal." She held out a hand for Darcy to shake.

Faith smiled.

"She's a smart cookie," Brandon murmured as Lara took Darcy's horse and led it over to where the others grazed.

"Yep." Darcy reached into the backpack and withdrew another bottle of water, passing it to Faith. "Take this one as well. You can never have enough water."

Her fingers brushed his as she took it, and a zing zipped through her. "Do you want me to return the float today?"

"No. I should be able to repair the pony club float by Tuesday and use it to take Lara's horse into town. We can do the swap then."

A shame. She wanted to see him again, wanted to hear what the sergeant in charge of the Retribution Bay police station had to say as well. "All right. Thank you for taking me riding and showing me your beautiful land."

"Any time." His gaze was serious.

For some it was a throwaway line, but he seemed to mean it. She felt she could call him and he would be there for her. Matt coughed, and she realised they were all waiting for her to move so they could get back to business. She blushed. "I'll see you later."

She mounted her horse, took Fezzik's reins from Lara, and headed towards the homestead.

She resisted the urge to look back.

When they arrived back at the farmhouse, Faith helped Lara with the two farm horses before she sent Lara inside to find Amy. She placed her own saddle over the wooden fence and brushed Spirit. "I'll give you extra feed tonight," she murmured. "You did well."

Spirit shifted back a couple of steps and her ears flattened. A small kangaroo hopped towards them. It wasn't shy, and there were no other kangaroos around.

"That's Maggie." Lara jogged over with Amy trailing after her. "She's a rescue. A car hit her mum and Granddad saved her."

How sad.

"She's a fan of almonds," Amy said. "If you want to feed her, I'll bring some out." She smiled. "Did you enjoy your ride?"

"It was wonderful. People would pay good money for a trail ride like that."

Amy pursed her lips. "It wasn't too hot?"

"We swam mid-way, so it was pleasant."

"Do you ever run trail rides?"

The question surprised Faith in how it mirrored her own earlier thoughts. "No, but I was considering it."

"I'll have to do some research," Amy said. "Lara mentioned you're taking our float?"

She nodded. "Darcy didn't like the state of the pony club trailer." Together they moved over to investigate it.

"It looks like it will rattle apart," Amy agreed. "Is he going to fix it for you?"

"That's what he said, but the pony club doesn't have many funds."

"We've got spare wood and metal around the place," Amy said. "It shouldn't cost much more than time, and Matt and Brandon will help." She pointed to the shed across the yard. "Can you back it in there? Our horse float is around the side."

"Sure. Thank you."

"Lara, can you put the kettle on while I help Faith with the trailers?"

"I was going to help her."

"All right, but put the kettle on first." When Lara was out of earshot, Amy asked, "How bad were the sheep?" The concern on her face mirrored Darcy's.

The question took Faith by surprise. "I'm no expert, but it didn't look good." Perhaps Amy would have some answers. "They called the police, but who would do something like that? I thought everyone supported each other out here."

"The locals do."

Lara returned. "Kettle is on," she announced.

Amy smiled. "Thanks, La La. Come inside when you're done, and I'll make you a drink."

Faith would have to get her answers later.

Faith finished taking care of Spirit and left her tied in the shade while she moved the float trailers around. She'd load her horse just before she left. Then she and Lara headed inside the farmhouse via the kitchen door.

Cool comfort. Faith lifted her face to the refreshing breeze wafting from the air conditioning. The long wooden table in the centre of the room spoke of family dinners and community. The kitchen was homely, even if all the cupboards had dated wooden doors and a beige Laminex bench top.

"Amy!" Lara called. She opened the fridge door and asked, "Want a drink?"

"Cold water would be nice," Faith answered.

Amy entered the kitchen. "How did you go?"

"The trailer's hitched and ready to go. Lara was a great help in directing me."

"La La's a good worker," Amy agreed, getting a tin out of the pantry. "Would you like a biscuit or a cuppa?"

The chunky choc chip biscuits looked too good to refuse. "Thanks."

"Have a seat. It's not often I have female company out here."

"Hey!" Lara complained.

Amy laughed. "Sorry, I meant people my age."

Faith sat. "You're the only woman out here with Brandon and Darcy?"

"And Matt. He lives in the shearers' quarters. Georgie visits when she can but since Beth died, it's been me and Lara keeping the men in line."

She was curious about this woman who seemed at home here. "You're engaged to Brandon?"

"Yeah." She twisted a simple ring around her left ring finger. "We're getting married next month."

"And now he's staying for good," Lara declared.

"They're letting him out of the army a couple of months early because of the circumstances," Amy said.

Faith's mother's friend, Lindsay had spoken about the army son who had returned in time for the funerals. "Do you work out there too?"

Amy laughed. "Only when they need me to. My role is taking care of our campsite guests and dealing with marketing and promotion."

"The campsite looks full," Faith said.

"It is. We're going to expand to a few more sites in the next month. It's a good revenue stream." She poured boiling water into a teapot. "Though it will become more work the more we offer our guests. That's why I asked about the trail rides. I'm investigating other activities to draw tourists to stay with us rather than one of the other station stays in the area."

She liked that Amy was considering options, and the work involved. Faith's father jumped into a new project without so much as a thought about what it truly entailed. "The biggest cost is the horses," she said. "You can't put them in a shed and forget about them like you could if you offered quad bike tours."

Amy nodded.

"Then you've got the tack plus food and vet bills and maybe a truck for transportation."

"Sounds like you've thought about it."

Faith shrugged. "It was an idea I had once." She wasn't ready to seriously consider it.

"How's the pony club going?"

She smiled. "That's more a labour of love. Most people are like Lara, a joy to teach."

Lara grinned at her.

"But there's always one," Amy muttered.

She was right. Lara's nemesis Natasha was one of the brattiest children she'd ever come across, not that she'd say it in front of Lara. She caught sight of the time on the clock behind Amy. She had borrowed her parents' car and promised to pick them up from the boat ramp this evening. "I'd better go." She placed her glass in the sink and Lara and Amy walked her out.

"Visit any time," Amy said. "The guys won't mind if you bring your horse and ride, but check in with me first so I know where you're going. It's easy to get lost, and you want to make sure someone knows where you are."

"Thanks. I appreciate the offer."

"You can also visit for a cuppa any time too," Amy added.

"I will." She was enjoying the opportunity to socialise with people her age in Retribution Bay. "Make sure you drop by when you're in town. I'm having dinner with Georgie and a few others on Wednesday night if you want to join us."

"Thanks. I'll let you know."

Faith loaded her horse and then checked all the

latches on the float. With a final wave, she drove out of the Ridge. Aside from the matter of the sheep, today had been one of the best days she'd had since coming to town.

If she had more like it, she could see herself staying. Imagine having the time to ride regularly, to build close friendships and live in a community that supported each other.

It was definitely something to consider.

***

Sergeant Dot Campbell took one look at the dead sheep and swore ripely. "Someone's got it in for you."

Darcy appreciated her honesty, but it snuffed out the minute hope he had that there could be another explanation. "Did you ever get any information from the guy who broke into the farmhouse?"

She shook her head. "He swore he'd heard about the funeral and thought it the ideal time to break in and steal some stuff."

Which made him a complete asshole anyway, but they were certain Stonefish was behind it. And the company had to be powerful for someone to go to gaol for it.

"Whoever it was brought their own dogs." Matt pointed back towards the gate. "Paw prints appear near the tyre marks by the gate, as if they jumped out of the car."

"Nice spotting." Senior Constable Nhiari Roe slapped her brother on the shoulder. He grunted.

"I'll take a look in a minute." Dot made a note in her notebook.

Matt was the best tracker Darcy knew. He'd grown up learning the traditional ways of the area.

"They got tired of waiting and shot some," Brandon added, pointing to the couple they'd found.

"You heard nothing?"

"Best we can figure it was the night of the thunderstorm," Darcy said. "I was out here on Tuesday to fix the trough and Matt delivered extra feed on Friday."

She made a note. "Stonefish haven't contacted you again?"

"Nothing we haven't told you," Brandon said. "We'd hoped they'd given up."

"Or maybe they were lying low," Darcy said. Some things were adding up. "Little things have been going wrong."

"Why didn't you mention it?" Brandon demanded.

Darcy held up a hand to calm him. "I'm just putting it together now," he said. "I was sure I'd fixed that water trough last week and Lara agreed, but it was broken again this week." He turned to Dot. "Might not sound like much, but we don't have water to spare and a leaking trough isn't something to ignore." He ticked items off on his fingers. "The parts delivery which went missing last Monday. The windmill which blew down in the thunderstorm."

"It was on its last legs," Matt pointed out.

"Maybe." He'd go over the remains later.

Dot sighed. "All right, make a list for me. Right now, let's focus on the sheep."

It took a couple of hours for Dot and Nhiari to document the site and take moulds of the tyre tracks. Darcy and Matt loaded a dead sheep into the back of the paddy wagon so Dot could search for a bullet. They found a couple of casings as well.

When they were done, Dot asked. "Where will you bury them?"

"Not sure." They couldn't be buried too close to the bores and he'd have to check with Matt's family to make sure it wouldn't interfere with them.

"Good luck. I'll let you know if I find anything else."

As she left, Darcy removed his hat and wiped the sweat from his brow. It was viciously hot now. This morning's ride with Lara and Faith seemed like a distant dream.

"I'll radio Danielle and ask if we can borrow their front-end loader." Matt went over to the ute to contact their nearest neighbour.

Darcy glanced at his brother. "We've lost part of next year's flock as well as this year's." Most of the dead ewes had been ready to give birth.

Brandon nodded. "We needed those funds."

Darcy's chest tightened, but then he remembered Faith's offer and hope sparked. Maybe she could find a clause which would help them recoup their lost investment. He'd have to take the contract to pony club next week. "We'll work it out," he said, trying to be optimistic. "While we have the front-end loader, we can clear more space for the campgrounds." And hope Amy performed a miracle at getting people in.

"Yeah. We don't have any other option."

Matt returned. "They're using it today, but we can borrow it tomorrow."

Darcy checked the time. It wasn't ideal to move a flock of sheep at this time of day, but he didn't want to leave them here where the smell would attract dingoes. "We should move the sheep."

His friend sighed. "You're right. Let's get the horses."

It would be a long evening.

Chapter 5

Faith arrived at the boat ramp as her father's tour boat pulled up to its mooring. She let out a sigh of relief that she wasn't late and then strolled down to the jetty while the tourists were transferred from the boat to the shore in a smaller inflatable dinghy. Her parents and their employees would stay behind to clean, and she'd get a lift out when the inflatable returned to pick up the second group of passengers. A couple of tour boats were already at the moorings and the sea breeze stirred the water, making them all bob.

Those who disembarked onto the jetty looked weary but were chatting about their day and what they'd seen. Sounded like they had a successful trip and had swum with a whale shark. She waved to get Gretchen's attention, and the red-haired woman waited for her to move down the jetty and join her on the boat.

"Good day?" she asked.

Gretchen winced. "Your mum had a fall." She put the inflatable into gear and motored them towards the larger boat. "Rob's been in a mood since it happened."

Nuts. "How bad?"

"It wouldn't have been bad at all, except she fell

against the edge of the bench and cut her arm. It bled a lot, but I don't think it needs stitches."

Gretchen had first aid experience and had worked in an aged care facility in the city, so she'd seen plenty of injuries.

"I convinced Rob she didn't need to be the first off the boat."

Faith prepared herself for her father's accusations. His gaze darkened when he spotted her on the inflatable, but he managed a cheerful goodbye to the remaining passengers as they left. Faith bypassed him and walked straight to her mother, who sat in the cabin inside, a white bandage wrapped around her upper arm.

"It's nothing," Milly said before Faith could ask.

"How mad is Dad?"

"Threatening never to let me on the boat again." Her mother sighed. "It was such a minor thing; anyone could have done it. We'll have to smooth the corner so it doesn't hurt any of the passengers."

"I told you it was a bad idea for her to come on the boat." Rob stood at the entrance to the cabin, his face a thundercloud. Through the window behind him, Faith saw the crew glance over and then hurry to go about their tasks.

"Rob, I'm fine."

"You're injured," he corrected.

"A scratch. One that wouldn't have happened if the bench didn't have such a sharp edge on it. You're lucky it was me and not one of our passengers. They might have sued."

The idea made him pause, and Faith seized the opportunity to speak. "Your clients seemed thrilled about their day."

"The whale shark was close to shore," he said. "Then we saw some manta rays when we went snorkelling."

"Sounds fantastic. Did you see them, Mum?" Her mother's hair had that mussed, been swimming look to it.

"I did. It was a real highlight. I'm so glad I came out today."

Her father's expression softened. "I don't like you getting hurt."

"But I love spending the day with you."

Rob hugged his wife and with his temper deflated, Faith slipped out of the cabin and went to help clean up. Milly had neatly defused the situation.

Neither of her parents were getting any younger. Perhaps she should suggest her father retire so he could spend more time with her mum.

Her parents sat side-by-side holding hands, talking to each other, their love obvious even after fifty years together. Would she ever find someone she felt that way about? The men she'd dated in the city had been too invested in their careers to want a serious relationship. Or they felt intimidated by her income.

Darcy's face came to mind. He wouldn't care about her job.

Maybe the next time they spoke, she'd invite him to dinner.

To see what could happen.

And have a little fun while she was here.

***

Darcy scraped up the last of the dead sheep with the front-end loader and dumped them into the hole he'd dug. Several hundred dead. His father would say "it is what it is", but Darcy refused to. This wasn't an act of nature, it was vandalism, or spite. A warning.

Fury and helplessness crashed together making him jerk the dump lever sharply. How could he fight a faceless entity? He had no idea how the Ridge would survive this setback. They were down to their last few dollars and the credit card was scarlet. They'd have to slaughter a sheep if they wanted meat, and Amy's vegetable garden wasn't big enough to provide for the whole family.

He exhaled, moving the loader to scoop sand and bury the animals. Brandon leaned against the ute, staring off into the distance, waiting for him to finish. They needed no words. The fury on Brandon's face mirrored his own.

Finally he finished and drove back to the farmyard, leaving Brandon to close all the gates behind him. One final task before he returned the vehicle—to clear more land for the campgrounds. Amy had given him a mud map this morning, showing him the area to clear. He had to hand it to her, she was savvy, keeping the sites grouped around the utilities but without making them feel on top of each other.

The next step would be creating the donkey showers, which they'd do when they had some free time. He almost laughed. That was a misnomer.

Then they had to install power to the sites, but they didn't have the funds to upgrade the generator or to buy more solar panels, let alone run the cabling. The windmill also needed fixing, and on further investigation looked as if it had been pulled down.

He waved to Jay, one of their long-term camp guests, as he came out of his caravan with a frown on his perpetually red face. His wife, Cheryl was right behind him. Amy had told the guests there would be noise around the middle of the day. She was always thinking of the little things which didn't occur to him.

It took little time to clear the area. As he drove towards the main road to return the front-end loader to his neighbour's, he spotted a ute down by the dry riverbed in the distance. Amy was filling the tray with rocks which would mark out each of the new camping bays. He appreciated that she wasn't afraid of hard work.

By the time he'd done another dozen things around the station and had finished for the day, sweat plastered his shirt to his chest and despair weighed on him. He trudged into the kitchen, hanging his hat on the hook by the door.

"Hey, Dad!"

He forced himself to smile, but when Lara ran over to hug him, his smile became genuine. He squeezed her tightly, and when she protested, he tickled her, her giggles shifting some of the darkness from his mood. "How was school?"

"OK. Natasha was being mean, but Mischa and I ignored her. She's stupid."

"Good idea." Natasha was the quintessential mean girl, and he hated that his daughter had to deal with her, but there was only one class of year fives at the school. "Got any homework?"

"I already did it when I got home, after I helped Amy with the rocks."

"Did you get all the bays set out?"

"Yep. Amy and I are going to paint the site number signs tonight."

He glanced at Amy. "When will you advertise them?"

She dished up a large slab of lasagne and handed him the plate. "Already done. Two are booked from people on our wait list. They'll arrive Wednesday and have paid a deposit."

Every cent counted at this stage. "You're the best, Ames."

She smiled. "Just doing my job."

A job they still couldn't afford to pay her for. "Thanks for being here for Lara. There was too much to do today with the sheep."

His mother had always been home when Lara arrived on the school bus, which meant Darcy could keep working until sunset. But since his parents' death, he'd been there, not wanting Lara to arrive home to an empty house.

"Any time."

After dinner he read Lara another chapter of the fantasy novel. Then, with her tucked into bed, he headed into his father's office. No, Brandon's office. He owned the Ridge according to their father's will, and they still needed to sit down and discuss what that meant.

His father had always said he would leave the Ridge to the oldest child, which left Darcy with nothing to leave Lara. Yet dividing up the property seemed like sacrilege.

Then there was the matter of his mother's will, which left all her possessions equally to the four children. Georgie and Ed had taken a couple of items of sentimental value, and Georgie had split their mother's jewellery between them, but Darcy had no money to pay them for any of the household furniture.

Not that either of them had asked for it, but it didn't seem fair for them to get nothing.

He closed his eyes. A problem for another day. He slumped in the office chair and turned on the laptop Ed had sent up. Ed owned a collection of old, working machines, but he'd upgraded to the latest shiny new thing. With money so tight, Darcy wasn't complaining if it took five minutes to boot.

Over the past two weeks they'd digitised much of the Ridge's information, particularly his father's meticulous spreadsheets. He scrolled through the emails looking for bills. A bunch of ads for hay and equipment, a fishing newsletter and an email address which made him freeze.

Tan Lewis, Stonefish Enterprises.

His hand shook as he clicked on the email. Son of a bitch. The rage built at the words. A new offer for the property, less than before, but the last sentence made Darcy shove his chair away from the desk. His hands clenched, wanting to grab the laptop and throw it across the room.

Sheep are riskier these days with the wild dogs in the area.

He was practically admitting to the crime.

"Problem?" Brandon stood at the door, a mug of tea in his hands.

Darcy gestured to the screen, unable to form words.

Brandon cursed loudly as he read. "Bastards."

They were vultures, no sharks—not waiting until the Ridge was dead before they attacked.

Stonefish knew they were getting desperate. "What do we do?"

Brandon glanced back at him. "Do you want to sell?"

Darcy jolted. Why would he ask? The Ridge had been all he'd ever wanted. But... maybe Brandon had changed his mind. If Darcy was the only sibling who wanted the Ridge, was it fair of him to hold on to it? "Do you?" He ran a hand through his hair and breathed out, trying to settle the anger.

"No. I told you that." Brandon perched on the edge of the desk. "But have you had enough, Darce? You were stuck here helping Dad while I was in the army. Do you want to leave and try something new?"

Darcy's immediate reaction was to refuse, but he took a second to consider it. Was he being closed-minded, somewhat provincial? Should he investigate other opportunities, something which might be better for Lara, for himself?

He'd been to the city once, when Georgie moved

there for university. His mother needed his support because she'd been emotional about her youngest baby moving out of home. He'd hated every second. The traffic, the noise, the people surrounding him, but not one of them acknowledging his existence with a smile or a hello. All the light and buildings everywhere made him claustrophobic, and he couldn't wait to get back into the car and drive home.

The station life was all he'd ever wanted, but he had Lara to consider too.

"Darce?"

He blew out a breath. "No. This is home."

Satisfied, Brandon said, "Then do we respond to this asshole?"

"Faith offered to read the cattle contract. She said there might be a way to get the money back." He smiled as he remembered her enthusiasm for Lara's tales of buried treasure. Maybe she could be his avenging pirate.

"That would be a miracle. Have you sent it to her?"

"Taking her a copy tomorrow."

"All right. Then let's ignore the email until we hear from her." He clapped Darcy's shoulder. "You all good?"

Darcy nodded, as nausea returned. When Brandon left, he reviewed the figures, the number of sheep, the feed and remaining fuel, and the nausea worsened. At best, they had three months. Then they'd have to sell their allocated sheep to the abattoir, which would give them another boost of funds, but they'd lost a lot of their next flock with the pregnant ewes being slaughtered. So they'd have to buy more, which would eat into any money earned. And oh, yeah, there was the bottomless pit of debt to pay back too.

He swore. Cattle was supposed to be their way forward—not as susceptible to predators and with a strong market. He'd done all the research, chosen the Droughtmaster breed, called a few people for advice. Livestock and Gear had the best value. He paused, goosebumps leaping to his skin. They'd sent him marketing material late last year, but someone later recommended it to him. Who? His heart beating fast, he made a list of everyone he remembered chatting to and then pored through his emails to find the recommendation in writing. Nothing.

All he found was the paid invoice with the multi-six-figure sum staring back at him. Darcy's father hadn't told him he'd bought the cattle. Brandon had discovered it when they'd gone through their papers and realised there was no money left.

He closed his eyes, the sick feeling in his gut returning as strong as when Brandon had rung the number on the website, and they'd realised they'd been conned.

He breathed past the nausea.

Whoever had recommended the company might have lost their order too. Perhaps they had a different contact.

Or maybe they'd been working for Stonefish like Taylor. He frowned. Had their ex-station hand recommended the site?

Damn it, he couldn't remember. He'd have to chat to Matt about it tomorrow.

He rubbed the ache at his temple. It was late. Nothing more he could do tonight.

With a sigh, he took himself off to bed.

***

On Tuesday morning, Darcy woke like a bullet being shot out of a gun when he suddenly remembered he had to fix the pony club float by that afternoon. It was still dark, but he dressed and trudged out into the cool morning air. On closer examination, the float wasn't in as bad repair as he'd thought. The floorboards were sturdy but the hinges on the doors needed tightening, some rust had to be removed and some cracks welded.

Still Faith never should have driven it out here. Though he'd never regret their trail ride together.

"What the hell are you doing up so early?" Matt stood behind him, dressed in only a T-shirt and shorts, with a scowl on his face.

"Lara needs the float this afternoon, and I forgot about fixing it." He stretched his legs. "Was I making too much noise?" The last thing they needed was the camp guests complaining and leaving a bad review.

"No, I'm just attuned to odd noises right now."

It didn't surprise Darcy, not with everything going on.

"What else have you got to do?" Matt asked.

"A bit of welding, and a coat of rust inhibitor."

Matt sighed. "Let me get changed and I'll help."

Darcy smiled. Matt had been his younger brother, Charlie's best friend, but Charlie had died in an accident when he was twelve. Matt had continued to hang around the station, and when he'd left school, he'd asked to be a station hand. He'd never let them down.

They worked in silence for more than an hour. Darcy scanned the trailer for anything they'd missed and kicked the tyres. Bald as a baby's bottom and he had no spares to replace them. It was a miracle Faith had made it to the Ridge without blowing a tyre.

He shuddered, the image of his parents' four-wheel drive on its roof flashing in all its clarity. The blood, his parents' bodies inside, and then Faith's face replaced his mother's. His hands clenched. No way was he letting Amy tow the float with dodgy wheels.

"I'll tow Starlight into town this afternoon," Darcy said.

Matt stood next to him, examining the tyres. "Good call. Take it easy."

He'd have to stop work far earlier than normal, but he wasn't taking any chances. "Let's get breakfast."

Darcy left for town not long after midday. He could drive at half the speed limit and arrive on time. Perhaps he was being paranoid, but he could visualise his parents' car in the bush clearly. After he dropped off Starlight, he'd drive past the tyre place and sweet-talk the owner into donating a couple of tyres to the pony club.

Jeff's daughter was in Lara's class, so he might be lucky.

As he reached the turn off to the club, his heartbeat increased. Stupid. Faith would be busy getting things ready for the session, or perhaps not be there yet.

But he would be lying if he said she hadn't been on his mind. Lying in bed after a hard day's work, the image of her brought him enough of a distraction to switch his mind off the trials of the station and to relax.

And there she was, setting out some cones in the middle of the arena, a wide-brimmed hat on her head, shading her face. He pulled up and got out, waiting for her to cross over to him, confidence in her stride.

"Did you get time to fix the float?" she asked, a smile brightening her face.

"Yeah."

"Thanks so much." She bit her lip. "How did things go with the sheep?"

"They're buried," he replied, not wanting to be reminded of it.

Faith crossed her arms. "Right. Well, when you've unloaded Starlight, you can park the float over there." She pointed to his float.

Hell, he'd been too abrupt. "Listen, I'm going to call

Jeff and ask if he'll donate tyres to replace these bald ones."

Her smile returned. "That would be great."

He unloaded Starlight and led her to the small stables where Spirit was stalled. He checked the time. If he was quick, he'd have time to get the tyres replaced before Lara arrived from school. Her friend, Mischa was giving her a lift. He dialled Jeff's number and a few minutes later had an agreement. Faith was across the yard erecting a couple of jumps and he wandered over.

"Jeff's going to replace the tyres if I head over now," he told her. "If Lara arrives while I'm gone, will you tell her I won't be long?"

"Sure." Her smile hit him in the gut, made a warmth spread through him, and he forced himself to walk away.

He drove into town and while Jeff changed the tyres, he grumbled about the cost of pony club and the horse he'd bought to keep his little girl happy. "You're lucky you've got all that land out there," he said to Darcy. "Don't have to find somewhere to agist Lara's horse."

"Where are you keeping yours?" Darcy asked.

"The pony club for now. Faith's feeding it, but I don't know what will happen when she leaves town."

He frowned. "She leaving soon?"

Jeff shrugged. "She's only here looking after her mother, and I heard Milly went out on the tour boat the other day. Faith's got a high-powered job as a lawyer back in Perth, so I can't imagine she'd want to stay."

No, of course she wouldn't. He had to remember that, not get too caught up in the joy her smiles made him feel. But it reminded him of the contract he had in his pocket.

"I'm done." Jeff stood and Darcy shook his hand. "Thanks, mate."

"No problem. I almost borrowed the float myself,

but didn't like the look of it. You've done a good job fixing it."

Darcy headed back to the pony club, parked the float where Faith indicated and then hitched his own trailer to the ute. Lara was already in the arena with a group of boys and girls her age.

She nudged Starlight into a slow canter and leaned forward as they easily cleared the jump in the middle. His girl was a natural on horseback. She circled around and spotted him, waving madly. He waved back, his heart full.

Some other parents sat on the seating around the arena, so he joined them.

"Darcy! How nice to see you."

He stifled a groan. He hadn't seen Kristy sitting next to Joan, otherwise he would have stayed where he was. Still, he tipped his hat. "Kristy. Joan, thanks for picking up Lara from school."

"It's never a problem, Darcy." Joan patted the seat next to her and he sat. "Lara's always a delight."

"I'd be happy to pick her up if you ever need me to," Kristy piped up.

"I'll keep it in mind." It would never happen. Kristy's daughter was Natasha, Lara's nemesis. From all reports she was like her mother who Georgie said was as shallow as the reef at low tide. Despite being married, she flirted with every male under the age of thirty, which unfortunately included him.

"Lara told Mischa you went riding with Faith on the weekend," Joan said.

He saw the desire for gossip in her eyes, but unlike Kristy, it wasn't malicious. Joan had been introducing him to every single lady in town since Lara had been in pre-school. "Yeah. Lara invited her, and we rode to the beach."

"Would have been a lovely day for it. Did you go

swimming?"

"Sure did." He wouldn't tell her about the dead sheep which had ruined the day.

"And then you fixed the pony club float as well."

"It was dodgy. I didn't want her to have an accident."

The glint in Joan's eyes faded. "Of course not." She touched his knee with the look of pity he'd become accustomed to since his parents died.

"I heard Faith deserted her mother to go riding," Kristy said.

Darcy gritted his teeth. "I believe her mother chose to go out on their boat." He never understood why some people felt the need to put others down or portray them in a poor light.

It was Lara's turn to jump again, and he watched, applauding as she made it over cleanly.

"She hardly needs pony club," Kristy said. "She can do it all already."

Darcy ignored her. Joining the pony club was the only thing Lara had ever pleaded for, and though money was tight, he couldn't refuse her. She didn't get to do a lot of after-school activities as she caught the bus home and no one near them had kids her age to carpool with. Lara didn't have the advantages of siblings like he had growing up.

"Mischa wants to have Lara over for a sleepover," Joan said. "The shire is putting on a screening of the latest Disney movie on Friday, so if it works for you, Lara could come with us and then stay over."

He hesitated. Lara hadn't liked being apart from him since the car crash, had insisted adamantly they continue their reading ritual. And he needed the comfort it provided too. "Let me chat to her about it."

"OK."

Darcy strolled closer to the rails to watch. Lara rode

Starlight next to Jordan and spoke animatedly to him. Darcy grinned. Lara had recently admitted to him that Jordan made her feel all funny in her tummy. Even from here, he could see Lara's cheeks were red.

He rubbed his chest. It wouldn't be long before he'd be explaining to her what boys were after. Was he ready for that?

When class finished, Lara rode over, flushed with her success. "Did you see me jump, Dad?"

"Yep. We might have to set up some for you at home."

"That would be awesome!" She rode over to the trailer and set to work caring for her horse.

Darcy followed her. "Joan asked if you wanted to go to the movies with them on Friday night and then sleep over afterwards."

Lara hesitated. "By myself?"

He hated her nerves. Before the car accident, she wouldn't have hesitated. "Yeah, pumpkin."

She bit her lip. "But what if something happens at the Ridge?"

He wanted to tell her nothing would, but she'd already seen the sheep. "Then I'll call you."

She glanced over to where Mischa was with her mother, laughing at something. He could tell she wanted to go. "How about you say yes, and then if after the movie you change your mind, I'll come and pick you up?"

"But it's a long way into town."

"No distance is too far for you, pumpkin."

She flung herself at him, knocking him back a step with her hug. "I love you, Dad."

"I love you more, pumpkin."

Lara raced over to her friend. "Dad said I can come to your place on Friday!"

He chuckled and brushed Lara's horse. Faith was

chatting to some parents, so he'd catch her before they left. Maybe she'd be free Friday night.

Lara returned and helped him load Starlight into the horse float. Faith was still surrounded by parents.

"Are we going home, Dad?" Lara asked.

"Yeah. I wanted to ask Faith something before we go."

"Are you going to ask her on a date?"

He jolted and stared at her. "What makes you ask that?"

"Natasha said the only reason Faith came riding with me was because she wanted to get into your pants." Lara frowned. "But your pants wouldn't fit her, so it doesn't make sense."

He thanked the Gods Lara was still innocent enough not to understand the phrase. "It means something else for people who are dating."

"What?"

He'd promised himself years ago he would answer all her questions honestly. He sighed. "It refers to having sex."

Lara's eyes widened. "Ew, gross. Does Faith want to have sex with you?" Her voice carried in the still evening air and Faith glanced in their direction.

Shit. His face hotter than the mid-afternoon sun, he shook his head. "No, pumpkin. Faith came to the Ridge because she wanted to go riding on the beach with you." He would have to check if Faith had overheard his daughter and explain.

"I knew Natasha was wrong." She slipped her hand into his. "Are we going to talk to Faith now?"

He would much rather avoid Kristy, who was the last parent talking to Faith, but he wasn't a quitter. As they joined the group, Natasha sidled around so she was next to Lara. Darcy placed a hand on Lara's shoulder in support as he smiled at Faith. "Could I have a word with you when you're finished speaking with Kristy?"

"Of course. We're done now, aren't we?" Faith asked the woman.

"Yes. I'll be back next week to make sure you've listened to my suggestions."

Faith's smile was forced. "See you then."

Natasha murmured something to Lara and his daughter stiffened. "Faith does not want to have sex with my Dad," Lara shouted. "She likes me."

"Your own mum didn't like you," Natasha sniped.

Outrage filled Darcy. Lara trembled under his hand and he wanted to throttle the smug smile from Natasha's face. Instead he channelled his father, the expression conveying his disappointment and anger while he kept his tone calm. "Natasha, it's not nice to spread rumours."

Her smile vanished, and she rushed to her mother's side. "Mum told me it was true."

He raised his eyebrows at Kristy.

She flushed and hushed her child. "What nonsense. Come, we've got to go." She dragged her protesting daughter over to the car.

Darcy wrapped his arm around his still trembling daughter.

"What are these rumours?" Faith asked lightly.

"Natasha said you only came riding with me on Saturday because you wanted to get into Dad's pants," Lara said. "I didn't understand what she meant until Dad explained it. But you wanted to go riding with me, didn't you?"

"Of course." Faith squeezed her hand. "I had a wonderful time planning our treasure hunt."

Lara nodded as if she'd known it all the time. Then she leaned into Darcy's side. "It's OK if you like my Dad too."

Faith grinned. "Well, that's good, because I do like your dad."

"He's the best," Lara assured her.

Heat filled his cheeks, and he cleared his throat. "As much as I love hearing you praise me, I wanted to ask if you could read through the contract we talked about on the weekend."

"Sure. Do you have it on you?"

He took it out of his back pocket and handed it to her.

She moved closer to the spotlight where the light was better and flicked through it. "It will take me a few minutes to go through it. If you've got time, we could get dinner in town and I'll go through it then."

"Yes!" Lara said.

Darcy hesitated. It would fuel gossip. Would it affect Lara further? He sighed. Funds were tight, but he'd be paying a lot more if he got another lawyer involved. "All right, my shout. Can I leave Starlight in the stables?"

Faith nodded, handing him back the contract. "I'll finish packing up here."

She strode away, her hips swaying, and his eyes lingered on her behind until Lara dashed in front of him to let Starlight out of the float.

He sighed. Faith wouldn't be staying in town, but maybe she could help him out of the mess he'd got them into while she was still here.

Chapter 6

On the drive to the country music themed restaurant in town, Lara was unusually quiet. She stared out the window, her expression serious. Concern filled Darcy. "You all right, pumpkin?"

Her face screwed up as if trying to decide what to say. He waited while she figured out the words. In a soft voice she asked, "Does Mum like me?"

The question stabbed him. What should he say? Sofia had barely been a blip in Lara's life. "I'm sure she does, pumpkin. She left me because she wasn't ready to settle down, and she didn't want to stay in Retribution Bay. She was very young."

"But you were the same age, and you stayed. You love me."

He squeezed her knee. "Yeah, I do. But when you were born, your mum was depressed, which is common amongst new mums. She wasn't diagnosed for a while, but that was part of the reason she left." The other part was because she refused to be trapped in Retribution Bay, but he wouldn't tell Lara that.

"But she's better now?"

"I think so. I haven't spoken to her in a while."

Georgie had called her when his parents died.

"Then why wouldn't she visit?"

"She lives over in Melbourne. It's a long way to come." As far as he knew, Sofia hadn't even been back to visit her parents. And after he'd refused to give them custody of Lara, they hadn't wanted to be part of Lara's life, as if their refusal would make him change his mind about custody.

Lara fell silent, and he pulled into the car park. "Do you want to talk about it more?" he asked. "We don't have to go to dinner with Faith." Though he wanted to spend more time with her.

"Faith likes me, right?"

"She does. You two had a blast on Sunday, didn't you?"

"Yeah, OK. Let's go." She thrust the car door open and strode towards the restaurant, determination in every step.

Darcy was so proud of her. He caught up to her at the door where she asked for a table for three. They were given a booth, and he slid in next to Lara and waited for Faith to arrive. She walked in only a few moments later, scanning the tables. He lifted a hand to catch her eye, and she smiled.

Damned if her smile didn't caress his insides.

"I love this place." She slid onto the seat across from them. "All the posters of country singers and the music playing."

He lifted his eyebrows. "You like country music?"

"Love it," she confirmed. "When I was about Lara's age, we spent a couple of years living on a farm in Queensland and all they played was country music. I fell in love with it and horses."

"But you live in the city now," Darcy said.

"Hard to be a corporate contracts lawyer elsewhere." She smiled.

The server came over to take their drinks order. "I'll have a glass of house wine," Faith said.

"The usual?" Darcy asked Lara.

She nodded.

"Chocolate milkshake and a coke," Darcy told the man.

When the server left, Faith asked, "You don't drink?"

"Not when I'm driving with Lara." He wouldn't risk it.

"Makes sense," she said. "Do you want to show me the contract?"

The nerves returned as he gave it to her, and while she read, he and Lara decided what they wanted to eat.

"It's not great," she said. "Whoever drew this up was definitely on the side of the seller."

The waiter returned with their drinks and they ordered burgers for dinner. Darcy waited impatiently for him to leave before asking, "Do we have a case?"

"You tracked down the parent company?"

"Yeah, Ed did."

"Great. There's a clause here," she turned the paper around to show him, "which means if they go out of business, their parent company is liable for their debts, which includes the delivery of your cattle."

His head spun. "We can still get them?"

She nodded. "Or your money back, but it won't be easy. If you can send me all the information you have, I'll go through it and prepare a statement for you to send to them."

He suppressed a grimace. "How much will it cost?"

She sipped her wine. "It's on the house. I haven't worked on anything like this in months. It will be a nice change."

Darcy hesitated. He didn't want to take advantage of her.

"Besides, I intend to take you up on your offer to ride on your property and that's priceless."

It didn't seem like a fair swap, but he wasn't in a financial position to argue. "Thank you."

"You're welcome."

"Does that mean the Ridge is going to be OK?" Lara asked.

He hated that she realised anything was wrong.

"We'll do everything we can to ensure it is," Faith assured her.

Not a promise it would be OK, but a promise to fight for it. It would have to be enough, and he was grateful for Faith's conviction. It made him hope as well.

Lara perked up and when the food arrived, she smothered her chips with tomato sauce before eating them. In between mouthfuls, she peppered Faith with questions about her childhood on the farm. "Do you have any brothers or sisters?" Lara asked.

"I have two brothers, but they're both much older than me. They'd left home by the time we lived on the farm."

"Did you have anyone to play with?"

Darcy's heart clenched. He did his best to keep her company, but he wasn't a replacement for a child her own age.

"I had the horses, and when the owner's children were home from boarding school, we'd play together."

"Why didn't you go to boarding school?"

Faith hesitated. "The school in town was good enough for me."

Perhaps her parents couldn't afford it. He'd chat to Faith later about what living on a farm was like for her and whether she had any recommendations for how he could make life easier for Lara.

He settled back, letting the country music tunes and

the sounds of Lara's chatter wash over him. He had his daughter by his side and a pretty woman to chat to. Right now he could pretend life was great and everything was all right. If only life could be so simple.

He caught sight of another woman across the room watching him. Dark hooded eyes, plump lips he used to dream about, and shoulder-length hair which was far more blond than it used to be. He blinked to rid himself of the mirage, but the woman stood and stalked towards him, those curves swaying in a way that had mesmerised him as a teenager.

She was real. Recognition slugged him like a high-voltage electric fence. Sofia.

What was she doing here? Did she think she could waltz in and surprise Lara like this? Surprise him?

Hell no. Fury shoved aside his shock. "I'm going to the bathroom," he said to Lara and strode towards the woman who had broken his heart.

"Darcy—"

He took her arm and spun her around, pulling her away from his daughter. "Walk with me."

He dragged her around the corner, out of sight. "What the hell are you doing?"

She wrenched her arm from his grasp. "I was going to say hello to my daughter."

He shook his head, trying to shut down the panic inside of him. "You think the best way to greet the daughter you haven't seen in ten years is in the middle of a crowded restaurant when she has no clue you're even here?" The woman was unbelievable.

"I planned to call. We only arrived today."

"Who's we?"

"My husband and two step-sons. We're visiting my parents."

He breathed slowly to calm himself. "A little warning would have been nice."

She glared at him. "I have a right to see my daughter."

"And I have a right to prepare her for the shock her mother is in town. What did you expect? That she would jump into your arms and be thrilled?"

Sofia crossed her arms, one hand going to her throat. "I didn't really think about it."

Of course not. It had taken him some time to realise how self-involved she was. "Here's what's going to happen," he said. "You're going to stay here until I leave with Lara. Then later you will call me and arrange a time to meet. That way I can prepare her."

"You going to tell her what a bitch I am?" Sofia demanded.

"No. I'm going to do my best to answer all her questions like why you want to see her now."

"I've matured, Darcy and have two beautiful step-sons. I want to get to know her, be a proper mother."

Fear gripped him. She was not taking his baby away from him. He unclenched his hands. "I can arrange for something after school, about three-thirty."

"Oh, we're swimming with the whale sharks tomorrow. Five would be better."

He wasn't hanging around in town for when it was convenient for her. "Then we'll make it a different day. You've still got my number?"

She nodded.

"Call me tonight. I'll take Lara home now, but don't let her see you. I don't think she'll recognise you, but I won't risk it."

Sofia opened her mouth as if to protest and then thought better of it. "All right."

On his way back to the table, he took a moment to control the fear and anger swirling in his blood. Across the room, Faith and Lara were laughing together. The sound lightened his heart, but he didn't sit when he reached them. "We'd better get going," he said to Faith. "It's a long drive home and we need to pick up Starlight still."

Her shoulders slumped, but she gave him a small smile. "Of course."

"Come on, pumpkin."

Lara pouted but slid out of the booth. "Who was the lady you were talking to?"

Damn, she was too observant. "An old school friend." He placed a hand on her back to keep her moving towards the cash register. He paid for Faith's meal despite her protests and ushered them all out of the restaurant. The warm night air soothed him.

"Thank you for your help tonight," Darcy said.

"You're welcome. Make sure you send me the info."

He nodded. "I'll call you later."

With a glance over his shoulder to make sure Sofia wasn't near, he said goodnight and hurried Lara to the car.

***

Faith lay in bed trying to concentrate on the book in front of her, but it was no use. Something had happened in the restaurant to spook Darcy, and she was certain it wasn't anything she'd said. She was tempted to call him, ask if she could help, but he wouldn't have been home for long and he might be tucking Lara into bed.

The haunted expression in Darcy's eyes was hard to forget. She picked up her phone and scrolled through her contacts until she found his.

Was she overstepping their relationship? He had family at home who would be there for him.

She sighed and placed the phone on the bed next to her. Maybe she should work on her lesson plan for pony club next week. It would keep her brain occupied at least.

She retrieved her laptop from her bag and powered it up. Outside her door, her parents chatted quietly as they got ready for bed. At least that was going right. Her mother had been on the boat the past couple of days and her father was relaxing. It helped that when he'd taken Milly to the hospital about the cut, the doctor had said it was a minor scratch and needed nothing except to be kept clean.

Faith reviewed her list of students. It was growing, but there weren't many horses in the area. Most were stock horses, not suitable for beginner riders. Her cursor stopped at Natasha's name. A nasty little girl, and her mother wasn't much better. Her list of suggestions for the pony club were ridiculous. They weren't trying to compete in dressage or show jumping here, it was fun for the kids, most of whom were interested in barrel racing and lassoing. The latter might be a rodeo event, but she didn't mind mixing things up to suit what the kids wanted to learn. She'd have to find someone who could teach them. Darcy might know of someone.

It might be fun to learn for herself.

The image of Darcy lassoing her made her smile as she worked through her list of students, making notes on where they were strongest and weakest. After she'd finished her review and packed her laptop away, her phone rang.

Darcy.

Her pulse increased as she answered. "Hi, Darcy."

"I hope I'm not calling too late." His honey tones slid over her skin.

"I just finished writing my notes on today's pony club session."

"You're a good teacher. Those kids listened to every word you said."

"Thanks." She'd never considered being a teacher, had focused on a job which gave her responsibility and power, leaning as far away from her father's flaky tendencies as she could. "I was going to call you. You seemed a little upset when you left the restaurant tonight."

He sighed. "I was."

"What happened?"

A pause. "I ran into Lara's mother and my ex."

Faith frowned. "But Lara didn't recognise her."

"Sofia left town only a couple of months after Lara was born. She hasn't seen her since."

Oh.

"Her brilliant plan was to walk over and introduce herself, right out in public." She'd never heard such pissed off sarcasm from him, but beneath it was something else—pain, fear?

"Has she had any communication with Lara in the past ten years?"

"She sends a card and a bunch of presents on her birthday and Christmas."

Faith remembered Natasha's nasty words. "So that's what Natasha meant today."

"Yeah."

That had to suck. It couldn't have been easy for Darcy. "So what does Sofia want?"

"To meet Lara. I spoke to her just now and we've arranged for them to meet after school on Thursday."

"Have you told Lara?"

"Not yet. I don't know when to tell her. I had to digest it myself on the drive home, and there's not a lot of time in the morning before she catches the school bus…"

And Lara was the type of girl who would process the news at her own pace. "Why don't you tell her tomorrow night? She'll be able to ask you questions, but not have too much time to stress about it."

"You're right. She counted the number of sleeps until you came out for our beach ride, so she's likely to obsess about this too."

Faith smiled, charmed.

"I'm worried." The catch in Darcy's voice pulled at her heart.

She switched off the light and slid under the covers, giving Darcy her complete attention. "What about?"

"Both that Lara won't want to meet with her, and that she will. She'll get her hopes up that it will be wonderful." He paused. "She's had so much to deal with over my parents' deaths. What if this is too much? What if Sofia wants custody of her? What if Lara wants to go? She's kept every single stuffed toy Sofia has ever sent her, and just today Lara asked if Sofia loved her."

Faith had studied family law as part of her degree. "The courts are unlikely to grant Sofia custody after all this time. At best she'd get visitation rights." She paused. "Where does Sofia live?"

"Melbourne."

The diagonally opposite side of the country, almost the furthest you could get from Retribution Bay and still be on the mainland. "Did she tell you much about her life?"

"She's remarried, has two step-sons." He cursed quietly. "Lara's always wanted brothers."

"Don't work yourself up, Darcy. They might be horrible little brats whom she hates."

He chuckled. "Thanks."

"Will you take anyone with you for support?"

"I don't know. Brandon and Matt will be busy on the Ridge."

"I can be there." What was she saying? "If you want me to be. I mean, I can be a friendly face." Ugh. Had she put her foot in it?

"We're meeting at Ningaloo Cafe at three-thirty." He sighed. "A friendly face would be welcome."

Relief filled her that he wasn't annoyed by her offer. "I'll be there."

"Thanks, Faith."

She liked the sound of her name on his lips.

"There was something else I wanted to ask you," he said. "Were you lonely on that farm when you were a kid? Is there anything you would have liked to make it easier?"

It took her a second to make the connection. He was asking for Lara, always considering his girl. "I was lucky. The farm wasn't far out of town and I could walk from school to activities and Mum would pick me up when they were over. I'd have regular sleepovers, and I loved horse-riding so I spent most of my spare time out with the horses. I remember those years fondly." She'd been devastated when they'd moved.

He sighed. "I worry about Lara."

"She seems happy to me, especially considering her grandparents just died. I suspect she'd tell you if she wanted something."

"Maybe. She knows too much about our financial status." He cleared his throat. "Listen, I've called Ed, and he's emailed me the information he has on Stonefish. I can forward it to you if you give me your email."

She told him.

A keyboard clacked in the background. "Done. There's something else you should probably know." He paused. "The parent company has been harassing us to sell the Ridge for the past six months. We suspect they're behind the dead sheep we discovered the other day."

She sat up. "That's a serious allegation. Why do they want to buy the Ridge?"

"We can't figure it out, but their actions are why you can't be on their radar. After you've reviewed everything, send me the draft letter and I'll forward it to them."

"It would have more authority coming from a lawyer."

"These people don't play fair, Faith. I don't want you to get hurt."

She was invested now but telling him that would only make him worry. "We can discuss the next steps after I've reviewed the documents."

Darcy growled. "That's not a promise."

"No, it's not. I wouldn't be a decent lawyer if I made promises when I don't know all the facts." She smiled at his annoyed groan. "But I won't do anything without your agreement, Darcy."

He sighed. "All right. I appreciate your help, Faith."

"It's my pleasure. I'll see you on Thursday." She hung up and smiled, snuggling down in her bed. He didn't know it yet, but she fought hard for the clients she believed in.

And she believed in him.

Chapter 7

Wednesday night arrived like a charging ram. Darcy still had no idea of the best way to tell Lara her mother was in town. He'd agonised about it all day, had considered picking her up from school himself, but that would only make her worry. So he waited anxiously in the kitchen for her to arrive home.

Amy sauntered in from the camp grounds reception, where she'd been checking in a guest. She clapped him on the shoulder. "You've got this, Darce. Don't stress."

She grabbed her hat from the hook and went to show the new guests where their campsite was. Outside Lara called, "Hey, Ames."

She was home.

Darcy busied himself putting on the kettle and getting biscuits from the cupboard so he wasn't just standing there like an idiot.

The screen door creaked open. "Hey, Dad! Did you see the new guests? That means all our sites are full!"

Her enthusiasm only further intensified his nerves. He forced a smile and opened his arms for her hug. And he held on for perhaps a moment too long, because she stepped back with a frown on her face.

"What's wrong?"

Damn. "Have a seat, pumpkin. I've got news for you."

She glanced around. "Did something happen? Is someone hurt?"

"No, pumpkin." He squeezed her arm. "You might like the news."

"Then why are you acting so weird?"

"Because I don't know how you're going to react." He took a deep breath. "Your mum called. She's in Retribution Bay and she wants to visit."

Lara's mouth dropped open. Silence. Finally she said, "She wants to see me?" The hope was clear on her face.

Darcy nodded. "Yeah. She's staying with her parents, and she's with her new husband and his two boys."

"Does that make them my brothers?"

"Step-brothers."

Lara opened and closed her mouth a couple of times as if not sure what to say. "Is she coming here now? What do I say to her? Should I get changed?" She started for the corridor.

Darcy hauled her back. "Don't panic, pumpkin." He squeezed her, feeling her jitters. "We're going to meet her after school tomorrow. At Ningaloo Café. If you want to see her."

"Why wouldn't I want to see her?" A pause. "Is she mean?"

Hell. He could hardly point out that some kids would be angry their mother had virtually ignored them for their entire life. He didn't want to plant those kinds of seeds if she didn't have them herself. "No, she's not mean."

"So what do I say to her?"

Good question. "You can tell her about school, and

about pony club. Then you can ask her about Melbourne and her husband and your step-brothers."

The tension melted from her. "I can do that."

He kissed the top of her head. "You'll be fine."

"Yeah. I'll write a list. Granny always says it's best to write a list so you don't forget anything." She bit her lip and her eyes glistened.

Darcy swallowed the lump in his throat and hugged her again. "Great idea, pumpkin. Do you need some paper?"

"I've got it." She rummaged around in her school bag and pulled out a notebook.

Darcy turned back to the kettle and closed his eyes. Lara would be fine, and no matter what, he would be here for her.

That night, after Lara was asleep in bed, Darcy was desperately trying to concentrate on the mystery show on the television, and not obsess about the Sofia meeting. His phone beeped, making him jump.

How'd it go?

Faith. Glad for the distraction, he said goodnight to Amy and Brandon, and headed to his bedroom. He briefly debated texting her back, but he wanted to hear her voice. He plugged in her number.

"Hey, Darcy. How's Lara?"

Her voice soothed some of the tension from him and he lay on his bed. "Coping better than me. She's asleep."

"You want to talk about it?"

"Yes, and no." He sighed. "She took the news well. She's written a list of topics to talk to Sofia about."

Faith chuckled. "I can't imagine Lara ever running out of topics to talk about."

He smiled. "You're right."

"So what are you worried about?"

"Everything," he confessed. "That it will go badly, and Lara will be devastated. Or that it will go well, and Lara will fall in love and want to move to Melbourne and be with Sofia." It felt good to vocalise all the thoughts running through his mind.

"OK, so let's take that one thing at a time," Faith said, her tone soothing. "If Lara's devastated, she's still got you and your entire family to support her. She's a strong girl. She'll get through it."

He knew she was right, but it didn't stop the fear that his baby would be hurting.

"Secondly, even if Lara falls in love, I can't imagine her wanting to move to Melbourne. She told me she hated Perth because it was noisy and smelly."

He straightened. "When did she say that?"

"At pony club," Faith replied. "She might want to visit Sofia, but Lara loves Retribution Bay. She loves Starlight, and the ocean, and she loves you. That will never change."

Darcy closed his eyes. To have her say that, someone who didn't know either of them particularly well, really helped. The fear settled into low-level white noise. "Thanks, Faith. I needed to hear that."

"My pleasure."

He exhaled. "So, how was your day?"

The next day, when Darcy waved Lara off to school, her face was pale and she clung to him a second longer than normal. "She will be at the café, won't she?"

"She will," Darcy promised. He'd hunt Sofia down and drag her there if he had to. "I'll meet you out the front of school and bring a change of clothes and your bathers in case you want to go swimming afterwards."

"Do you think she'll swim with me?"

"I don't know, pumpkin." But he'd suggest it. The café was right on the beach front.

Finally she climbed on the bus and waved at him as it drove down the road.

Darcy spent all day worrying that she would be worrying and had returned to the house with plenty of time to shower and get ready. He called Sofia, but it went straight to voice mail. He swore. "Sofia, it's Darcy. I'm heading into town to pick up Lara and wanted to confirm you were meeting us at Ningaloo Café at three-thirty. I'm taking Lara's bathers if you want to swim after the café." He wouldn't have reception on most of his drive into town. "Text me when you get this."

It was the best he could do. On his way out of his bedroom, he checked the mirror. He spent so much of his life in work gear that it was odd to see himself in normal clothes. The blue T-shirt was old, but he wore it so rarely it was still in good condition and he threw on his best jeans. Sofia wouldn't have a reason to turn her nose up at him, and he wanted to look nice for Faith as well.

He smiled. She was so easy to talk to, and they'd talked long into the night about things from their childhoods and her love of riding. She hadn't sounded excited about going back to Perth, but he refused to get his hopes up.

On his way through the kitchen, Amy stopped him. "You all right?"

He nodded. "It's what Lara wants." He hoped it would be good for her.

"I can come if you need a back-up."

His face heated. "Faith's going to meet me at the café."

She grinned at him. "That's great."

At the door he reached for his Akubra and hesitated. He didn't need it if he was sitting in a café, and Sofia used to tease him that he wouldn't go anywhere without it.

But why did he care what she thought? She'd made it clear he wasn't good enough for her ten years ago.

"Wear it," Amy called. "The sexy cowboy look suits you." She winked.

He rolled his eyes but grabbed the hat. He didn't feel whole without it.

Darcy did his best to keep himself from worrying about Lara on his drive into town, but he failed miserably. There were some things he couldn't protect his daughter from, could only support her. He arrived at the district high school with plenty of time and scored a car park right outside.

"Hey, Darcy!"

He braced himself as he turned and then relaxed. "Julia, how's things?" He hugged his high school friend. "Here to pick up Lachlan?"

"Here to drag him away." She laughed. "He loves pre-primary."

"That's great."

"Hey, did you know Sofia's in town? I ran into her at the bakery yesterday and almost died of shock."

There was no malice in her question. Julia had been best friends with Sofia in high school and had been almost as devastated as he'd been when she'd left. "Yeah. Lara and I are going to meet with her after school."

"How's Lara taking it?"

"She's a little nervous." Though Julia wasn't a gossip, he didn't want to talk to her about it.

The bell rang and Julia gasped. "I'd better run. I'm supposed to meet Lachlan outside his classroom. Good luck today." She waved and was gone.

Darcy smiled. She'd visited him and Lara a few times after Sofia had left and always spoke to him when she saw him in town.

The kids poured out of their classrooms, a sea of

yellow and brown uniforms, and he scanned the crowd for his daughter. She was one of the last to come out, walking slowly, chatting to Mischa, her feet almost dragging on the ground.

Crap. Had she changed her mind about meeting Sofia? This was going to be tough. He waved, and she changed direction towards him, pulling Mischa with her. "Have a good day, pumpkin?"

"It was all right."

"How's it going, Mischa?"

"Is Lara still allowed to sleep over tomorrow night now her mum is in town?"

The question took him aback. Did Lara not want to stay at her friend's place?

"Please can I, Dad?"

"Of course. You're walking home with Mischa after school."

She beamed and high-fived her friend.

"Do you want a lift home?" Mischa only lived around the corner, but he was happy to drop her off.

"That would be great! Thanks."

Both girls climbed into the back seat of his ute and he drove the short distance to Mischa's house. "Your mum is going to love you," Mischa said as she climbed out. "And if she doesn't, then she's an idiot." The door shut, punctuating her sentence, and Darcy felt a wave of love for the girl.

"You want to hop into the front seat?" he asked.

"Yeah." Lara trundled around and strapped herself in.

"What's bothering you?" He drove slowly, taking the long way around to the beach so she had time to talk.

"What if she doesn't like me?"

"Then as Mischa said, she's an idiot."

"What if I don't like her?"

"Then all you need to do is say you have homework

to finish and come over to me. I'll be in the café waiting for you."

"Will you stay with me?"

Sofia had requested time alone with Lara, but, "If you need me to, I will."

"We should have a secret signal," Lara said. "Like they do in the movies. If I'm in trouble, I'll bang my fist three times on the table and you can rescue me."

He bit back his smile, pleased she was back to more of the Lara he knew. "I'll keep my eye out," he said. "And I'll swoop in and save you."

"Thanks, Dad. You're the best."

There weren't many cars parked outside Ningaloo Café when they arrived, but he recognised Faith's red Prius. He smiled. "I brought you a change of clothes in case you don't want to wear your school uniform."

She pursed her lips. "What did you bring?"

He reached over to the back seat and grabbed the bag he'd packed. It included bathers and her favourite horsey T-shirt.

"I'll get changed." She hurried across to the change rooms which faced the beach and only took a couple of minutes before she was back, thrusting her uniform into the back seat.

"Ready?"

She let out a deep breath and nodded.

On the way across the car park, she slipped her hand into his and he squeezed it.

Across on the sand, a lone photographer crouched, taking photos of something that had washed up on the shore. Darcy frowned. Was that Lee, a camp guest they'd had when his parents had died? He'd said he was going to Perth.

The man spotted Darcy and hesitated only a moment before he waved.

"Darcy! Lara!" Lee walked towards them. "Nice to

see you again."

The man had always been friendly, and Darcy had seen him walking miles to get the perfect photograph.

"What brings you back to town, Lee?"

Lee grinned. "I've been commissioned to take photos for a coffee-table book," he said. "They specifically want shots from this area. I was going to call Amy and ask if there's room at the Ridge for me."

"There should be. If we don't have a site, tell Amy you can stay in one of the shearers' quarters until we get space." Lee had been a long-term guest and they could do with the money.

"Thanks, mate. That's nice of you."

"No worries. We've got to get going."

"See you out there."

Next to him Lara hadn't said a word, which showed how nervous she was. Lee had taught her how to compose photos, and she'd spent a couple of afternoons wandering around the grounds with him.

The café was beach themed with shells and starfish decorations covering the walls outside. Several tables were set out on the pavement in front of the ocean, shaded by large umbrellas, and a couple of families sat at them, but Sofia wasn't amongst them. "Ready?"

Lara nodded.

Inside was a little cooler with the air-conditioning blaring. He spotted Faith first, sitting in the far corner, next to the wall where she could see the entrance and everyone inside. He smiled. At the table next to her were Jay and Cheryl. Though retired, Jay occasionally helped around the station. They were chatting to another couple, probably some tourists they'd befriended. They seemed to make friends everywhere.

"Is she here?" Lara whispered.

He kept scanning. Sofia hadn't replied to his voice mail message, but she sat at a table by the window, next to a man who was possibly her husband, and two young boys, maybe five years of age. Darcy cursed to himself. Why had she brought her entire family with her? It would be difficult enough for Lara to meet her, let alone the people who had replaced her.

"Dad?"

"Yeah, she's here, pumpkin. She's at the table by the window."

Sofia spotted them and waved. Lara pressed closer to his side. "Who's with her?"

"I'd guess it's her new husband and his sons."

Lara looked up at him and frowned. "Does that make him my dad?"

He winced, not liking the surge of jealousy. "Step-dad I guess. Do you want to go over there?"

She straightened. "Yes. You remember the sign?"

"Three bangs on the table," he replied.

Sofia had taken a couple of steps towards them and now she waited as they approached. Her eyes glistened. "Lara. I can't believe how much you've grown." She held out her arms.

The woman was clueless.

"Lara, this is your mum, Sofia."

Lara dived into her arms and hugged her.

Hurt pinned him to the spot. He shouldn't be surprised. Lara loved everyone and had the kindest heart around. He swallowed down his pain.

"You must be Darcy." The man at the table held out his hand. "I'm Josh."

He forced a smile and shook his hand. "G'day." Lara was still buried in her mother's arms and Sofia was crying. "These your boys?"

"Twins. Todd and Trevor."

The boys barely acknowledged him, too busy slurping their milkshakes.

Lara pulled back and wiped her eyes. Darcy handed

her a tissue. "You OK?"

"Of course she is," Sofia said, pulling out the spare seat. "Have a seat, baby. What would you like to drink?"

Darcy ignored Sofia, waiting for Lara to nod in response to his question. "All right. I'll be right there with Faith."

She hugged him and whispered, "I love you."

"I love you more." He kissed her head and walked over to where Faith waited. She stood. "You look like you need a hug."

Her arms came around him before he could answer and he leaned into her, drawing comfort from her softness. "Thanks." She smelled like the ocean and her hair was a little damp. "You been swimming?"

"Yeah, I had a quick dip before I came in." She gestured to the chair she'd been sitting in. "Take that one so you can monitor things."

He smiled his appreciation as he sat. "Where's your mum?"

"She's visiting a friend."

Lara was talking, her hands gesturing like they did when she was excited. So far, so good.

"Darcy?"

Faith still stood, her eyebrows raised as if she'd asked him a question.

"Sorry?"

"Can I get you a drink or something to eat?"

His stomach wouldn't handle food right now, but there was a bottle of water on the table. "Water's fine."

She sat across from him and twisted so she could also watch Lara. "She looks OK."

"Yeah." He should be pleased, but had she been pining for her mother, and he hadn't known about it? Was he wrong not to have made an effort to keep in touch with Sofia?

"You want to talk about it?" Faith asked, pouring him a glass of water.

"I'll cope." His eyes didn't leave his daughter. Couldn't risk missing her sign.

Faith chuckled. "Maybe a little less intensity with your staring, Darcy. The tourists will think you're a stalker."

It took a second for her words to sink in, and then he glanced at her. Her smile was sympathetic. "It's a little creepy."

His cheeks heated. "She arranged a signal with me. If she taps her fist three times, then she needs rescuing."

Faith nodded. "OK. How about we both keep watch then?" She shifted the table and shuffled her chair so she could see Lara without turning.

Her support warmed him. He had lost touch with most of his school friends after Lara had been born, as they'd either moved away or they hadn't wanted him hanging around with a new baby. He'd received all of his support from his family.

Lara was chatting to her brothers. Todd responded, but Trevor stared out the window at the ocean.

"Are they her brothers?" Faith asked.

He blinked. "Step-brothers. Josh is Sofia's new husband." Josh sat back listening but not taking part in the conversation, though when Lara got going, it was hard to get a word in edgewise. He looked like a decent enough bloke. Had that kind of refined wealthy look about him with the Ralph Lauren polo shirt and boater shoes. Would he think Lara was too common for his family?

"Darcy, chill."

He glanced at Faith. "What?"

"You have a million thoughts going over your face. Whatever the last one was, it wasn't nice. You practically burnt a hole through Josh."

He rubbed his face. "Sorry, I'm a little stressed."

She covered his hand with hers. "It's understandable, but you need to have faith in your relationship with your daughter. It's strong and her having other family won't change that."

He wished he could be as certain as she was.

The waitress brought over an iced coffee and a large slice of carrot cake. Faith thanked her and asked Darcy, "Want some?" She held out her fork with some cake on it.

His stomach had settled a little. "Sure." He leaned forward, opened his mouth and she put the cake inside. The intimacy of the action struck him, and he stared at her as he tasted the delicious moist cake. They barely knew each other, but it felt so natural.

She broke the eye contact and cut herself a piece of cake. "Is it good?" As if to answer her own question, she tasted the cake and shut her eyes as her lips closed around the fork that had just been in his mouth. He shifted, unable to look away from her. He could visualise those lips on him. He dragged his gaze away. The sight of his daughter across the café doused all of his inappropriate thoughts. Lara still chatted, but her hands clutched the milkshake glass in front of her and her shoulders were hunched.

Sofia spoke now, and he wished he could hear what she was saying, but the hum of other voices drowned her out. "What do you think she's saying?"

"I'm sure Lara will tell you all about it afterwards."

"I want to go swimming!" Trevor's shout rose above the noise of the café.

Josh said something to his son, but Trevor shook his head and banged his hand on the table. A tantrum was coming.

Lara spoke, and the boy glared at her before saying

something that made Lara stiffen and lean back. Her hand clenched into a fist.

Darcy moved his chair back and Faith covered his hand again. "Give it a minute," she said. "She needs to figure out this new relationship with them without you barging in."

His muscles relaxed when Lara's hand relaxed. He blew out a breath.

"Siblings don't always get along," Faith reminded him. "And a child his age won't quite comprehend how he's suddenly got an older step-sister. It will take time for them to get to know each other."

Sofia patted Lara's hand and gestured to the drink, which Lara quickly finished. Then the family stood. Lara hurried over to him. "We're going swimming. Is that all right, Dad?"

Sofia should be the one asking him, even if he had mentioned Lara was bringing her bathers.

"Come on, Lara," Sofia called.

"Do you want to go?" he asked.

She nodded, though the concern in her eyes showed she wasn't convinced.

Sofia came over.

"Where are you going?"

She sighed and gestured outside. "Just down there. You can take our table if you want to spy."

Annoyance made him press his lips together. Just because Sofia was Lara's mother, it didn't mean she was experienced at taking care of a child and he wasn't risking his daughter. "I'll get your towel out of the car," he told Lara.

Sofia seemed surprised and then said, "Thanks." She held Lara's hand and led her out of the café.

"Sofia seems as nervous as you," Faith commented.

His annoyance faded with her observation. Neither one knew what to do. He needed to remember that.

"I'll be back."

Faith stood with her drink and cake. "There's a table out the front under the umbrella."

He smiled at her. "Thank you."

By the time he delivered the towel to Lara, Josh and the boys were already in the water and Lara had stripped to her bathers.

"Are you coming, Mum?" Lara asked.

Sofia shook her head. "No, I don't swim."

Lara stared at her. "I can teach you."

Sofia laughed. "I can swim, baby. I choose not to."

"But it's hot and the water's lovely."

"I don't like the saltwater," she said. "Join the others." She waved towards the water.

Lara glanced at the ocean. "I'll stay here with you, if you'd like company."

So generous. Perhaps Sofia didn't realise what a sacrifice the offer was for Lara. "No. I'm fine. I need to speak to your dad."

Darcy stiffened and then nodded at Lara. "Go on, pumpkin. It looks like fun." Josh was throwing his boys in the water.

She grinned. "OK."

Darcy waited until she was in the water before he asked Sofia, "What's up?"

"There's a movie playing in town tomorrow night and we'd like to take Lara with us."

He shook his head. "She's already got plans. She's going to the movies with her friend and then sleeping over."

Sofia flung her hair over her shoulder. "Surely she can cancel. It's not every day I'm in town."

Darcy raised his eyebrows. "No, it's not, but you can't expect Lara or me to jump to your bidding because you graced us with your presence."

"I'm only here a week."

"Yeah, and if you'd given me some notice, I would have made sure Lara was available. But she's made a commitment to her friend and breaking a commitment because something else comes along is not a behaviour I want to encourage." When Sofia pouted, he added, "She's had a rough time since her grandparents died. This is the first sleepover she's had, and it's important for her confidence that she do this."

Sofia placed a hand on his arm. "I was sorry to hear about your parents. They were always so kind to me."

He nodded, not wanting to bring up those emotions now.

"Maybe Lara can come out to Turquoise Bay with us on Saturday." Sofia continued.

"I usually pick her up from her friend's mid-morning."

"We wanted to get out there before the crowds."

No consideration for what was best for Lara. "She'll be tired from the sleepover anyway." In the water Josh was still throwing his boys around and Lara hovered nearby as if waiting for her turn. "How about you bring Josh and the boys out to the station on Sunday? The kids can go for a ride, pet the animals and go swimming in the bay. I'm sure Lara would love to show you her barrel racing skills."

Sofia's mouth dropped open. "Is that dangerous?"

He chuckled. "You've been away too long, Sofia. She learnt to ride almost before she could walk and now she takes lessons from Faith." He glanced over his shoulder to where Faith sat under the umbrella waiting. It felt so good for her to have his back.

"I'll talk to Josh about it."

Josh still hadn't included Lara in the game he played with his boys. She glanced towards the shore at him. Hell. He wouldn't let her feel left out. He should have brought some bathers, but he hadn't wanted to intrude.

"Is there a reason your husband is ignoring Lara?"

"He's got a bad back. Lara's too big for him to throw."

"There are other ways to include her." Would that be Lara's life if she spent time with her mother? He stripped off his hat and T-shirt and pried off his boots and socks.

"What are you doing?" Sofia asked.

"You might want to waste this time with Lara, but I don't." Without another word, he jogged towards the ocean. Lara's huge grin was all he needed as he waded in up to his knees.

"Dad! You're in jeans."

He shrugged. "They'll dry."

She swam over to him and he met her halfway, the water up to his waist. Swimming in jeans was not pleasant. Josh frowned at him. "Think you can throw the boys further than I can throw Lara?" He cupped his hands and Lara placed her foot in it. "One, two, three." On three he pushed, and Lara backflipped into the water. She came up laughing.

"That was awesome."

Darcy glanced at Josh, whose boys were demanding he flip them like that.

That would teach him to ignore Darcy's girl.

Chapter 8

Faith fanned herself with a napkin as she watched a half-naked Darcy throw his daughter into the water. The afternoon's heat had nothing to do with why she was so hot. Nothing was sexier than a man who cared that much for his daughter.

She'd been watching Lara grow more and more despondent as her stepfather ignored her. Sofia hadn't seemed to notice, but then again, she'd been having an intense conversation with Darcy. It wasn't easy for either of them, but Faith was Team Darcy all the way.

The way the water glistened as his back muscles bunched and he launched his daughter into the air. Those wet jeans moulding to his butt.

"Nice view, isn't it?"

Faith jolted, glancing at the speaker and smiled. "Sure is." Dot held a take-away coffee and wore her police uniform. "Coffee break?"

"Yeah, needed a top up." Dot's gaze didn't leave the beach.

A little frisson of jealousy skittered down her spine. "You interested?" She liked Dot. They had fallen into an easy friendship when Dot had started taking the adult horse-riding classes Faith offered.

Dot laughed. "Not like that. Darcy fell into the friend zone when I dated Brandon in high school," she said. "But I can still appreciate a body like his." Her radio squawked with instructions of where she was needed. She sighed. "I'd better get back to it. See you Saturday."

Faith waved and when she returned her gaze to the beach, she found Sofia walking towards her. "Are you Darcy's girlfriend?" she asked.

"We're friends," she replied, holding out her hand. "I'm Faith."

Sofia shook it and sat under the shade. "The horse-riding instructor?"

Lara must have mentioned her. "Yes."

The woman sighed as she shifted her chair so she faced the ocean. "I used to hate how Darcy had so many female friends at school," she said. "He was so charming and all my friends fancied him."

"How old were you when you had Lara?" She'd figured they must have got married quite young.

Sofia seemed surprised by the question. "Seventeen."

Wow. Practically a baby herself. "Were you in the same class?"

She nodded. "Hasn't Darcy told you?"

"No. It's none of my business."

Lara's laughter rang out over the beach. Sofia sighed. "I knew he would be a great dad," she said. "It was the one thing I didn't fear when I left. He adored our child from the moment he held her in his arms." Sofia looked at her. "My only thought was I finally had my body back."

It was difficult not to judge, but Faith tried. She'd never been pregnant, but her friends and sisters-in-law either loved or hated the experience.

"My plans after high school had never included having a baby and staying in the Bay, but when I got pregnant, Darcy painted such an idyllic picture of our life together. Reality was nothing like his image." Sofia studied her. "I'm not telling you this for sympathy, but so you know I understand how my choices appear. Seeing Josh with his boys awakened a desire to meet my daughter and she's so very sweet."

"Do you want her to live with you?"

"I want what's best for her." Sofia hesitated. "I'm not sure what that is yet."

The woman was blind if she couldn't see Darcy was best for Lara. They still played in the water and Darcy even threw the twins around, much to their delight. "How long are you in town for?"

"Until Monday. Darcy's invited us to the Ridge on Sunday."

"I'm sure the boys will enjoy it."

She nodded. "Probably. I don't know them very well. They spend most of their time with their mother."

Faith wanted to know more. "Have you been married long?"

"Almost six months. It was a whirlwind romance." Sofia smiled. "He literally bumped into me on the street. Spilt coffee down my blouse and then insisted on taking me into the nearest store to buy a new one." She waited for Faith's reaction, so Faith said, "Cute."

"It was."

Sofia struck Faith as a woman who needed to be the centre of attention, who had to have the ideal life. Testing the theory, she said, "Lara's doing well at pony club. She's a natural at barrel racing."

"Is she? Horse-riding never appealed to me, though some of my friends loved it."

Faith waited for a follow up question about Lara, but it didn't come.

"What do you do in Melbourne?"

"I used to be a receptionist, but Josh earns the money now. I play tennis and organise a book club."

Maybe they had something in common. "What do you read?"

"We're working our way through the Stella shortlist at the moment."

Faith preferred a good romance to literary fiction.

They sat in silence watching the antics in the water and Faith relaxed, breathing in the fresh, salty air. She enjoyed the more laid-back lifestyle in Retribution Bay. She hadn't realised how the long work weeks had drained her until she didn't have to face them anymore. Caring for her mother had had other challenges, but she liked having time for her own interests.

The idea of staying here equally thrilled and scared her. It was so like her father, embracing a new life without considering the practicalities it involved. She'd worked hard to become a lawyer at one of the top law firms in Perth. She'd be able to slot back in when she returned.

Whenever that was.

Back to starting work at seven and not getting home until way after dark, as well as working from home most weekends. She sighed.

Her mother went on the boat every second day now, and when she was at home, she visited her friends. She still couldn't drive, might not ever be able to, but it was a short walk from their house to the shopping area and Faith was happy to drive her around.

Was Faith needed as a carer any longer? Faith had a sneaky suspicion she was actually glad her father still insisted on it, because it gave her a chance to delay making the decision about returning to Perth.

When she'd first arrived, she'd been so caught up in her mother's rehabilitation she hadn't had a moment to think, but when she had, she'd realised she hadn't missed the city. She'd missed the challenge of writing a well-structured contract, but since she'd started volunteering at the pony club, and working on the occasional legal matter for people in town, even that had faded.

Her phone rang and when she saw the caller, she excused herself to answer it. Walking away from the table she said, "Hey, Donna. What have you got for me?" She'd called in a favour with one of her colleagues who had access to a couple of databases Faith couldn't access from here.

"Stonefish is huge, Faith. I wouldn't go up against them without a hefty legal team behind you."

Not the news she wanted to hear, but she'd been expecting it.

"Based in Singapore but with links in China and all over south-east Asia and the south Pacific," Donna continued. "I've emailed you the details I could find. You want to send the initial letter to the subsidiary company I've highlighted but if you get no response, take it up the chain."

She knew how it worked. "Thanks."

"Henry says if you want to use the firm's letterhead, you have to charge our rates. Without a law firm behind you, you won't have much clout."

Her boss, Henry was ruthless. "Yeah. I know. Not much I can do about it. The family can't afford it."

"You always were a bleeding heart, chicky. I've missed you at our boozy Friday drinks."

Faith felt a twinge of guilt. She hadn't missed those at all. Her colleagues had used Friday night to blow off steam and get plastered, while Faith stayed sober so she didn't feel like crap if she went riding Saturday morning.

"When are you coming back?"

Faith grimaced. "Not sure yet. Mum's getting better,

but it's still early days."

"It's been eight months."

"Yeah, well rehabilitation takes time."

Donna lowered her voice. "Just so you know, Henry's making noises about hiring someone new. You might want to get your butt back here sooner rather than later, or you might not have a job to come back to."

Damn it. "Thanks for the warning."

"Any time. Call me if you need anything else. I've got to go, my next client just arrived." Donna hung up. Life at the firm was like that. Each minute recorded so a fee could be allocated to it. Faith had hated it. But something Donna said resonated with her. She needed a law firm name behind her. No way Darcy could afford her firm's rates, but did she have another option?

She scanned the area. The blue ocean sparkled in front of her as the sun edged towards the horizon behind her. Tourists and locals alike sat in the café enjoying the warm weather and tasty food. While she'd been here, her parents' friends had asked her to review a contract or talk about a legal issue they had.

Could Retribution Bay sustain a law firm of one?

Would she be satisfied with the kind of work she would deal with? She wasn't interested in criminal law, but she could do contracts and estate planning. And if the work wasn't there, she could explore expanding the pony club and her idea of trail rides. Would it be too much to juggle two new businesses?

Did she really want to stay?

Darcy and Lara walked out of the water, done for the day. Darcy brushed his wet hair out of his face, and the grin he gave his daughter made her own heart flutter. He'd be another reason to stay, but he couldn't be the only one. She wouldn't be happy without her own job and her own challenges.

Sofia had returned to the towels and handed them to Josh and his children.

Faith wandered over, taking her damp beach towel from her beach bag. She gave it to Darcy. "It's a bit wet still."

"Thanks. I appreciate it." He rubbed it against his chest and she looked away. She might never wash it again.

"Did you enjoy your swim?" Faith asked Lara.

"It was nice." She wrapped the large beach towel around herself. Sofia was talking to Josh.

Darcy spoke in a low voice. "Are you ready to go home, pumpkin?"

Lara glanced at her mother and then nodded.

He put his T-shirt and hat back on and collected his boots and socks. "We'd better head off."

Sofia nodded. "What time should we come on Sunday?"

"It's nicest early in the morning—say eight o'clock."

"All right."

Darcy placed a hand on Lara's shoulder. "Do you remember the way?"

"Yes."

"Bye, Mum." Lara stepped forward to hug Sofia, but Sofia held her at a distance.

"You're all wet, baby." She air-kissed Lara's cheeks.

Faith heard Darcy's grunt of disbelief. Lara slipped her hand into Darcy's and Faith walked with them across the sand to the car park. Lara dumped her things in the back seat of the ute and then climbed in the front, staring out the window.

Darcy sighed.

"Give it time," Faith suggested. "It won't be easy for any of you."

"I know." He turned to her. "Thanks for coming today."

"Any time." She hugged him and kissed his cheek. He turned his head, their faces only inches apart. Heat shot straight to her core. Kissing his lips would take this to the next level and would be difficult to come back from. The temptation was so strong. She stepped back, glanced down, swallowing hard, and then smiled at him. "I've, ah, got an update on the contract," she said. "When you've got time, I'd like to go through it with you in person."

"How about tomorrow night?" he suggested. "We could do dinner in town."

She shook her head and noted the disappointment cross his face. "Tomorrow night would be great, but we should discuss the details in private."

"Lara's got a sleepover at her friend's place," Darcy said. "You could come out to the Ridge and share the details with Brandon too. If we finish late, you can bunk in the shearers' quarters."

She'd rather bunk with him. "All right. What time?"

"How about six?"

"Great." She waited on the footpath while he climbed into the ute and drove off.

It was definitely time for her to consider her priorities and what she wanted next in life.

Because Darcy was definitely on the want list.

Darcy was changing the oil on the ute when the radio inside crackled. "Darce, are you there?"

He grunted as he shuffled out from under the car and reached in through the open window to answer. "Yeah, Ames. What's up?"

"I've got Joan on the phone. She said Lara didn't come home with Mischa."

He jolted. Had she been injured? No, the school would have called. Had she been kidnapped? No, Retribution Bay was safe—except with Stonefish around. Fear froze his voice, as sweat sprang to his skin, but Amy continued. "Mischa told her Sofia had picked her up. Did you know about that?"

Relief made him slump against the doorframe, and he swore ripely. "No." He gasped for air. Lara was all right. Then the enormity of what Sofia had done filled him with fury. "I'll be right in." How dare she take Lara! He'd told her Lara wasn't available. He ran for the house, and Amy met him at the door with the phone. He snatched it from her. "Joan?"

"Darcy, I'm so sorry. What do you want me to do?"

His brain was stuck on the fact he didn't know exactly where his daughter was. "Can I ask Mischa about the woman who picked Lara up?" Lara wouldn't have gone with a stranger. He was almost certain of that.

"Sure." He heard her telling Mischa to explain what happened.

"Hello?" The tremble in the girl's voice made Darcy take a deep breath before speaking.

"Hey, Mischa. Your mum tells me Sofia picked Lara up from school. Can you describe her for me?"

"She was fancy," Mischa answered. "Such pretty blonde hair and she wore a summer dress with yellow flowers on it and really big high heels."

Sounded like Sofia. "And what did she say to Lara?"

"She said you agreed she could take Lara shopping for a new dress before the movies. She's going to drop Lara off by five."

Darcy bit down on his growl. "OK. Thanks, Misch. Can you put your mum back on?"

"You OK?" Joan asked.

"No. I'll call Sofia now. I'll call you back." He hung up, his hand shaking.

Amy pressed him into a chair. "Take a second to calm the anger, Darcy. Sofia was wrong, but yelling at her isn't going to help matters."

It was a damned good thing Sofia wasn't in front of him right now…

Amy placed a glass of water on the table. "Drink."

His whole body vibrated with rage. That brief moment of thinking Stonefish could have taken his girl was etched in his brain. He sipped the water, trying to control the tremble. He closed his eyes.

"Do you want me to call her?"

He nodded. Nothing he said to Sofia would come out well. He watched while Amy dialled Sofia's number. After a minute, she hung up. "No answer."

The fear crept into his soul again. "Let me find her parents' number." He leapt to his feet to find his mother's address book which lived by the phone.

The phone rang and Amy answered. "Hi, Faith. Yeah, he's right here."

He didn't have time to speak to her, but Amy pressed the phone into his hand and took the address book from his other one. "Faith, can I call you back?" He winced at the harshness of his tone.

"Oh. Sure. I just wanted to tell you I ran into Lara just now—"

"Where?" he blurted.

"I'm at the shopping centre with Mum. Lara's shopping with Sofia, but when I said I thought she was having a sleepover with Mischa, she mentioned it was a surprise." Faith paused. "I know it's probably none of my business, but I wanted to make sure you knew about it."

He exhaled. "I didn't. Joan just rang me to tell me Lara hadn't come home with Mischa."

Faith gasped.

He closed his eyes as his pulse slowed. "Thank you for calling. Can you still see them? Sofia's not answering her phone."

"She went into the newsagency. I can go in if you want."

"Please. I need to speak with her."

"Give me a minute."

Darcy waited, willing himself to be calm when he spoke. He heard Faith speak to Sofia and then Sofia say, "Sweetness, why don't you tell your dad what a great time you're having?"

Lara came onto the phone. "Dad! This is the best surprise ever! Mum's bought me a new dress for the movies, and we're going to get our nails done. Just us girls."

He gritted his teeth as her joy radiated down the phone. How could he disappoint her? He kept his tone light. "Sounds great. Are you still going to Mischa's at five?"

"Yeah. Of course."

"Can I speak to your mum now?"

"Sure. Love you!"

The scuffle of sounds as the phone was passed back to Sofia. "Darcy, we're having such a wonderful time." She laughed.

He clenched his hand. "If you *ever* pull a stunt like this again, I will have you arrested for kidnapping."

"Darcy, don't be so upset." She'd lowered her voice and placated. "It's not a big deal. I just wanted to spend some mother-daughter time with Lara."

"You have no fucking idea," he growled. "For a few very long minutes, I had no idea where she was. That terrified me."

She gasped. "But how did you know?"

"Because Mischa's mother, Joan is a decent human being. She knows I would have *never* changed plans without telling her, and so she called when Lara didn't turn up after school."

"But Mischa knew she was with me. Honestly,

Darcy, you need to know when to let go. I'll be spending more time with my daughter from now on."

What did she mean by that? She lived in Melbourne, she could hardly pop in for a visit every weekend. Unless she wanted custody... The fear returned and he lashed out. "Have Lara back at Mischa's at five o'clock exactly, or I *will* call the police." He hung up before she could argue otherwise.

"Darcy—" Amy began.

He thrust the phone at her. "Call Joan and tell her Lara will be there at five. If she isn't, to call me back. I need air."

He strode out of the house.

***

Darcy fought to let go of his animosity towards Sofia as he dressed for dinner Friday night. Joan had called at five to say Lara was with her, and a few minutes later, Sofia had texted to say sorry.

He reminded himself she didn't know about Stonefish, and she'd grown up in the Bay where kids often roamed the town after school without their parents knowing exactly where they were.

He clutched his aftershave bottle in a death grip, and slowly placed it on his dresser. It was over. Lara was safe, and Faith would arrive in twenty minutes.

Nerves helped to push the remaining anger away. He hadn't spoken to Faith after he'd hung up, had needed time to cool down and by the time he had, she would have been on the way to the Ridge and out of reception.

He was fairly sure she would understand, and he was looking forward to seeing her. That moment on the beach yesterday when she'd kissed his cheek, and he'd been so close to kissing her had stuck in his brain.

The only thing stopping him was his daughter in the

front seat and his fear it would give Sofia ammunition to take Lara from him.

He shook his head. Don't think about Sofia.

He towel-dried his hair a final time and checked the mirror. His best jeans were still in the wash after their impromptu dip in the ocean, but these black jeans looked all right. The simple grey T-shirt showed off his lean muscles. He was as ready as he would ever be.

In the kitchen, Amy tossed together a salad.

"Need a hand, Ames?" he asked.

"Nope, all sorted here. Steaks are marinating in the fridge and the potatoes are almost done. All we need are drinks, but I'll wait until Faith arrives to see if she wants to share a bottle of wine."

He stood by the table, not sure what to do. If he went outside, he'd get sweaty and it wasn't the look he wanted. His gaze caught on the Akubra hat. What had Amy called it—his sexy cowboy look? He needed all the help he could get. He reached for it and Amy laughed. "Leave it off, cowboy. Let her see your pretty face."

He rolled his eyes and turned to her. "Yesterday you said to wear it."

"That was when you had to show your clueless ex what she was missing," Amy said. "Tonight, you're trying to charm Faith and you can do it better if she can see your eyes."

"She's coming out to help us with Stonefish."

"Sure she is." Amy pursed her lips, failing to hide her smile. "That's why you've showered and put on aftershave."

His face heated, as his brother walked in, still scruffy from the day's work. "Who are you trying to impress?"

Darcy shook his head. As pleased as he was that his brother was back, he didn't need the teasing right now.

"Faith," Amy answered for him.

Brandon grinned at him. "The pony club instructor,

huh? Nice work."

"Shut up, Bran." The sound of a car outside gave him an excuse to leave. Faith pulled up behind the house. Bennet barked, and Darcy hushed him as Faith opened the door and her long, tanned, naked legs exited wearing some pretty black sandals. The rest of her followed, and he almost swallowed his tongue. He hadn't seen her in a dress before. It was sleeveless with a neckline which showed her plump cleavage. The cut tapered to her waist before the skirt fell to just above her knees. The bright red colour made him think of roses. She waved and then bent to get something out of the backseat, giving him a nice view of her backside.

Kicking himself mentally, he strode over to help. "Drive out was OK?"

"Yeah, no problems." She shut the door, tucking a thick folder under her arm. "Are you all right after this afternoon? Amy called me back to explain."

He'd have to thank Amy. He blew out a breath. "Yeah, but let's not talk about it otherwise it'll just make me angry again."

"Sure."

They walked back to the house and Amy crossed to give Faith a hug. "It's great to see you again," Amy said. "Put the folder on the bench and we can go through it after dinner. We're waiting on Brandon," she continued. "Darcy, why don't you take Faith up to the dunes to watch the sunset?" She was all innocence as she added, "It's so breath-taking. You don't want to miss it." She handed Darcy an insulated backpack with drinks in it.

Darcy smothered his smile at her smooth moves. "Would you like to?"

"Ah, sure. Is what I'm wearing all right?"

"Yeah. The path isn't rough." If he'd been less distracted by Sofia's antics, he might have thought of taking Faith up there himself. The red sand dunes were located to the east of the property only a ten-minute walk away. They offered a slightly elevated view over the station across to the Ridge. The Ridge would have been a better spot to take her if they had time, but the sun was already low in the sky.

"What did you get up to today?" Darcy asked.

"Before we went grocery shopping, Mum and I spent the day cleaning out cupboards. She's decided to go through everything they've accumulated over the years."

"She's mobile enough?"

"Yeah. She's just a little slower than she was."

"That's great." Did it mean Faith wouldn't be staying for much longer? How could he get an answer without being obvious about it? "Do you miss Perth?"

"Not as much as I expected to," she admitted. "At first there was too much to do helping Mum with her exercises and keeping the house running." She glanced at him. "I miss the challenge of the work, but I've had more opportunity to ride my horse here in the past couple of months than I did all of last year."

They reached the start of the dunes and he took her elbow to help her up them. The sand was firmer than beach sand, but too dusty to take off her sandals. At the top he let go and she turned in a circle, surveying his land. "It really is beautiful," she said. "You're so lucky to live here."

He studied her. Not many people thought that. They saw the red dirt and dry scrub and considered it hell on earth. Sofia had. But there was nothing in Faith's expression which made him think she was lying. "I always thought so."

"You've lived here all your life?"

"Yeah. Stokes have lived on this land for over a hundred and fifty years."

Faith nodded. "That's right. The Retribution."

He smiled. "Lara loves the story, though I've caught her adding her own embellishments."

"So the mutiny and the flood never happened?"

"They happened from all reports. It was a cyclone which forced the ship into the gulf, and it crashed on the reef around the island. They managed to save some items from the ship and some livestock, but after they got on the mainland, there was a mutiny, and many were killed before the culprits were hanged."

"And after all of that, there was another cyclone and a flash flood?"

"Information is sketchy," Darcy told her. "There was definitely a flood, but it might not have been caused by a cyclone." He pointed to an area where gum trees were bunched together. "When we get rain, that becomes a river. The low land over there becomes a wetland for a short while and if the rain comes down really heavily, we get a flash flood in the valley by the ridge."

"Sounds dangerous."

Darcy shrugged. "The house and yards are built in an area away from the flood plains, and we have plenty of warning from the weatherman to make sure the stock is on high ground. There are showers forecast for next week, so we're monitoring the situation."

"It's hard to imagine," Faith said. "The ground is so dusty and dry. It doesn't look as if it ever rains here. Why anyone would decide it was the ideal place to set up a station is beyond me."

The words hit him like a punch. For a moment he'd thought she understood the appeal, but he'd been wrong. "We should get back to dinner."

"But the sun hasn't gone down yet." She turned to him, the blonde streaks in her hair picking up the sun. She frowned. "I've upset you." Taking his hand, she said, "What did I say?"

"It doesn't matter." He gave a self-depreciating smile. "I've got issues."

"It does to me. I don't want to hurt you."

Darcy ran his hand through his hair, wishing he had his hat on so he could pull it low over his face.

Faith moved closer, inside his personal bubble, but he had no desire to step away. "In case you hadn't noticed, I like you, Darcy."

The words cracked the plating he'd placed around his heart. Her blue eyes stared earnestly up into his. He couldn't resist the pull. Slowly, he lowered his head. "I like you too." His lips brushed hers. Warm, soft. She pulled him closer, and he wrapped his arms around her, needing to touch, to hold. Her tongue touched his lips, and he opened for her, dancing, taking the kiss deeper. His body sprang alive. Even after a dry spell longer than an Australian drought, he couldn't ever remember kissing being this good, this encompassing. His hands roamed over her bottom, pulling her against him, and she gasped.

"Darcy."

The way she said his name made him feel like a hero. He wanted to lay her down on the sand and touch every inch of her. The thought reminded him where they were. Sand rash wouldn't be pretty. Reluctantly he pulled back, breathing heavily, and rested his forehead against hers.

"Wow," she said.

"Wow," he agreed.

They stood in silence for a moment before Faith said, "Lara's having a sleepover tonight, isn't she?"

"She is." He smiled. "You want to have our own sleepover?" He held his breath, hoping that was what she was hinting at.

"I'd love to." She kissed him again and then turned

towards the sun, which was halfway below the horizon, and slipped her hand into his. "You haven't told me what I said to upset you."

It took him a moment to remember, and he rubbed the back of his neck. "It's really not a big deal."

She lifted her eyebrows. "Then tell me."

He slid his arm around her waist, needing her comfort. "It was what you said about this land not being ideal for a station. Sofia hated it here, the dust and the heat. It was one of the reasons she left, and it's kind of a sore spot."

"I don't hate the land," Faith said. "But I was picturing it from your ancestors' point of view. They came from England, right—land of green hills and rain. This," she gestured around, "is about as far from the mother country as you can get. When they arrived, nothing would have been here, no buildings, no town, no roads. It would have been a huge culture shock and a massive gamble, particularly if they'd lost stock and supplies in the wreck."

He hadn't considered it from that point of view before. It gave him a lot more respect for his ancestors.

"I like this land, Darcy. I've always preferred warmer weather, and the harshness has a beauty all of its own." In the fading light, her eyes shone with sincerity.

"OK." He kissed her again, long and slow, and then took her hand. The sun was below the horizon with only its final rays giving a last farewell to the day. "We seem to have missed most of the sunset."

"Maybe you can show me the sunrise tomorrow." She smiled at him.

Yeah, he'd like to do that. Perhaps they could even go for an early morning ride if he could convince Brandon to do the morning chores. "We'd better get back before we lose all the light. It does get dark out here when there's no moon."

Hand in hand, they descended the dune and walked along the path back to the homestead. It was fully dark by the time they arrived, but the light on the porch was a beacon. Brandon stood in the garden cooking meat on the barbecue. He raised his tongs in greeting as they walked in. "I figured you wouldn't be long after sunset. Grab a drink and I'll be in soon."

Darcy had become used to his older brother being home, but every now and then it hit him that Brandon was back for good. This was one of those times. He rubbed his chest as he opened the kitchen door for Faith. Amy grinned at them. "Had a nice walk?"

"Yeah." He turned to Faith, who gasped and then laughed.

"You've got a bit of lipstick there." She rubbed around his mouth.

No wonder Amy was grinning at him. "Maybe I like it there," he said, pulling Faith close. "I think I need some right here." He caught her lips with his, swallowing her gasp of surprise.

When he pulled away, Amy said, "We've got beer and wine." She showed Faith the bottle.

"A glass of wine might be nice."

He'd forgotten about the drinks Amy had packed for their walk. He returned them to the fridge and got himself a bottle of beer.

Brandon brought the meat in and set it on the long table. Only four settings were out. "Where's Matt?" Darcy asked.

"Gone into town. I think he has a date, but he wouldn't admit to it," Amy said. "He's staying with his parents this weekend." She raised her glass. "We need to toast," she said. "To new friendships." She clinked her glass with Faith.

That was something he could get behind. "To new friendships."

Chapter 9

Dinner was a friendly, chatty affair with Amy and Brandon talking about their upcoming wedding as well as asking Faith about the pony club. Through it all, Darcy sat by Faith's side and his presence made it difficult for her to focus on the conversation. Her thoughts constantly went back to their kiss.

She hadn't been expecting it, had been bowled over by the intensity and passion. She'd been tempted to rip his clothes off. But she could wait for tonight. She'd sent her parents a message to say she was staying at the Ridge so she didn't have to drive home in the dark. It was a good excuse, but she doubted she fooled either of them.

Faith helped clear the table and do the dishes and then Brandon said, "You want to tell us what you've found?"

She'd forgotten about the point of her visit. Darcy was a great distraction. She retrieved the folder from the bench and carried it over to the table, flipping it open. "Don't get too excited," she warned. "The biggest issue is there's not a lot of proof linking Stonefish to the company Darcy bought the cattle from."

"But they bought the domain name," Brandon said.

"Someone used their name when buying a domain name," she corrected. "That's probably the defence they will use."

Amy got up to put the kettle on and then said, "Do we need whisky for this?"

Faith chuckled. "Tea is fine. I spoke with a colleague and she sent me some details about Stonefish. They're a vast company with a lot of money behind them. They have the time and the funds to drag this out."

"We can't afford that," Darcy said. "With them slaughtering so many sheep and our funds low, we might not survive the season."

She squeezed his knee. It was worse than she'd thought. "What about a loan from the bank?"

Brandon shook his head. "They refused."

All three of them looked at her as if praying she had an answer. She hated to disappoint them. "From all reports, Stonefish values their reputation. Any time there is a hint of a scandal, it's swept under the rug or they make a show of hunting down which part of the business is responsible and then fixing it." It wasn't how she normally operated, but it might be their only choice. "I'll send an official letter stating a breach of the contract terms and requesting an immediate refund of your money. According to the contract, they have seven days to respond to the letter."

"But you've said they'll draw it out," Brandon said.

She nodded. "We then put a claim in with the Australian Competition and Consumer Commission. Stonefish don't want to be on their radar. If that doesn't work, we go to social media. The Aussie battler, the poor farmer who has been taken advantage of by the big corporation, will be a story no reporter will want to miss." She wasn't sure how they'd feel about that.

"Won't it make us look bad?" Brandon asked. "We're relying on tourists to keep the money flowing in and this might cause them to stay away."

Amy spoke. "We can spin it to our advantage. Show how we're still managing even though times are hard. Welcoming people in." She glanced at him. "We could arrange some kind of fund-raiser. How about a Bachelor and Spinster ball?" She clicked her pen and began writing notes. "We'd need a band, lighting, more toilets, food and drink. People could stay the night in the shearers' quarters, or camp in the sheep pens."

Brandon got up to finish making the tea. Faith smiled. "That's something we can consider, but the first step is the letter to Stonefish."

"If you write it, we'll sign and send it," Darcy said.

She shook her head. "It has more weight if it's signed and sent from a lawyer."

"You aren't practising," he countered.

His concern warmed her. "It doesn't matter. It will make them sit up and take notice."

Darcy squeezed her hand. "No. It will just put you on their radar."

She chuckled. "I'm used to big companies not liking me." She thanked Brandon as he placed the mugs of tea on the table and then took his seat.

"I'm worried what they might do to scare you off," Darcy admitted.

"They know nothing about me," she said. "No point going after the messenger." She tried to sound more confident than she felt. "It will be fine."

He scowled.

"I don't like it any better than you do," Brandon said. "But it's us they're after, not Faith. She can't give them what they want."

Faith cleared her throat before asking what she'd been so curious about. "Why do they want the station so badly?"

"We can't figure it out," Darcy said. "One guy said they had a connection to the Retribution but then wasn't interested in the history I offered to share with him."

She chewed on her lip. "Could there be something valuable on the land—a mineral deposit or something?"

Brandon shook his head. "They surveyed the land in the sixties and found nothing of real value."

"Do you have a map?" It wasn't likely she'd spot anything.

"Yeah." Darcy left the kitchen and returned a few minutes later with a large A2 sized map of the property. A red line marked the border which stretched almost the entire way to the coast in the west, with access to the bay in the north.

"Are there any towns on the east side of the gulf?"

"No. Closest is Onslow."

She studied the map, but nothing unusual stood out to her. "What about the rumours of buried treasure Lara told me about?"

Darcy smiled. "She made those up."

"Could someone have thought they were true?"

He shook his head. "I doubt it. Besides, there's so much land, they could look for it and we probably wouldn't know they were there."

Good point. She handed Darcy the draft letter she'd written. "With your permission, I'll email the letter to Stonefish tomorrow and also post a registered letter to their head office."

After Darcy read it, he handed it to Brandon. "Can't anyone else send it?"

"No. If they decide to follow up, they need to contact me."

"We'll tell Dot what we're doing," Brandon said. "She's as involved in this as we are."

Having the police aware of the circumstances was comforting. "So do I send it?"

Amy squeezed Brandon's hand and nodded. Brandon and Darcy exchanged a glance, and Darcy huffed. "All right. But you need to keep alert."

She smiled at him. "I'm either with Mum or I'm at the pony club. It will be fine."

Amy pushed back her chair. "Thanks for your help, Faith." She placed a hand on Brandon's shoulder. "You'll discover farmers are early to bed, early to rise, and we're off to bed."

Brandon glanced up at her as if surprised and then stood. "Yeah, of course."

It wasn't subtle, but soon she was alone with Darcy and nerves tickled her belly. She gathered the empty mugs and took them to the sink to wash. Darcy dried them and then asked, "Do you still want to stay the night? I can make up the bed in Ed's old room if you don't want to stay in mine."

Such a gentleman. She couldn't resist him. Sliding her hands around his waist, she pulled him close, the memory of their kiss at the front of her mind. "I'd very much like to stay in yours." She kissed him, giving him no room to misinterpret what she wanted. His hands squeezed her butt, pressing her up against his erection.

"Good," he murmured, taking her hand and leading her down a corridor. She paid little attention to the rooms they passed, but she heard the sound of a shower down the opposite end of the house. He flicked on a light and pulled her into his bedroom.

Masculine and minimalist. A navy-blue bedspread and matching pillows covered the queen-sized bed. No clothes on the floor, but a shirt lay over a jarrah tallboy and a bunch of childish drawings had been framed and hung on the wall.

That was all Faith took in before Darcy shut the

door and pulled her back into his arms and kissed her. "I want you so much it hurts."

The admission sent a shot of lust through her. "I've been fantasising about you since the first time we met." She slipped her hands under his T-shirt and pushed it towards his neck. He stepped away to shed it and then he stood there in all his naked man chest glory. She hummed in appreciation, running her hands over his firm pecs.

The zip at the back of her dress crackled as he slid it down and then pushed the straps off her shoulders. She stepped out of it, toeing out of her sandals, pleased she'd opted for her matching white bra and pantie set tonight.

"You're so beautiful, Faith." Before gathering her into his arms again, he took off his shoes. Then he cupped her face in his hands as if she was precious and kissed her.

She was drowning in sensation. The warmth travelled through her body, setting her on fire. She hooked one leg around his waist to drag him closer. She wanted to consume him.

The buckle of his belt pressed into her and she shifted, slipping her hands between them to unbuckle it and his black jeans. Her bra loosened as his hands swept across her back, and then he bent to take one breast into his mouth.

Her head fell back. "Yes, Darcy."

He shifted her around, backing her towards the bed, pressing kisses against her neck. When her legs hit the edge, she scrambled on to it and he stripped off his jeans and underwear.

Holy moly. The naked Darcy was more than she'd ever imagined. Firm lean muscles and a cock which stood to attention, capturing her gaze. She slipped her hand around it and took him into her mouth. His swear words sounded more like a prayer of thanks. She smiled as she licked him, liking his fresh musky taste.

With a groan, Darcy pulled away and then pushed her back onto the bed. "My turn."

His wicked grin flipped her heart. He lowered to his knees and ran his hands over her thighs, caressing and then following the touch with a path of kisses, slowly getting closer to her core. She squirmed, wanting him to hurry and not wanting him to stop.

Finally his lips brushed her clitoris, and she moaned.

"Did I hit the right spot?" Darcy asked, a picture of devilish innocence.

"Yes. More."

He responded, giving her the attention she craved as her arousal built. "Darcy, please. I need you inside me."

He gave one last lick which almost sent her over the edge then took a condom out of a drawer and slid it on. He covered her body with his, kissing her until she forgot her name. Then he slid inside her with a sigh. "Faith."

She clung to him as he thrust, shifting a little so he rubbed the right place. Their movements sped until her orgasm shattered over her and he called her name again in release.

***

It was dark when Darcy woke, as it was every morning, but today something was different. He wasn't alone. He smiled and shifted, unable to resist snuggling into Faith before he started the day. Last night could have been a dream if she wasn't here next to him.

Faith mumbled something in her sleep.

He didn't want her to wake alone and be uncomfortable in his house. "Faith, honey. I need to feed the animals, but I'll be back in a couple of hours."

Her voice was full of sleep. "It's dark."

"Sun will be up by the time I finish breakfast," he said.

She turned to him. "Do you need a hand?"

The offer touched him. Sofia had always grumbled about him being too noisy when he got up. "I've got it. Brandon will be up too."

"Will it be quicker if I help?" She ran a hand over his chest.

She might be more of a distraction, but he liked the idea of her helping him. No, it was selfish to want her to rise so early, and he hadn't asked Brandon to cover for him. He must have been silent too long because she sat and rubbed her eyes. "Does Amy have some clothes I can borrow?"

He was powerless to resist. The idea of her coming with him was just too appealing. "Georgie leaves a change of clothes in her room." He slipped on his jeans and went down the hall to his sister's room and found a pair of jeans and T-shirt. When he came back, Faith had turned on the lamp and sat in bed with the sheets pulled up around her breasts, her short hair sticking out in every direction, her lips a little swollen from the night before. He hardened and passed her the clothes and then threw on a T-shirt and gathered his boots.

He kissed her chastely. "If I stay here with you looking as sexy as you do, we won't get out of the house until long after sunrise."

Her smile stayed with him as he entered the kitchen where he found his brother making coffee.

"Rain's forecast for Tuesday," Brandon said as a way of greeting.

It gave them a few days to prepare. They'd moved most of the flock closer to the house after the sheep had been slaughtered, but one flock still remained in a low-lying paddock. "We'd better move the sheep in the wetlands to higher ground."

"What time do you have to pick up Lara?"

"About ten."

"How about we do it when you get back?"

That was fine. Lara would need a nap because she would have stayed up later than normal.

"Morning," Faith said as she entered the kitchen. Georgie's clothes fit her, and she'd found a comb to tidy her hair.

Brandon's eyebrows raised, and he smiled. "Morning. You're up early."

"I offered to help Darcy."

Brandon glanced out the window. "The back side of the ridge should be checked for stray sheep. If you two hurry, you could take the horses and make it up to the ridge by sunrise."

Darcy covered his surprise. He'd been out there a couple of days ago.

Brandon poured the coffee into a thermos and placed it in a backpack. "Looks like a nice morning for a ride."

Love for his brother filled him. "You be right with the rest?"

His brother nodded. "Yep." He added some of Amy's biscuits to the bag and handed it to Darcy. "Have fun."

"Thanks." Darcy added a portable radio and held out his hand to Faith who took it. His heart expanded. Chores always came first in his father's eyes. Then relaxation. But he wasn't giving up this opportunity. He owed his brother one.

Over at the horse yard they saddled two horses. Faith could handle his father's gelding, Reg. The horizon was a thin glow of orange, but they had time yet. He swung onto his horse and they rode out of the yard side by side.

Birds flittered around the bushes in the cool

morning air. Over near the taller gum trees, cockatoos screeched the morning wake up alarm. None of the campers had stirred yet.

Next to him, Faith inhaled deeply. "This is lovely. It was nice of Brandon to suggest it."

"Yeah. I'm glad you offered to help, otherwise I'd be off in the ute somewhere."

She chuckled. "Glad I could help."

Her laugh entwined around his heart like a vine. If he wasn't careful, he'd get used to having her around. But she hadn't said whether she was staying. Too chicken to ask, he said instead, "It will take about twenty minutes to get to the top of the ridge. We might miss some of the sunrise."

"It doesn't matter. I'm happy being out here with you."

The vines gripped tighter. "Do you have plans for the weekend?"

"Adult riding classes today at four," she said. "Most of my students have kids who have activities in the morning."

"Is the pony club solely your responsibility?"

"I'm trying to put together an official committee, but some members have strong opinions about how things should be."

"I can imagine." He tried for casual as he asked, "Will you take any of the executive roles?"

"If no one else wants them. I'm conscious I'm an outsider so I don't want to take over."

"You're the one who revived the club," he commented.

"That wasn't exactly my choice," she said. "I wanted to agist my horse there, and the condition was that I try to encourage the town to use the area. One of the shire councillors said they'd been getting requests from property developers to buy the land and turn it into a housing estate."

"Retribution Bay has plenty of housing."

"Maybe it's meant for the tourists. I figured it was a cheap deal for me, so I agreed."

The trail sloped upwards and the sun's rays peeking above the horizon behind them brightened the dark land to more of a grey. Another few minutes and colour would return.

"Lara seemed happy spending time with Sofia yesterday." Faith's voice was low as if she was afraid to disturb the peace surrounding them.

Darcy's mood plummeted. "Yeah. She was so disappointed Sofia didn't swim with her on Thursday, and then Sofia pulled her stupid stunt." He glanced at Faith. "Lara sounded thrilled."

"And how do you feel?"

The urge to say he was fine was on the tip of his tongue, but he stopped himself. "When Joan called to say Lara hadn't come home with Mischa, I was terrified. And then to discover Sofia had picked her up when I'd told her Lara had plans…" Even now the thought brought with it a simmering anger. "I was furious. Not only did she suddenly appear and blindside me, but then she kidnapped our daughter. And I couldn't do anything about it without upsetting my girl."

"You are such a good father," Faith said. "Lara's lucky to have you."

He smiled. "To think, for the first year after Sofia left, I kept thinking she'd be back, and I'd fantasise about us being one happy family again." He shook his head. "Now, I'm so glad she didn't."

"Do you still love her?"

Had he ever? He remembered the teenaged infatuation with Sofia, of feeling so good about himself because he was with the hottest girl in their year. When she'd told him she was pregnant, he convinced himself he loved her, but she'd never given him the thrill one of Faith's smiles gave him. They'd never spent time together in comfortable silence, and their love-making had been immature. "No."

Around them, the land took shape. The bushes morphed from blobs to branches and the sand blushed with the first colour of the morning. He shifted to look behind them. The top curve of the sun was above the horizon. They wouldn't make it to the top in time, but they were a fair way up its slope. "Let's watch it from here." He pulled Fezzik around so he faced east, and Faith did the same. He poured Faith a cup of coffee before he poured his own.

"The way the colours come to life is magnificent," Faith said with a sigh.

It had been some time since he'd taken a moment to appreciate a sunrise. Most of the time it symbolised the start of the workday and a race to get the hardest work done before it became too hot. Fezzik snorted and flicked its tail, but otherwise the silence encompassed everything.

The sun crept above the horizon slowly but with determination. It was his turn to shine.

Soon the final curve breached the horizon.

Faith let out a breath as if she'd been holding it. "Glorious."

Her appreciation mirrored his own. He took her now empty cup and returned it to his backpack. "The path is a little rough to the top." He turned his horse back around and they climbed the rest of the way to the plateau. From here they saw the ocean and all over Stokes' land. Lights were still on in the homestead and Brandon drove the ute south towards the animals. To the west of the ridge sat another rocky outcrop which helped form a valley at the bottom.

"Is all this yours?" Faith asked.

"Yeah," he replied.

She nudged her horse to the other side of the ridge and looked down at the valley. "Is that another dry riverbed?"

"Not really. It collects the runoff from the ridge when it rains and funnels it south to the low-lying areas I pointed out yesterday. It's pretty amazing to see the amount of water and how quickly it gathers. Every few years there's enough rain to cause a flash flood."

"So that's why we need to check this area for livestock?"

He'd forgotten the excuse Brandon had given. Normally he would have taken the ute and driven around the ridge. It was longer, but faster. Still, it was best to double-check. "Yeah. We'll ride down this side and there's a trail up the other." He pointed it out.

He took the lead down the trail, which was only wide enough for one horse. The ground was a mixture of rock and sand, and he let Fezzik have his head so he could pick his way. As a kid, he'd raced Charlie down the trail after they'd watched *The Man From Snowy River*. His dad had been furious they'd endangered the horses going so fast on the rough ground. Now every time he came out here, he filled in any gullies in the trail to maintain it. And because he still felt guilty about his recklessness.

"Is that a cave over there?"

He twisted to where Faith pointed at a cave at the bottom of the opposite ridge. "Yeah. We often see rock wallabies there." He smiled. "Lara believes it's where the mutineers hid the treasure they stole from the Retribution."

"Weren't the mutineers hanged?"

"The details are vague depending on which account you hear." And which version you preferred to believe.

"So have you looked?" Faith asked.

"Not personally. Lara came up with the theory recently, and the wallabies had babies in their pouches. We didn't want to scare them away by traipsing into their home. I'll take her when they're weaned."

"Mutinies and treasure sound all very much like high seas pirate shenanigans," Faith said.

"Mum had started investigating the truth of the history, at Lara's prompting," Darcy said. "I'm not sure how far she got. There are some old trunks in the shed, but whether they go back that far, or are just junk some of our other ancestors left there, I don't know." Maybe he should see if Lara was interested in reviewing it with him.

"Do we need to check the cave for sheep?"

"No, they don't come down in the valley, not as much food."

They reached the bottom and crossed the hard surface of the valley bed. Larger trees grew here, probably because of the way the water collected during a rain. Branches and twigs lay against them, evidence of a flood which had pushed debris down the valley and had caught on the trees. Occasionally he drove the ute down into the gully and gathered the debris for firewood.

They rode side by side, towards the cave and the trail which led up to the other side.

Faith sighed. "This would make a lovely trail ride," she said. "If you wanted to diversify your income a bit more."

She was right. Especially at this time of the morning. It was cool, and the walls of the ridge shaded the gully from the morning sun. They could offer morning tea or even breakfast, but at this stage they had no one to lead the tour. Amy wasn't a confident enough horse rider yet. "I'll keep it in mind." It would keep the horses exercised as well.

At the top of the other side, the land was flatter. Aside from an emu pecking at a nearby bush, the land was still. No sheep, not that he expected any.

"Can you access this area with a car?" Faith asked.

"Yeah. There's a gate near the main road." Darcy pointed. "And another further south where the ridge ends."

She raised an eyebrow. "So it would have been quicker to drive?"

He smiled. "But nowhere near as pleasant." He shifted his horse closer to hers and kissed her.

"I didn't pick Brandon as a romantic," she said.

"He surprised me as well."

But he was thankful for it. Spending time with Faith was just want he needed right now.

Chapter 10

On their way back, Brandon radioed Darcy to tell him a fence was down. From the sounds of it, Faith guessed it would take a lot of work to fix. "I've got to cut this short," Darcy said apologetically. "I need to get the fence done before I pick up Lara."

"If you need me to pick her up, say the word."

"Thanks." He hesitated and looked down the gully in the opposite direction to where they were headed.

"Do you need to go that way?"

"Yeah, but I'll take you back to the house first."

She didn't need to be coddled. "The trail's pretty clear, Darcy. I can make my own way back. You go."

"I'm not leaving you alone."

"Then give me the radio and make sure you check in when you reach Brandon." She held out her hand.

He sighed. "You are wonderful." He gave her the whole backpack, kissed her, and then pointed out the path.

"I've got it."

He smiled, kissed her again, then turned his horse and cantered down the gully.

Sometime last night or this morning, he'd captured

her heart. If she returned to Perth, she wouldn't escape this without pain. With a sigh, she headed back to the homestead.

Halfway back to the house, the radio came alive. "I'm with Brandon. Where are you?"

"In sight of the house," she said. "Should be back in about ten."

"Roger that."

The ground was flat, so she kicked her horse into a canter, enjoying the rolling motion and the wind brushing by her face. At the horse yard she radioed Darcy to tell him she'd arrived, and then groomed Reg and returned him to the yard. It seemed natural to walk back into the house through the kitchen door. Amy sat at the table in front of a laptop with a couple of notebooks scattered around her. She smiled. "Have a pleasant ride?"

"It was beautiful," Faith said. "We rode down into the gully beyond the ridge."

"I haven't been down there yet. The slope scares me, though Brandon tells me it's not as bad as it looks."

"It isn't," Faith agreed. "But if you're not comfortable on a horse, then it would be scary."

"Actually, that's something I wanted to ask you about," Amy said as she filled the kettle with water. "We have four horses out here. Would they be suitable for trail rides?"

She hadn't seen them all in action, but, "Possibly. Darcy would be the better person to ask as he knows their temperament. And it would depend on the skill of the rider as well." She considered the options. "If you just went to the top of the ridge, it would be suitable for a beginner, but you could also do rides to the beach or around the sand dunes."

Amy made some notes. "How much would you

charge?"

Faith named the going rate. "If you offer a picnic lunch or breakfast with it, you could charge more."

When the kettle boiled, Amy filled a teapot and set it on the table. She rubbed her forehead. "My brain hurts with all the numbers," she said. "But it's my job to make the camp grounds as lucrative as possible."

Faith hesitated. It wasn't any of her business, but she wanted to help. "How bad are the finances?"

"Bad," Amy said. "We're running low on feed and the slaughtered sheep were pregnant, so we've lost next year's flock as well. Brandon's hoping for rain because new growth will sprout and provide more food."

"Is there anything I can do?"

"If you can recoup the money they lost on the cattle, it will help." She held up a mug. "Tea?"

"Yes, please." She sat, and a notebook caught her attention. "These wedding plans?"

Amy nodded. "It's a simple wedding here, but I've been cross-checking a bunch of wedding lists in case I've forgotten anything." She marked items off her list. "We've got a celebrant and food organised. The invitations will be sent the next time I go into town, and Ed's bringing up the rings from Perth."

"Wow, that's quick."

Amy nodded. "Brandon's teammates are being deployed next month and Brandon wanted them at the wedding, so it was either bring it forward or wait for months." She grinned. "And we didn't want to wait.

Faith could understand that. "Are you having a photographer?"

"One of our camp guests, Lee is back in town and he offered to take them." Amy went over to a basket of envelopes and sorted through them. She handed one to Faith. "Here's your invitation."

Faith blinked. She hadn't expected one. "Thanks.

When is it?"

"Next month. Aside from Brandon's army buddies and Ed, everyone we want to invite is up here."

"What about your family?"

Amy pursed her lips.

Nuts. "What's wrong?"

"It's complicated. I haven't seen my brother since I was fifteen, but it turns out he's one of Brandon's teammates."

Awkward. "And you don't want him here?"

Amy sighed. "I don't want to visit those emotions around my wedding." She tapped her pen. "He was supposed to come this month but cancelled. I shouldn't be surprised. He probably won't even make it to the wedding." She sounded defeated.

"What makes you say that?"

"Do you have a good relationship with your family?"

Faith thought about it. "I was an oops baby," she said. "Both my brothers are over ten years older than me, so they'd moved out of home when I was young and I don't have a close relationship with them." She considered her parents. "My father is like a bower bird, always after the shiny new thing, and we moved from town to town as he bought business after business which would make him rich. That meant my parents were the only constant in my life, and after Mum's stroke we've grown closer." Faith took the biscuit Amy offered.

"I get that," Amy said. "My brother followed my father into the army as soon as he was old enough." She played with her pen. "Then Mum became addicted to painkillers and overdosed when my father was overseas. Arthur stayed less than a week, even though I was only fifteen. I packed my things and left and haven't heard from them since."

How horrible. Faith covered Amy's hand. "It must

have been difficult for you."

Amy nodded. "I want to talk to Arthur, find out why he acted the way he did, but not right before my wedding."

"I get that," Faith told her. "Perhaps start with an email, see if you get any response. Or video chat before the wedding, so it's not so confronting if he comes." She didn't enjoy seeing this normally cheerful woman so sad. "He might not know what to say to you. It sounds like he's the one who did wrong by you."

"Maybe," Amy agreed. She changed the subject, and they chatted about things happening in town until Darcy arrived back around nine.

He hung his hat on the hook by the door and leaned over to kiss Faith. "I'll go wash up."

He was a little sweaty, but the sight of him made her heart skip a beat. She watched him leave the room.

"Darcy is about the nicest man I know." Amy grinned. "Aside from Brandon, of course."

"He is, isn't he?" Faith was tempted to follow him to help him wash up. She swallowed her smile. When he returned, she asked, "Did you get the fence fixed?"

"Most of it," he said. "Brandon's doing the last bit now." He took a biscuit from the plate Amy offered him. "I have to pick up Lara."

Faith stood. "I should go anyway. I've got a few things to do before my class this afternoon." She looked down at herself. "I'll take these clothes home and wash them. Then I can drop them off at Georgie's." She hugged Amy. "Thanks for the tea. If you want to chat wedding, or other stuff, call me."

"I will."

Darcy walked her to her car and then pulled her into his arms. "I haven't seen nearly enough of you today."

How could she resist such comments? She kissed him. "We both have things we need to do," she said.

"Are you free tomorrow?"

He shook his head. "Sofia's coming out. But I'll call you later and maybe when she's gone, we can do something?"

She smiled. "All right."

His kiss sent tingles right down to her toes. "I'll follow you into town."

A few minutes later she was on the road, with the man who'd captured her heart behind her.

***

When Faith arrived home, she found her mother sitting in the lounge room alone. "Mum, what are you doing here?"

"I live here," her mother said with a smile.

"Where's Dad?"

"He's out on the boat." Before Faith could ask her next question, her mother added, "I told him you would be home at eight so he would leave."

Faith sank down on the couch next to her. "Is everything all right?"

"I'm tired of being coddled," she said. "I need time to myself, *by* myself. Your father doesn't understand that."

"He's scared, Mum."

"Yes, but it doesn't change matters." She gripped Faith's hand and the wrinkles in her hand and the slight shake reminded Faith her mother wasn't getting any younger. "You need to help me convince your father it's time to retire."

Surprise made her blink. "Dad always said he'd work until he died."

Her mother scowled. "He came home last night and said he'd had enough of the boat and he wanted to sell the business. He's decided a café in town will be easier and more lucrative."

Faith groaned. "He never learns."

"He's got itchy feet," she agreed. "Never was one to settle for long. But I want to spend more time with him. My stroke made me aware of how little time we have left. I want to sell everything and buy a caravan, join the grey nomad brigade."

Concern filled Faith. "Are you mobile enough, Mum? Caravans are pretty small."

"I'm fine," she insisted. "Can't you see how happy your father would be? We could move on to the next place when the desire struck, he'd get to yarn with new people every day and if he had the urge, he could sell things from the van."

Her mother had a point. The freedom to move on when he had the urge would appeal to his gypsy soul. "What do you need me to do?"

They brainstormed ideas and after lunch while her mother napped, Faith got out her laptop and sent the letter to Stonefish. Step one done. She expected them to ignore the letter completely, so she prepared the details for a claim to the ACCC. Again, it was a long shot. She doubted the Stokes would see the money again, which left the option of a public relations attack on the company. They weren't playing fair, so neither should she. But it felt good to be doing law work, considering her words and argument.

When her mother woke, she joined Faith at the table and began researching caravans. It was lovely to see her mother enthusiastic about something again. Since the stroke she had been full of determination and grit and it was a side Faith had never seen.

Finally, Milly closed her laptop lid. "I'm going to be dreaming about caravans."

Faith grinned. "Find any you liked?"

"Too many," she said. "I don't know how I'll

choose." She tried to stand and struggled to push back her chair. Faith rose to help, and Milly waved her away. "I'm fine. I need to do these things myself. You're not always going to be here." She stood and switched on the oven. "We should discuss that. What will you do after I've convinced your father to retire?"

Faith shifted. "I'm not sure yet."

"Don't think I'm not grateful for you coming up here to care for me. I won't ever be able to repay you."

"I don't need payment, Mum. You needed me."

She nodded. "I did. Will you be able to slot right back in with your law firm?"

Should she talk to her mother about her ideas? "I'm not certain I want to move back to the city."

Milly raised her eyebrows. "Why not? You love your house and job."

"I haven't missed it much. I've enjoyed having more time to ride."

"You always were obsessed by horses. It broke my heart seeing you so devastated when we moved away from the farm."

"Dad had to move on."

Milly covered her hand. "I know moving around was tough on you."

"What about you?" Faith asked. "Did you want to move all the time?"

"To be honest, I'm happy if your father is happy. Home was never a building or a town for me, it is when I'm with Rob."

Faith stared at her mother. She'd never considered it that way. All she'd seen was her father's restless feet and her having to negotiate a new town and a new set of friends. "But Mum, you always gave in. You never got what you wanted."

Milly frowned. "Is that what you think?"

Her sharp tone made Faith hesitate before she

nodded.

"I didn't realise you had such little respect for me."

Faith started to speak, but her mother cut her off. "Just because I don't yell and argue, doesn't mean I don't get my own way when it's important to me. Didn't I convince your father to take me out on the boat the other day?"

Faith shut her mouth. She had, without any real argument. And she'd defused Rob easily after she'd been injured on the boat.

Faith thought back through her childhood and remembered other times when her father had wanted one thing and they'd done another. Her eyes widened in realisation. "I'm sorry," she said. "You were so subtle I didn't realise what you were doing." That grit and determination she'd seen in her mother when she'd done her exercises had been there all along. "Does Dad know?"

Her mother smiled. "I'm sure he does. He likes to be the protector and provider for the family, so it's the little dance we do."

With her mother the planner under it all.

"You'll understand when you fall in love." Her eyes twinkled. "How was your evening with Darcy Stokes?"

Heat flooded Faith's cheeks at the change of subject. "I went out there to help them with a legal matter."

"Your father was pleased you stayed overnight rather than drive home. He was worried about you driving in the dark."

"Seemed like the sensible thing to do," Faith agreed, knowing her mother wasn't fooled in the slightest.

"If you don't go back to the city, what will you do?" Thank goodness her mother returned to the original topic.

Faith hesitated. "I'm not sure." She wasn't ready to voice her ideas yet.

She still needed to consider her mother's bombshell. It put everything into a new perspective. Now she had no doubt Milly would convince Rob to retire and buy a caravan. Which meant she had a lot to think about. She stood. "Will you be all right if I go for a walk?"

"Yes, darling. I'll be fine."

Faith left the house, inhaling the warm air. It was time to rethink her entire plan.

Chapter 11

By Sunday Darcy had let go of his rage for Sofia. He could be civil to her for a few hours for Lara's sake, and then he'd say goodbye. This time he was on his turf and Lara was with him. He had control.

Lara had been up early and had insisted on baking scones ready for when her mother arrived. Then she'd cleaned her room without him even needing to ask.

"Will she want to go riding?" Lara asked. "Or should we go to the beach? Does she like dogs? Should I put Bennet inside?" She hopped from foot to foot.

Darcy placed his hands on her shoulders. "Relax, pumpkin. Remember, she used to live here. She knows all the places, but Josh and the boys might like to ride."

Lara bit her lip. "I forgot."

He hated seeing her so uncertain. "Maybe you could show her your room."

She nodded. "I can show her the box where I keep all her cards and show her where I put everything she bought me on Friday."

Aside from a new dress, Sofia had bought Lara more fancy clothes which would be impractical for anything Lara did, as well as jewellery and a new riding hat that

Darcy hadn't been able to afford yet. Darcy forced a smile. "Great idea."

Amy walked in and filled the kettle. "They're due at eight, right?"

"Yeah." Five minutes to go. The scones were due to come out of the oven right on the dot.

When the timer rang, Lara retrieved the tray, placed it on the bench, and moved the scones onto a plate. The table was set for an early morning tea.

Fifteen minutes later they were still waiting. Lara kept walking to the kitchen door and peering outside in case she'd missed the car arriving. Darcy checked his phone, but there were no missed calls or messages. Sofia had never been a morning person, so maybe they'd slept in, or perhaps the twins were difficult to wrangle into the car.

"Dad, what if they've had an accident?" The genuine fear in Lara's eyes killed him. He hugged her. "I'm sure they're just a little late. When you were Todd and Trevor's age, it took me ages to get you ready to go into town because you were always wanting to play."

"Really?"

"Yeah." Outside a car rumbled and Lara pushed away from him and ran to the door.

"They're here!" She flung open the door and then hesitated. "Are you coming, Dad?"

"Right behind you, pumpkin."

She waited for him to put on his hat and then slipped her hand into his and they walked out into the cool morning. Sofia waved and then opened the back door to get one twin out of the backseat. Darcy shook his head. She wore a long flowing skirt, sandals with barely any sole and a strappy tank top—not dressed for riding.

Darcy exhaled as anger tickled his skin. Let it go.

The boy she lifted out took off the moment she let

go, running at full speed towards the horses. "Todd!" Sofia called.

Shit. The horses were pretty placid, but if the kid startled them, he could be in trouble. Darcy ran after him. "Todd, wait up."

The kid didn't slow down.

Darcy increased his stride and grabbed the back of Todd's T-shirt just before he scooted under the railing into the yard. "Wait a minute, mate."

Todd struggled against him. "I want to see the horses."

"You can, but there are rules." He kept his hold tight as he glanced behind him. Josh had a firm grip of Trevor and Sofia spoke with Amy and Lara, her back turned to him. Perhaps she'd seen him grab the boy.

"Todd, I told you to get permission from Darcy before you could go to the horses." Josh gave an apologetic smile. "Thanks for the fast footwork."

"No worries. The horses are good, but a missile like Todd might startle them." Todd had stopped struggling.

Lara gestured for her mother to follow her and they walked towards the horses. Good. "If you stay on this side of the fence, I'll fetch Lara's horse, Starlight. I'm sure she'd like to meet you."

"Lara has her own horse?" Todd's eyes widened. "Can I have one too, Dad?"

"We've got no room at the house," Josh said.

Confident the boys would stay put, Darcy ducked under the railing and took the halter and lead rope from one of the posts. Starlight was across the yard, but she trotted over when she spotted Lara. Darcy suspected Lara fed her extra treats. He slipped the halter over her head and led her to the boys.

"This is my horse, Mum," Lara said, ducking under the fence to join him. She rubbed Starlight's neck and murmured to her. "Isn't she beautiful?"

"She is," Sofia agreed.

"Can I ride her?" Todd asked.

"I made scones," Lara said. "We could eat those first."

"We just finished breakfast," Sofia said. "Maybe later."

Darcy should have considered that. Not wanting Lara to be too disappointed, he said, "I'm sure Sofia would like to see how well you ride. How about I get the tack while you show the boys the right way to approach a horse?"

"OK." Lara went through the instructions and Darcy jogged over to the tack room. When he returned, both boys and Josh were stroking Starlight.

"Who wants to brush her?" Darcy asked.

Todd laughed. "Why do you brush a horse?"

"Because she gets dusty," Lara told him and launched into an explanation on how to care for a horse.

Darcy smiled through the pang of loss. He could hear his father's words as she spoke. Bill had always insisted each of his children knew how to care for the animals.

When Starlight was saddled, they stood outside the yard while Lara demonstrated barrel racing. Next to him, Sofia gasped. "Isn't she too young for this, Darcy? It's dangerous."

"All sports can be dangerous, Sofia," he replied. "But see the joy on her face." Lara finished the course and slowed Starlight, trotting over to them.

"Can I do that, Dad?" Todd asked.

"I think it takes practice," Josh answered.

"I can lead them around the yard if they want a ride," Darcy offered.

"That would be great. Thanks, mate."

On the opposite side of the yard, Lara's pet sheep trotted under the fence towards them. Lara dismounted. "Did you see, Mum? Uncle Brandon and Faith are teaching me how to go faster."

"Brandon's back?" Sofia asked.

"Yeah," Darcy said.

"Sheep!" Trevor hollered.

Lara took his hand. "Come on, I'll introduce you to Flotsam and Jetsam." Todd joined them and the boys exclaimed over the oily wool. When they returned, Sofia asked, "Do you still lasso?"

"Not as part of a competition." But he liked to practise because every now and then, he needed to catch an animal to treat it.

"Are you a real cowboy?" Todd exclaimed.

Darcy chuckled. "I wouldn't call myself that."

"But he kind of is," Sofia stage whispered.

Darcy's face heated.

"You should show them, Dad. Lasso one of the sheep."

The boys jumped up and down, pleading with him to show them, and Darcy couldn't disappoint them. "Let me get a rope." He grabbed some from the tack shed, tying the knots and looping it through. He hadn't lassoed anything for an audience in a good long while, and nerves hummed over his skin as he swung the rope, getting the rhythm with his wrist to make sure it flattened at the right place.

"You've got this, Dad."

He chuckled, loving her encouragement. With the next rotation, he let go and the rope sailed over the sheep's head and he pulled it tight. The sheep trotted a few steps away and then stood still. The boys applauded and Darcy released Jetsam.

"Can I have a go?" Todd asked.

Both boys were a bit young to get the wrist motion,

but Darcy spent a few minutes showing them and giving them a go. When Todd got frustrated, Josh said, "Did you want to try riding?"

The distraction worked, and Darcy lifted Todd into the saddle and showed him how to hold the reins.

"Dad, can I show Mum my room?" Lara asked.

"Sure." Maybe there was something in there they could bond over. While they went inside, Darcy did a couple of laps around the yard and then lifted Todd down and gave Trevor a turn. Josh walked with him.

"Darcy, I'm sorry about Friday," Josh said in a low voice. "I had no idea Sofia hadn't asked to take Lara."

Darcy grunted, as the tension stiffened his skin again.

"She came home all indignant, and when she told me what happened, I backed you all the way. If my ex had just taken the boys without me knowing…"

Darcy blew out a breath. This man got it. "I've never been so damned scared."

Josh clapped him on the back. "She won't do it again. She has a tendency to only think about what she wants, but she's getting better." The real affection in his voice showed Josh's love for her.

Darcy studied the man. "Does she want Lara?"

The man glanced at him, his eyes shuttering. "She wants a relationship with her, whatever that looks like." He gestured around. "How much land do you have?"

Darcy respected that Josh wouldn't talk behind Sofia's back, so didn't push the topic. "A quarter of a million acres," he replied, smirking at the shock on Josh's face. People never believed him.

"That's incredible. So you run sheep?"

They spoke about the farm as Darcy took both boys around the yard again, before Trevor said, "I'm hungry."

Josh sighed. "He's got a bottomless stomach."

"Then he's lucky Lara baked fresh scones this morning. Why don't you all head inside and I'll unsaddle Starlight? Holler out and Lara will hear."

As he crossed the yard to the house, his gaze caught on the frame of a house in the distance. The house he'd been going to build for Sofia. He hadn't got far before she'd walked out and he'd never got around to tearing it down. Had hoped one day he'd have a reason to build his own place. Now, with Brandon and Amy getting married, he should probably plan a rebuild. They would want the main house to themselves, especially if they had kids.

He sighed and continued into the kitchen, where Amy had served drinks and the kids had their mouths stuffed with scones, jam and cream. Sofia's plate had a single biscuit on it. She'd always been conscious of her weight. She'd hated how big she was during pregnancy and often complained about his mother baking so much.

Funny how he'd forgotten the little details.

As they ate, Lara regaled Josh and her stepbrothers with stories about the Retribution wreck while Amy made small talk with Sofia. It was strange to have Sofia at the kitchen table again. He remembered being excited to come home after a day's work and find her sitting there with Lara in her arms. He'd always made a beeline to his baby girl, needing to hold her after so long away, seeing how much she grew each day.

That image was clear, but what wasn't clear was him greeting Sofia, asking her about her day. Had he forgotten to do that?

"Can we go see the island, Dad?" Trevor asked, his eyes wide with excitement.

Josh glanced at Darcy. "We'll have to ask Darcy."

The twins both turned to him with pleading eyes. He chuckled. "If you've got time, we can head to the beach. It's about an hour's round trip. The road's bumpy."

Josh turned to Sofia and Lara said, "Do you remember how lovely our beach is, Mum?"

Sofia sighed. "We can go, but I didn't bring beach towels."

"We've got plenty if the boys want to swim," Darcy told her. They'd finished eating, so he stood. "I'll bring the ute around. Lara, can you put bathers on and then get enough towels for everyone?" He glanced at Amy. "Want to come?"

She smiled and shook her head. "I've got a couple of guests coming in this morning."

Right. By the time he'd driven the ute over to the house, everyone waited outside.

"We won't all fit in there," Sofia said.

"There's plenty of room in the tray and your hire car won't make it down the road," Darcy told her. "Lara, what are the rules for riding in the tray?"

Lara climbed in. "No standing while the car is running, no leaning against the tail gate, and always hold on to the side." She demonstrated.

The twins jumped up and down and Josh helped them into the tray. "Boys." He waited until he had their full attention. "Anyone who breaks the rules will ride in the front with Darcy, is that clear?"

They both nodded and Josh climbed in, making sure each child was tucked next to him. Sofia hesitated and Lara held out her hand. "Come on, Mum."

With a sigh, Sofia climbed up.

Darcy took it slowly, keeping an eye in his rear-view mirror to check the boys were behaving themselves. When he saw a couple of emus, he stopped for them to have a better look and then continued to the beach. Lara helped the boys down and then she raced them over the sand, helping them take off their shoes and shirts before heading into the water with them.

She'd make a great older sister.

The image of Faith holding a baby accompanied the thought, and he reined it in with a jerk. What the hell was he thinking? That was moving way too fast.

"This must have been a great place to grow up," Josh said as they walked at a slower pace over to where the kids had dumped their clothes and towels.

"I loved it," Darcy said.

"And Lara loves it too." Sofia stopped him. "You've done such a good job with our daughter."

Darcy's chest tightened as Josh continued walking to give them privacy. "Thanks."

"I am sorry for Friday, and I'm sorry for how I left. I know I hurt you and Lara, but honestly, seeing her now, such a confident and happy girl, I believe I made the right decision. I would have been miserable here and that misery would have rubbed off on you both." As if to punctuate her words, the wind blew a small willy-willy around them, coating them in red dust, and Sofia sneezed, brushing at her clothes.

Something clicked in Darcy's head. It had never been about him or about Lara, it had been about the place and Sofia's own needs. He'd been so caught up in what he wanted, in his dreams, he hadn't considered she might not share them, might not love the land as he loved it. An acceptance settled over him. "I get that now. It looks as if you're happy."

She nodded, watching Josh join the kids in the water. "I've still got a lot to learn about being a mum, but they make me happy."

"And Lara?"

She was silent a moment. "When I arrived here, I had ideas I would sweep in and rescue her from this place," she admitted. "We would be the perfect mother-daughter pair."

His chest constricted, and he opened his mouth to refuse when she laughed. "But taking her from the Ridge would be as bad as me staying here."

His angry words fizzled, and he was left a little dizzy. She wasn't taking Lara from him?

"I'd like to stay in touch, though. Maybe we can set up regular video chats, and perhaps during the school holidays she could visit us in Melbourne."

The idea of Lara flying across the country by herself made his muscles tense, but he relaxed them. "I'm sure we can sort something out." This was the best outcome for all of them.

"Thanks, Darcy. For everything." She kissed his cheek and then went to sit at the towels.

Darcy stayed where he was, free of the fear that had sat on his shoulders since he'd first seen Sofia across the restaurant. She wasn't taking his baby away from him. And better yet for Lara, she wanted to have a relationship with her. Hot, happy tears blurred his vision, and he brushed them away. Lara would be thrilled. He couldn't wait to share the news with Faith. But right now Lara was calling for him to join them.

And he wasn't letting his girl down.

***

After lunch, Darcy and Lara waved as Josh and Sofia drove away. Darcy slipped an arm around Lara. "How are you feeling, pumpkin?"

"Sad," she said. "But good."

"Want to talk about it?"

"I understand why Mum didn't stay now," she said.

Interested in what she would come up with, he asked, "Why's that?"

"Are you kidding?" Lara raised her eyebrows. "She hates dust and the ocean, and doesn't much like horses. She'd make the worst farmer, and she'd be unhappy."

His daughter was observant. "Are you all right with that?"

She twisted a strand of hair around her finger. "Yeah. She saw the doll I crocheted and said she wanted to learn, so I'm going to teach her when she video calls."

He loved the idea they would have something to bond over. "Sounds perfect."

They walked inside.

Amy was still in the kitchen doing dishes. He took the dishcloth from her. "I've got this, Ames. You deserve a break. Why don't you take the afternoon off?"

Amy smiled. "I don't mind the work, Darce."

"I know, but you've been working hard for us and you've got your wedding to plan."

"It's all planned."

He shook his head and shooed her away from the sink. "Then hang out with your fiancé for a couple of hours." Brandon had been muttering something about doing maintenance on the equipment in the shed.

She laughed. "All right. Thanks. Call me if you need anything."

He finished the dishes and then heard someone yelling outside. He went to the door. Jay sprinted towards the house, fear on his red face, pointing and shouting. "Fire!"

Darcy wrenched open the door and dashed out. Smoke rose into the air right above the area where their bales of hay were piled.

Fuck.

He stormed towards the sheds where they kept the water truck filled, ready to go. "Brandon!" His brother appeared at the entrance to the shed, glanced behind Darcy, and sprinted back inside. Seconds later, the truck's engine roared.

Darcy jumped aboard and Brandon drove towards the smoking pile. The horses in the nearby yard were pacing nervously as they smelled the smoke. If they panicked and tried to jump the fence, they'd be hurt.

Shit.

The haystack wasn't completely alight, thank God, maybe the bales were packed too tightly together. Brandon parked as close as was safe and Darcy unwound the hose before Brandon turned on the water.

The smoke came from the bottom of the stack and flames licked towards the scrubby grass nearby. He sprayed the flames, dousing those closest to him and preventing them from spreading further. As he did, he scanned the pile. No way of telling how far in the fire had spread. They'd have to take the whole pile apart to check. The last thing he needed was for it to combust in the middle of the night.

Brandon had dragged the waterproof cover off the wall of bales and Amy and Lara ran up. "I've rung the fire brigade," Amy called.

Fat lot of good that would do. If they didn't have the fire out by the time the fire truck arrived, they were screwed.

"Can you both move the horses to the sheep pens?" Darcy yelled. "They're stressing out. Get Jay and Cheryl to help you."

"On it!" Lara said and pulled Amy away.

Brandon climbed on top of the wall and threw bales down, away from the flames. Lee joined him and soon a few of their guests had joined in, moving the bales which had been thrown down further away.

The heat scorched Darcy's face, and he glanced at the water tank. Half empty. He needed to get it out before he ran out of water.

His livelihood, hopes, and dreams were going up in the flames. If they couldn't feed the sheep, they'd lose everything. He kept the water directed at the smoke, unable to see the flames over the water. That was good, wasn't it?

"Over there." Brandon pointed from the top of the pile.

A lick of flames was spreading out along the grass towards the now empty horse yard. Darcy redirected his spray, before scanning the rest of the ground around him. A bush was smoking right next to one of the gum trees, and he doused it.

The haystack still smoked and smouldered. The stench of wet hay and smoke stung his nose and he turned the hose back on the stack.

Across the yard, Lara ran towards him with Amy, Jay and Cheryl. Beyond them the horses were calmer in the sheep pens.

Good.

When Lara reached him, he said, "Be my spotter. Search the area in case the fire spread without me seeing."

She nodded, her expression serious. "OK."

There was far too much smoke on the haystack to see the damage. He kept the water focused on the middle.

Only a quarter tank to go.

The water pressure decreased and the water came in fits and starts. Shit.

"Dad, the fire's out." Lara tugged on his arm and he blinked.

He shut off the hose, ready to turn it back on at any sign of flames. The scent of wet hay and smoke wafted towards him.

"Are we out?" Brandon called from the top of the stack.

He moved closer, heart racing, and prodded the bales. "Looks like it." But now the hay was soaking wet and would go mouldy if it wasn't dried. They would have to move the whole lot.

More work. More risk of damage.

Brandon jumped down, while Amy thanked all of those who'd come over to help. "What started it?"

"No idea." It could have been a stray cigarette butt. He called to the guests still congregated. "Did anyone see anything?"

They all shook their heads.

There was a real possibility it could have spontaneously combusted, and wouldn't that just be their luck? Exhaustion whispered to him to give up, give in, to stop fighting what was inevitable.

Lara slipped her hand into his. "What do we need to do now, Dad?"

Her simple question and the absolute confidence on her face that he would know what to do almost scuttled him. But he would not let her down. Drawing on a strength he didn't know he had, he straightened. "We need to sort the bales, pumpkin. Make sure the wet ones dry." Only a few puffy white clouds deigned to mark the blue sky today, but rain was due mid-week. They needed to get the bales dry and covered again before then.

"How about over there?" Brandon pointed to a flat piece of land only a few metres away but it would be far enough should the stack start burning again before they finished the transfer.

Darcy nodded.

"Right." Lara marched over to a bale and struggled to lift it.

She killed him with her kindness. "Pumpkin, they're a little heavy for you."

She jutted her chin as if she was about to argue.

"But it would be a huge help if you filled our water cooler with water and ice, and brought some plastic cups out so everyone has something to drink. Maybe bring some biscuits too."

"Yep, I'm on it." She ran towards the house.

He kept thinking he couldn't love her more than he did, but she kept proving him wrong. "Bran, can you go fill the tanker?"

He nodded.

In the end, about a dozen guests help shift the stack, leaving the bales which were soaked to one side so they would dry in the sun. The fire truck arrived and investigated the point of ignition.

"Darcy!" Jeff, the officer in charge, waved him over.

"What's up?"

He crouched and showed Darcy a blackened section of bale separate from the rest of the stack, and then another one. "There are multiple ignition points." He glanced up, his expression serious. "This wasn't a case of spontaneous combustion."

Fury stormed into him. Son of a bitch. "How long for the fire to take hold?"

Jeff shrugged. "No more than five minutes."

In the middle of the day. They were getting more brash.

"Who spotted the fire?" Jeff asked.

"Jay." He was resting on a bale, drinking a cup of water. Darcy strode over to him with Jeff by his side.

"How did you discover the fire?" Darcy asked.

The man frowned. "I came out of the caravan after having lunch," he said. "I was going to read my book, but I noticed the smoke and ran to get you."

"Did you see anyone around the haystack?" Jeff asked.

"No one."

His caravan was the closest. "What about anyone walking past while you were having lunch?"

He shook his head. "Do you think it was deliberately

lit?"

"Just checking all options," Darcy said. The last thing they needed was for the guests to be worried about their safety. But it was something he should consider. Would Stonefish's tactics escalate to hurting their guests?

He and Jeff moved over to the fire truck. "I'll call Dot," Jeff said. "She'll need to come out so leave those bales where they are so she can look at them."

"Will do."

The fire crew stayed and helped for a while before they headed back into town. A red car pulled in and Darcy's heart lifted. "Faith, what are you doing here?"

She smiled. "I called and Lara told me what had happened. I figured you'd need some help."

He pulled her into his arms, needing her comfort.

She stroked his back. "How bad is it?"

"Could have been worse. Jeff thinks it was deliberately lit." Which meant it almost had to be a guest at the Ridge. Who hadn't come to help?

"Have you called Dot?"

"She's on her way." He shifted away.

"We've got this." Her words gave him strength, even though he knew they weren't necessarily true. "What can I do to help?"

He scanned the area. Lara sat by the water cooler, staring at them, a look of uncertainty on her face. Crap. He hadn't spoken to her about Faith. She'd been so nervous about Sofia's visit, he hadn't wanted to add to that. "Ah, can you check the wet bales, rotate them if they've dried? I'd better talk to Lara."

Faith followed his gaze. "You didn't mention us?"

"Not yet. She was preoccupied with Sofia's visit." He kissed her again. "I'll be back."

When he reached Lara, she said to him, "You kissed Faith."

He nodded. "I did. Does it upset you?"

Lara picked up the water cooler. "I need to fill this."

He winced at the non-answer and walked with her back to the house. When they were inside, she said, "How long have you been kissing Faith?"

"Since Friday."

"Does that mean Natasha was right?" The question was so quiet, Darcy nearly missed it. It took him a second to remember Natasha's taunt at pony club about Faith only being nice to Lara because she fancied Darcy. Damn.

"No, pumpkin. Your relationship with Faith is different from my relationship with Faith. You were friends with her before we even met."

"I thought we were a team." She turned on the tap to fill the cooler.

This was going to be harder than he realised. "We are a team, but I like Faith a different way from the way you like Faith."

"Do you want to get into her pants?"

He cursed Natasha to the ends of the earth and back. Reaching over Lara, he turned off the tap and pulled her around to sit at the table next to him. "Remember when you told me Jordan made you feel all warm and funny in your tummy?"

Her cheeks reddened and she nodded.

"That's how Faith makes me feel. I like her and she likes me. It's completely different from the way I love you to the moon and back. That won't ever change no matter what happens between Faith and me."

"Will Faith stop teaching me riding if she stops liking you?"

"I don't think so, pumpkin. Faith's not that kind of person. She liked you before she even met me."

Lara pursed her lips and then nodded. "OK."

Darcy breathed out a sigh of relief. "Are we good

now?"

"Yeah. I'd better get this water out to everyone." She hefted the cooler out of the sink.

"I've got this, pumpkin." He took the cooler from her and together they walked back out to the haystack.

Chapter 12

Faith's back and arm muscles ached by the time the salvaged bales had been transferred to a new pile and the wet bales had been turned. With so many people helping it took only a couple of hours and Darcy told his camp guests he'd give them the night free of charge as thanks.

"Here you go." Lara held out a cup of water to Faith.

"Thanks, Lara." The cold water relieved her parched throat. What had Darcy said to Lara about them? All he'd said when he'd come back from talking to her was that they were all good. Not helpful.

A police car rumbled into the yard and they both turned to watch Dot and Nhiari get out of the car.

"What're they doing here?" Lara asked.

Faith had the same question. "I don't know."

Amy wandered over. "Why don't we go inside?" she suggested. "I don't know about you two, but I need a shower and something more substantial to eat."

"Sounds good," Faith said, still watching Darcy and Brandon greet the police, her gut churning. The fire must have been deliberately lit. It was the only reason they would have called the police. Someone really had it in for the Stokes. Could Stonefish be responsible? If so, they were odd tactics for a large company to resort to.

"Dad?" Lara called.

Darcy waved at her. "It's all good, pumpkin. We'll be inside shortly."

Lara harrumphed but followed Amy and Faith back inside. Amy popped the kettle on. "Do you want the first shower, Lara?"

"I'll wait," she said. "I need to talk to Dad when he comes inside."

Faith smiled. She liked the girl's determination.

"All right," Amy said. "I won't be long." To Faith she said, "Help yourself to anything."

Lara got out a tin of chocolate chip biscuits and offered it to Faith.

"Thanks." She grabbed a biscuit and sat at the table, too tired to stand. This was her first real taste of farm life. Having to get things done whether or not you had the energy for it. "Did you have a nice morning with your mum?"

Lara nodded. "The boys rode Starlight, and then we went to the beach. Mum doesn't like the farm, but I'm going to teach her to crochet."

Faith blinked. "Is she staying in town?"

"Nah, she's going to video call me from Melbourne."

Faith hoped that meant Sofia didn't want custody of Lara. She'd ask Darcy later.

Lara studied her biscuit. "So, you like my dad."

Faith flinched. The statement shouldn't have surprised her. "Yeah, I do. He's a pretty great guy."

"He is," Lara agreed. Then she asked, "But we're still friends, right?" She met Faith's eyes briefly before looking away.

Faith's heart caught. "Absolutely." She moved down

the table to sit next to Lara. "Of course. Who else am I going to search for buried treasure with? I hope we'll be friends no matter what happens between your dad and me."

"Promise?"

"Promise."

"OK." The phone rang and Lara jumped up to answer it. "Hey, Georgie. No, the fire's out. Dad's talking to Dot." A pause. "I don't know. Brandon's talking to her as well." Another pause and Lara rolled her eyes. "Amy's in the shower. It's only me and Faith here." With a sigh, she handed the phone to Faith. "Georgie wants to speak to you."

She wasn't sure if she could help. "Hi, Georgie."

"Faith, what the hell is going on out there?" Georgie demanded. "The first thing I heard when I got off the boat this evening was the fire truck was sent out to the Ridge."

"The haystack caught fire," Faith explained. "It was out by the time I got here and we spent a couple of hours moving the bales to ensure nothing was smouldering and to dry them."

Georgie swore. "How much burned?"

"About a quarter."

More swearing. "This is bad. The hay was all we've got left to feed the sheep."

Faith frowned. "So what will they do?"

"I don't know," Georgie said. "Tell Darcy and Brandon to call me if I can help."

She liked how supportive this family was. "I will." She hung up and switched on the kitchen light. "Everyone's going to be starving when they finish out there," she said. "Shall we make something for dinner?"

Lara grinned. "Yeah. Amy was going to make a vegetable frittata."

Faith could manage that with the help of the

internet. "All right. Let's get to it."

***

Darcy waved goodbye to Dot and Nhiari, the effort of it just about doing him in. His entire body ached and the weight of the additional loss made him drag his feet.

"We're going to have to factor this in," Brandon said.

He nodded. "Yeah, but not tonight. My brain won't focus on the numbers."

Brandon clapped him on the shoulder. "We'll get through this. Danielle might be able to loan us some feed."

He was right. Neighbours always looked out for neighbours. Matt drove into the yard and his friend hurried over. "What the hell happened?"

"Haystack fire," Darcy told him. "Lost about a quarter."

Matt swore. "I've got to stop visiting my parents. Shit always seems to happen when I'm away."

Suspicion raised its ugly head and Darcy slapped it away. Not Matt. Never.

"We'll sort out what we're doing tomorrow," Brandon said. "But right now we need showers and food."

Darcy followed them into the kitchen and his heart stopped. Lara and Faith were frying onions on the stove and laughing at something. The beautiful picture almost made him weep after the day he'd had. Lara grinned at him. "Dad! We're making frittata for dinner."

"Sounds great, pumpkin. Have we got time for a shower?" He was still damp and itchy from moving all the hay.

"Yep. We'll have a beer waiting for you."

He chuckled. "Just what I need." On his way past Faith, he gave into his urge and pulled her close to kiss.

"Also what I need," he murmured and then continued out of the kitchen with the hollering teasing of both Brandon and Matt behind him. He had a little more of a spring to his step as he passed Amy in the hallway and ducked into the bathroom.

About ten minutes later he returned to the kitchen. Faith and Amy were cutting up a salad, and the frittata was in the oven. Lara handed him a beer, and he sank down at the table next to Matt, who sliced tomatoes.

"How are your parents?"

"Pretty good. They're preparing for the rain next week."

"They can come here if they have any problems."

"Yeah, mate, they know." He slid the tomatoes he'd cut into the salad bowl. "What did Dot and Nhi say?"

Darcy didn't want to think about that now. "Only thing we can do is be alert. Dot suggested we stop taking camp guests for a while, but we can't afford not to."

"Did someone start the fire, Dad?"

Damn. "Looks like it, pumpkin. We're lucky Jay spotted it in time."

"He was pretty quick," Lara said. "He said he had a haystack fire at his farm once and it made a big mess."

At least Jay didn't have to worry about such things now he'd retired. Though he helped them often enough on the farm that maybe it should be called semi-retirement. Some people weren't born to completely relax.

When Brandon returned from his shower, Darcy realised Faith still wore the clothes she'd arrived in. "Faith, do you want to borrow more of Georgie's clothes?"

She smiled. "I brought a change, just in case. It's in the car."

"I'll walk you out to get it."

As he stood, Matt murmured, "Darcy and Faith sitting in a tree, k-i-s-s-i-n-g…"

Real mature. He shoved Matt lightly and went outside with Faith. The air still smelled of smoke and his muscles tensed.

Faith held his hand. "How are you coping?"

"I can't think about it tonight," he said. "If I do, it will do me in."

"Do you think it's Stonefish?"

"Who else would it be? There were too many ignition spots for it to be someone being careless with a cigarette butt."

"What about your neighbours? Anyone in competition with you?"

He shook his head. "We help each other. The market is big enough for all of us and we know how hard it is."

At her car, she slipped both arms around him and held him. He closed his eyes, leaned his head on her shoulder. He'd forgotten how it felt to share his troubles with someone. If he could stay like this forever, he'd be happy. She stroked the back of his head. "We'll get through this, Darcy."

His heart tripped over itself and fell. Foolish, but he wouldn't regret loving Faith. It was too soon to say the words, so he showed her instead. He turned his head, kissed her cheek and then found her mouth. Slowly he teased and caressed her lips, pouring his emotion into the kiss. Her arms tightened around him and she met him with an equal passion. This. All of this. They were matched, two parts of the one whole, but instead of sinking further into her, he forced himself to pull away. "Stay the night."

"Yes." She kissed him one more time and then got her bag from the back seat of her car. "I brought back Georgie's clothes. She called earlier and said for you or

Brandon to call her if you needed anything."

"Thanks." Georgie didn't have time to worry about what was happening at the Ridge.

They walked back inside and the smells of dinner permeated the room.

"Can I have a shower?" Faith asked.

Lara glanced at the oven. "Yep. I'll show you to the bathroom."

Faith squeezed Darcy's hand. "That would be great."

Lara didn't need to know Faith had stayed the night Friday.

"You and Faith, huh?" Matt said.

"Yeah." He smiled as he sat and took a swig of his beer. It was early days still. He'd have time to convince her to stay.

"She's nice."

Lara returned to the kitchen. "Do you want me to suss out the camp guests, Dad?"

Darcy blinked. "What?"

"One of them must have lit the fire. I could go around, ask them if they want to meet Maggie or Starlight, see if they're bad people. People never suspect kids."

He shook his head, smothering his smile. "No, pumpkin. It might have been someone driving on to the property."

"Bennet would have barked, or Mum would have seen them when she left."

Good point. He'd call Sofia after Lara went to bed. "Promise me you'll leave the investigation to Dot. She knows what she's doing." He didn't want Lara to be on Stonefish's radar.

She pouted. "All right."

They sat chatting until Faith returned and dinner was ready.

Afterwards, Darcy tucked Lara into bed, but only got halfway through a chapter before Lara was asleep. He smiled, brushing a kiss on her forehead and pulling the covers over her. Then he returned to the kitchen where the others waited.

"Have you sent the letter to Stonefish?" Brandon asked Faith.

She nodded. "Yesterday. I doubt I'll hear anything from them, so I've prepared a letter for the ACCC."

Darcy wrapped his hands around his coffee cup. These guys were in the big leagues and the Ridge was an annoying fly that wouldn't go away. Perhaps it was time to pretend to be dead. "We should do a deal."

All heads turned towards him and Brandon spoke. "You want to give in to them? Are you crazy?"

"Hear me out," Darcy said. "For the past six months, they've been trying to buy the property. We don't know why, but it's got to be something significant for them to stick around and not move on to the next property."

"Has anyone asked your neighbours if they've had offers?" Faith asked.

She had a point. It wasn't too late, so he phoned Danielle.

"Darcy, what do you need?"

He smiled at the easy offer. He should invite her family over for dinner one day soon. "Danielle, have you had anyone approach you to buy the station?"

"No. Have you?"

"Yeah, some mob from Singapore."

"They want to pay you decent money for it?" She sounded interested.

"Seems decent."

"You going to sell?"

"We haven't decided yet."

"Well, if you decide not to, send them my way. I

could handle retiring right about now."

He chuckled. "Will do. Talk to you later." He hung up. "She hasn't been approached, but she's interested in selling."

"Should we direct Stonefish to her?" Amy asked.

Darcy sat. He didn't want to divert Stonefish's violence on a friend. "No. If they wanted her land, they would have already given her an offer." There were a lot of variables in his suggestion, but he was tired of sitting around waiting for the next thing to go wrong. "We should set up a meeting with them."

"To what end?" Brandon asked. "They won't admit they're behind the damage."

"No, but right now they're an anonymous business. Tan hasn't been seen since before the accident. We need names and faces."

Brandon leaned back and smiled. "I like your thinking."

"Why would they believe you're willing to sell now?" Faith asked. "You've been adamant about it."

He glanced at his brother. "The station has been moved into Brandon's name. He's spent the past month playing farmer—" He held up a hand to stop Brandon's protest, "and has decided it's too hard. He wants to get rid of it, but he knows I won't agree, so he needs to meet with them in town in secret."

"Then we'll have someone we can follow," Brandon said. "It might work."

"Will they send someone important?" Matt asked. "They were using Taylor before, and the guy who had a petty thief rap sheet."

Faith spoke. "If you imply you're ready to sign the contract, they'll send someone who can countersign it and get it witnessed immediately. They wouldn't want to lose the opportunity."

"We should bring Dot in on this," Amy said. "She

deserves to know what we're planning."

Darcy could already hear Dot's pissed off tone in his head, but Amy was right. "Let's set up the meeting first. They might not agree to it. Then we can tell her."

"Let me get the laptop," Brandon said. "I'll write the email now. It's the perfect timing with the haystack fire. The straw that broke the farmer's back."

For Darcy, it was the straw that made him determined to fight fire with fire.

It took over an hour for them to agree to the wording of the email. Faith pointed out a few things to change, so the wording was vaguer, less like a promise to sign. "If you're not careful, they could use the email as an unofficial contract and take you to court. You'd have nothing left by the time they were done."

Darcy wanted to be sick. He wasn't cut out for contracts and legalese, but having Faith there gave him a measure of comfort. She'd steer them right.

Finally Brandon was ready to press send.

"Do you want to wait a couple of days first to see if they respond to my email?" Faith asked.

He was ready to take action, but if they could settle this in a civilised way, there would be less danger to those around him.

"We could wait until Friday," Brandon said.

Darcy sighed. "All right. You'll call me as soon as you hear something?" he asked Faith.

"Us," Brandon corrected.

Faith smiled. "Of course."

He stood. "I'm heading to bed." He held out his hand to Faith, and she took it. "Night everyone."

As they walked down the corridor, Faith asked, "Will Lara be upset if she finds me sharing your bed?"

He hesitated. "I don't know. She doesn't normally wake before me, but we'll cross that bridge if we come to it," he said. "I need you in my bed tonight."

"All right."

He closed his bedroom door behind them and stripped off his shirt. Faith ran her hands over his chest. "You look exhausted." She led him over to the bed. "Lay down and let me take care of you tonight." She undid his jeans, and he helped her slide them off. Then she showed him just how much she cared for him.

Chapter 13

The next morning, Faith's shoulders were tense as she prepared coffee in the kitchen. Her ears strained for sounds of Darcy and Lara's conversation, but she heard nothing. Darcy had decided it was best if he explained to Lara that Faith had stayed the night when he woke her. That way he could answer any questions she might have like where Faith had slept.

What if Lara was upset about it?

Faith couldn't wipe the memory of Lara's uncertainty from her mind. If Natasha hadn't said nasty things, Lara probably wouldn't have thought Faith could have ulterior motives for befriending her.

"Morning, Faith!" Lara's cheerful greeting wiped Faith's concerns away.

"Morning. Would you like a hot chocolate?"

"Yes, please."

And just like that, everything was fine. Lara got her own cereal while Faith made hot drinks and Darcy made lunches, not only for Lara, but for him and Brandon and Matt to take out on the station.

"Want me to drop you at school, Lara?" Faith asked. She'd already discussed it with Darcy.

"That would be great."

When they were done, Lara hugged Darcy and gathered her backpack. Faith hesitated, but Lara was already out the door, so she kissed him. "I'll call you tonight."

"Looking forward to it."

On the drive to school, they discussed the supposed buried treasure. Faith suspected Darcy was right, and it was all a figment of Lara's imagination, but it was still fun to plan.

"We should go on an expedition this weekend," Lara declared as Faith pulled up in front of the school.

"Sounds like fun. Count me in."

Lara jumped out and waved. "See you at pony club, Faith."

"I can't wait," Faith called back and then drove the short distance to her parents' house. Her father's raised voice sailed out of her parent's front door. That wasn't good. He should already be on the boat by now. Fear gripped her, and she ran inside to find her father pacing and her mother sitting calmly on the couch. He whirled around and gestured wildly towards her. "And here she is."

"I told you she would be home," her mother said. "I'm perfectly capable of being alone, Rob."

"She should be looking after you, not having her pipes cleaned," he growled.

Faith gasped. "Excuse me?"

"You heard me. Don't think we don't know you're sleeping with Darcy."

Outrage filled her. How dare he judge her relationship? "What I do in my own time is none of your business."

"Your time should be spent with your mother."

No, that was it. She'd had enough. Her mother might like the subtle way, but it didn't work for Faith.

"Sit down." Rob stumbled back at her tone, landing on the couch, his mouth open in shock. Her hands shook, and she clenched them. "So you're telling me I'm not allowed to have any free time?" she asked. "I have to be glued to Mum's side whenever you're not here?"

His nod was a little uncertain.

"It's not enough that I put my very well-paid career on hold, moved several thousand kilometres from my home and have entirely given my life over to helping her rehabilitate?" He opened his mouth to speak, but she cut him off. "While you've continued your life, business as usual, with Mum's stroke being barely a speed bump in your life."

"Now, Faith," her mother said.

"No, Mum," she said. "It's time someone pointed out how hypocritical Dad is being." She turned to him. "Mum said you're thinking of selling the business and buying a café. What will you do then? Am I expected to move with you, or will you prop up Mum at a corner table so you can keep an eye on her?"

"She could have died!" her father yelled. "I can't risk losing her again." The pain and fear in his eyes extinguished her anger.

Faith let out a breath. "Yeah, she could have, but the doctors think she's doing well. Having a babysitter twenty-four seven won't prevent a second stroke." She sighed. "Have you even asked Mum what she wants?"

His guilty expression was all the answer she needed.

"Then you two need to talk, while I go for a walk." She didn't wait for a response.

Outside, the day promised sunshine and hope. She inhaled deeply, letting the last of her frustration fade. No matter what her parents decided, it was time she figured out what she wanted. She wouldn't be moving with them even if her father got his way about the café. Her steps took her towards the centre of town. Her decision revolved around whether she wanted to stay here or return to the city.

"Morning, Faith!" Gretchen's son, Jordan waved at her as he zoomed by on his bike on his way to school.

She grinned and waved back. "Morning!" It wasn't a difficult choice. The Bay and the Ridge had captured her heart.

Yesterday when everyone had pulled together to help move those bales, she'd seen the community in action. Darcy looked as if he was ready to drop from exhaustion and despair, and yet he kept going, never giving up, even managing a smile and a cheerful word to Lara.

That took incredible strength.

He was always taking care of everyone else, which was why last night she'd wanted to look after him. Her body tingled as she remembered their slow love-making and the way he'd wrapped her in his arms afterwards and held her. This relationship wasn't about 'cleaning her pipes' as her father had so crudely put it. She wanted to explore where they could go, and to do that she needed to stay here.

On her way past the shopping complex, she ducked in and bought a notepad and pen and continued to the bakery where she ordered coffee and a muffin. Then she took her time writing her ideas for work if she stayed in town.

It took an hour to brainstorm options. Her parents had had plenty of time to talk things through. On her way home, she stopped by the real estate agency's window. A townhouse by the marina would be nice. If she sold her place in Perth for what it was worth, she'd be able to afford it easily enough. There was also a sign in a nearby building declaring it was available to rent. She peered inside. A decent size, though the walls needed painting and the carpet replacing. It would make a good office space.

At her parents' place all was quiet, and she almost knocked. Instead, she let herself in and found them sitting in the lounge with a cup of tea.

Her mother smiled. "Your father is retiring. We're selling the business, buying a caravan and travelling around Australia."

Relief swept through her and Faith grinned. "That's great."

Her father nodded, looking quite chuffed by the idea. "I reckon we could become one of those Youtubers who film their trips. Become influencers."

She stifled a chuckle. "You could." And he'd probably succeed as well.

He stood. "I'm sorry for what I said to you. I appreciate what you've done for your mother and me." He clasped his hands together and shuffled his feet.

Milly cleared her throat.

He glanced at her and cringed. "And I'm sorry for my comments about you going out to the Ridge. I'm sure Darcy's treating you right."

"He is." But she wasn't discussing her relationship with him. "When are you putting the business on the market?"

"As soon as I've got the paperwork in order. I'll organise some of my team to take over my shifts and then your mum and I will fly to Perth to buy a caravan." He headed out of the room. "I'll check the flights now."

She had to give him credit, when he decided on something, he worked fast. Maybe that's where she got it from.

"What will you do now?" her mother asked.

Faith took a deep breath. "I'm staying here. I enjoy running the pony club."

"The pony club doesn't pay much."

She busied her hands making a cup of tea. "I could set up a law practice. I'd need to brush up on a few different areas like wills and estates."

"Would you have enough business even with the fees lawyers charge?"

Faith didn't know, but voicing her other idea would give her plans more weight. She sighed. "I was considering setting up a trail riding business," she admitted. "But the start-up costs will be high and there might not be a market for it. People come up here to swim and snorkel." Now she'd started, she couldn't shut up. "Though the Stokes might agree for me to do something out at the Ridge. And I'd have to research all the licences I need and insurance." Her mother nodded, and Faith asked her the real question bothering her. "Does it sound like something Dad would do?"

Milly burst out laughing. "Darling, is that what's worrying you?"

Faith nodded.

"It doesn't sound the least bit like your father. Firstly he wouldn't consider licences and insurance until after he'd bought the business and I don't think he even knows what market research means. Horse riding is your passion, you know far more about it than Rob ever knew about whale sharks or running a boat."

"It seems just like Dad to throw away one good job because something else caught my interest."

"No." Her stern tone made Faith sit a little straighter. "Your father changed jobs because he was bored, yes, but it was because he'd worked through all the challenges. We never, ever sold a business for a loss. He always increased the profit."

Faith sat back. "Really?"

"Absolutely, and I'm sorry you didn't realise that. Your father has restless feet because he's smart. You get your intelligence from him. And if you're not following your heart because you are worried about being like him, then you should be ashamed."

She gaped at her mother.

"I brought you up better than that," Milly continued. "I thought you loved and respected him."

"I do love him."

Milly waited for her to continue. Perhaps she hadn't respected him. She'd considered him flighty and with no drive. She sighed. "I'm sorry. He never stuck with anything for long."

"That's because he'd achieved everything he wanted to achieve."

Hell. It appeared as if she was wrong about both of her parents. She closed her eyes. If she'd asked questions about their constant moving, and about the businesses, perhaps she would have realised it earlier. Foolish that she assumed she knew everything. "I'm sorry."

"For what?" Rob asked as he returned with his laptop.

"For making assumptions." Telling her father would only upset him. "I was just telling Mum, I'm thinking of moving here permanently." The words made her shiver with anticipation. She was really going to do this.

"And do what?" Rob asked.

She smiled. "Law and horses."

***

By Wednesday Faith had crunched her numbers and booked an appointment with a real estate agent to look at the vacancy in the main shopping complex. She hadn't mentioned moving here permanently to Darcy when she'd seen him at the pony club the night before. What they had was too new, and she didn't want to put any pressure on him. She was staying in Retribution Bay for herself first and foremost.

Cindy waited for her outside the office. "Lovely to meet you, Faith." Her handshake was firm, though her skin was soft.

"Likewise."

Outside, the space was nothing to rave over. Simple large glass windows in the brick frontage. Cindy struggled with the lock. "I'll make sure it's fixed if you decide to lease the premise," she said.

Inside the walls were an ugly grey and covered in picture hooks. The carpet might have been beige sometime in the eighties but was now a dusty red-grey colour and there was a single door leading to another space.

"The air conditioning is reverse cycle," Cindy said, going over to the panel on the back wall. "Not that you'll need heat much up here." She switched it on, and it groaned to life before settling into a relatively quiet hum. "Through here is a small kitchenette with running water, but you'll need to provide your own equipment. You'll share the bathroom around the back with the other tenants in the building, but it's kept locked, so the public doesn't get in."

Faith slowly turned, examining the space. It wasn't likely she'd have any drop-in clients, but people valued their privacy. They may be put off if shoppers walking past could see them inside. Then everyone would wonder why they needed a lawyer. "Can I erect a wall here?" She indicated where she wanted it.

"I have no issues, as long as it's removable when you leave."

"Is there anyone in town who could do it?"

"I can give you the name of a builder," Cindy said. "Otherwise you'll need to look at Carnarvon or Karratha."

Would she need a receptionist? Maybe not at first while things got started, but she'd leave space for a desk. "Who pays for new flooring?"

They negotiated the details until both were satisfied. Faith's skin tingled as she shook Cindy's hand. "I'll take it."

She left Cindy to sort the contract and ducked into the bakery where she'd promised to meet her mother for lunch. Milly sat at a table with a cup of coffee in front of her.

"Sorry, am I late?" She slid in the seat opposite her.

"Not at all. It didn't take me as long as I thought to walk here." Milly beamed.

"That's great." They ordered lunch and then Milly asked, "Did you like the place?"

"I did. I can make something nice of it," she said. Though it may take a little longer than she'd like to get the work done if she couldn't find a local to do it.

"Wonderful. Your father's booked us flights to Perth on Friday evening and we won't be back until Tuesday. I insisted on catching up with your brothers while we were in town."

"Say hi to them for me."

She was pleased both her parents seemed happy with their decision. Her mum looked a lot more vibrant than she had in the past few weeks, as if having something to look forward to had given her a new lease on life.

After they ate, they wandered along the verandahs of the shops and then out into the sun. So much for the weather forecast of rain. She enjoyed this kind of weather for winter, but the summers were scorching. It had been a shock to the system when she'd first moved here to help her mother, but she would get used to it.

As they crossed the road, a black ute drove towards them. Her mother stumbled, falling on Faith, and Faith almost dropped her. "Oof, sorry darling," Milly said.

Faith glanced down the road. The ute still came towards them and if anything had increased its speed. The windows were too dark to see the driver. "Quickly, Mum." She pulled on her mum's arm, heart racing as the car barrelled towards them.

"It'll stop," her mother said.

Faith wasn't so sure. "He hasn't seen us, Mum." With more strength than she knew she had, she yanked her mother forward, and they both stumbled to the edge of the road, tripping on the curb and falling in a heap on the ground. The ute raced past.

Heart racing, she dusted the dirt off her palms. "Are you OK?"

"Bloody tourists," her mum grumbled. "No respect."

Faith rubbed the goosebumps on her arms. The vehicle was too far away to get the number plates. A normal person—whether a tourist or not—would slow down if people crossed the road in front of them. Perhaps she was being paranoid. She helped her mum to her feet and then helped her brush the dirt from the back of her pants. Faith gave her mother a tissue to stop the bleeding on her palms.

They kept to the footpaths as they walked home, with Faith looking for a black ute in any of the driveways they passed. She stopped to get the mail while her mother continued into the house saying she was going to wash up. In the letterbox was a plain white envelope with her name on it. No stamp. No address.

She scanned the neighbourhood, but no one was in their garden. Her hand shook as she slid her finger under the flap and pried the envelope open. Inside was a single piece of paper. The typed words sent a chill down her spine.

Next time we won't miss.

Chapter 14

Darcy hung up the phone after speaking with Faith, his hand shaking with rage. Very carefully he put the receiver back on its charging station rather than slam it down like he wanted to. Stonefish had gone too far.

"Is something wrong with Faith, Dad?" Lara was getting biscuits out of the kitchen cupboard for afternoon tea.

Yeah, something was wrong. Someone was threatening her, and if he caught the bastard, he'd kill him. Instead, he forced a smile. "No, pumpkin. Faith's coming to hang out here for a couple of days. She wants to go through some ideas she had with Amy."

At her name, Amy glanced up. "Horse-riding stuff?"

Darcy nodded. It hadn't been difficult to convince Faith to stay at the Ridge, and that told him she was scared. "Have you done your homework?" Lara's pout gave him her answer. "Go get your school bag."

The second she left the room, Amy asked, "What gives?"

"Faith and her mum were almost run down today," Darcy said, his hands clenching. "A letter addressed to Faith said next time they won't miss."

Amy swore. "She OK?"

"Shaken. She took the letter to Dot, but there were no prints. Faith's parents are heading to Perth for a few days, and she's convinced them to go a day early."

"Rain's forecast on the weekend," Amy blurted.

He frowned, but then Lara walked in. Ah. Well spotted.

He helped Lara with her homework while Amy finished making dinner.

A car arrived as Lara returned her school things to her room. Darcy strode outside and was at Faith's door before she'd switched off the engine. Opening it, he pulled her into his arms and breathed in her scent. "You're all right?"

"Yeah. A scrape on my palm is all."

He turned her hand over and pressed a kiss against the red scratches. "How are your parents?"

"Dad didn't want me to stay, but Mum and Dot convinced him. I told Dot about the email we've drafted to Stonefish and though she doesn't like it, she wants to be included."

He nodded. "Sure." He retrieved her overnight bag from the back seat and then slipped his hand into hers. "I told Lara you're here to help Amy with trail ride ideas."

"That works."

Inside the kitchen, Amy was dishing up dinner. Lara came back in and grinned. "Hey, Faith! Dad said you're staying a few days. We can plan our expedition."

"Sounds like fun," Faith agreed.

"What's this?" Darcy asked.

"We're going treasure hunting," Lara said, a huge grin on her face.

It would keep her distracted and if a few of them went, they should be safe, especially if Brandon sent the email this evening telling Stonefish he was considering selling. That might be enough to keep them from trying anything else until after the meeting.

Matt kicked off his boots outside and came in, his face a thundercloud.

Now what?

"What's up?"

Matt shook his head. "Nothing. Just my folks."

Odd. Matt normally had a solid relationship with his parents. "They OK? No one's sick?"

"Nah, nothing like that. It's fine. Just community stuff."

"The bush tomatoes should be ripe soon," Lara piped up.

"Sure will," Matt replied. "We'll go looking for some on the weekend if it doesn't rain."

"Yes!"

"What are bush tomatoes?" Faith asked as she sat at the table.

"I was wondering the same thing," Amy said.

"A native plant which grows out here," Matt told them. "Used to live on them as kids."

"Could I go with you?" Faith asked.

"Sure," Lara said, sitting next to Faith and hugging her.

Darcy smiled. He would be screwed if Faith and Lara didn't like each other. They kept the chat light until it was time for Lara to go to bed. "Which book are we starting today, pumpkin?" he asked as he tucked her in.

She pressed her lips together. "Do you think Faith would like to listen too?" she asked. "If she's staying a few days, she might like a story."

"How about I ask?" At her nod, he returned to the kitchen and said to Faith, "Lara asked whether you'd like to join us at story time tonight. We're starting a new book."

Faith smiled. "I'd love to."

His heart filled as they walked back to Lara's room. Lara had already made room amongst her stuffed toys and patted the bed each side of her. "We should all fit."

He chuckled. Two adults and a child on a single bed would be a squeeze. "How about you sit on my lap?" he suggested.

"All right."

He and Faith took turns reading a chapter each of the fantasy story about a princess assassin. When they finished, Lara said, "Can we have one more chapter please?"

"No, pumpkin. You've got school tomorrow."

He shifted her off his lap and brushed a kiss on her forehead. "Sweet dreams."

Faith kissed her as well. "Thank you for sharing story time with me."

"You're welcome."

Darcy switched off the light and followed Faith back to the kitchen. Would this be what life could be like if he convinced Faith to stay?

"What's the plan for Stonefish?" Brandon asked.

The joy of story time vanished as reality intruded.

"It's time to send the email we drafted," Faith said. "Today's incident made it clear they aren't interested in giving back any money."

Brandon nodded. "I agree. I can add I don't want anyone else getting hurt."

"Would they buy it?" Darcy asked. "You're ex-army. Wouldn't they expect you to go on the offensive now they tried to run Faith over?"

"Not if they think I got out because I burned out." Brandon brought up the email on the laptop and showed them. "Do we change anything?"

Darcy read it and then looked at Faith. "What do you think?"

"It's stronger if we stick with one message. Brandon's had enough of farming, and he wants to get out. If they agree to meet with you, you can say you want to give Darcy options to change his life, or something like that." She squeezed Darcy's hand.

He hated even the thought of pretending to sell the land, but if it identified someone to investigate, it was worth it.

"Ready for me to sell?" Brandon waited for them each to nod before he pressed the button.

It was done.

Now they had to wait for the response.

***

On Thursday and Friday Faith helped Amy with the campgrounds. The plumber was due next week to do the piping for the new showers, and so they sorted the scrap metal to make sure they had the supplies for the frame. It was such a great idea, and Faith couldn't wait to see it finished. Then they pored over options for offering horse-riding and priced up costs to add powered sites. The isolation was a problem. Equipment was more expensive, would take longer to arrive, and then installing the utilities was a task. So they kept exploring options.

Faith also sent her boss a resignation letter and spent time on the costings to refurbish her office. The builder in town could do the work, but the supplies were more expensive than she'd expected.

When Lara arrived home from school on Friday, Faith helped her and Amy work on their riding technique in the yard. The activity caused interest amongst the guests and they came over to watch. Jay joined in, using Matt's horse, Wesley. He'd had horses on his wheatbelt farm and was keen to do more riding. While they were brushing their mounts, Faith remembered a question she'd been meaning to ask Lara. "Do you know anyone who is good at lassoing?"

"Dad is. He showed the twins last weekend. Lassoed one of my sheep. Why?"

"A couple of the kids at pony club want to learn and I need to find an instructor."

Lara grinned. "Dad would be great. He's been trying to teach me, but I'm not very good. Sometimes he goes on his knees with his hands up so I have a stationary target." She demonstrated.

An appealing visual, but not one she should think of with Lara around.

"Can we go on our treasure hunt tomorrow?" Lara said.

Faith blocked the image and glanced at the sky. Still blue skies despite the forecast for rain over the weekend. She couldn't imagine it eventuating. "We'll have to check with Darcy, but I can't see any issues."

Lara stood on tiptoes to see Jay around her horse. "Do you want to come, Jay?"

"I'd love to, Lara. Maybe you can point out some of the edible plants you were telling me about." He retrieved a gadget out of his pocket similar to a swiss army knife and flicked on the light to have a closer look at something on Wesley's coat. "There's a cut here."

Faith came closer. Nothing too bad, just a scratch, but she'd put some antiseptic on it.

"That's neat," Lara said, pointing to the gadget.

"It's been a lifesaver on more than one occasion." Jay showed her the knife and other tools it contained. "I don't go anywhere without it. You never know when you might need a light, or a knife, or a flint."

It would be handy on a farm. Perhaps Faith should get one for herself if she started trail rides. She finished brushing Fezzik and turned him loose in the yard. After her riding lesson tomorrow, she might bring Spirit out.

Georgie and Dot were taking turns feeding her at the pony club, but she'd have more opportunity to ride here.

She said goodnight to Jay and then walked back to the house with Lara. "Have a shower and then you'd better do your homework," she said.

"Yes, Mum." Lara slapped her hand over her mouth, eyes wide, cheeks red. "I mean, Faith. Sorry." She hurried from the room.

Faith had no words. The warmth spreading through her was as unexpected as it was pleasant. It didn't matter that it was a slip of the tongue, or that Lara had her own mother, suddenly Faith could see herself as a mum and she'd never really considered that.

"You all right?" Amy asked. She opened the slow cooker and stirred the soup.

Faith nodded. "That got me right in the gut."

"Lara is the loveliest kid," Amy agreed. "How are things going with you and Darcy?"

"It's easy," she said. "I don't know if that's good or bad, but it's like he's always been part of my life."

"I'd say it was good. Have you told him you're staying in Retribution Bay?"

"Not yet. I'm nervous. I don't want him to freak out. I'm staying for myself first."

"I get it, but I don't think it will bother him at all."

Faith sighed. Amy was right. Faith was more nervous that he wouldn't care either way. She'd talk to him tonight.

"It would be nice having another woman around here again," Amy said and winked.

Was that an option? They hadn't discussed how long she would stay at the farm. At least until her parents got back from Perth, but afterwards? It might not be wise to be so far out of town for her law firm, though she could always work school hours and take Lara to and from school.

She was getting too far ahead of herself.

The kitchen door opened, and she spun around, hope in her heart. As Darcy walked in and hung his hat on the hook, a grin spread over her face. She hurried over and kissed him. "How was your day?"

"Better now you're here." His expression was weary.

"What happened?"

"A bore stopped working. It took us most of the day to fix it. Looks like more sabotage."

She swore. "I thought Brandon's email would have put a stop to that."

He shrugged. "Might have happened before it was sent. We haven't been out there in a few days."

Brandon and Matt followed him in.

"Dinner's about ready," Amy said, kissing Brandon.

Faith moved back to let them go wash up and heard Lara greet her father enthusiastically. She set the table, and when Darcy returned, he arranged drinks for everyone. It wasn't long before they were eating, and Lara was regaling everyone about the trials and tribulations of Year Five.

Faith grinned. Everyone was so supportive of her and each other. Matt might work for the Stokes, but he was family too. She was struck by how comfortable and casual it was. Amy might do most of the cooking, but the others helped either by setting the table, getting drinks or cleaning up afterwards. She felt as if she was one of them, part of the family almost. Would this be what it would be like if she moved here? Would she tire of sharing a house and want her own space?

"Dad, can I go treasure hunting with Jay and Faith tomorrow?"

"Depends on the weather, pumpkin. It's still supposed to rain." He glanced out the window. "But if it's fine, you can."

She cheered.

After dinner, Lara got ready for bed and came back to the kitchen to say goodnight. "Faith, will you read with us again?"

Faith smiled. "Absolutely." It was such a simple thing, but the inclusion warmed her.

The moment she and Darcy returned to the kitchen, she knew something was wrong. Brandon, Amy and Matt all looked tense and unhappy. "What's happened?" Darcy demanded.

"They've responded." Brandon gestured to the open laptop. "They want to meet tomorrow morning in town to discuss terms."

Nerves clashed with relief. Maybe now they could put this behind them. "What did they say?" She leaned over him to read the email. Very basic, spoke about the terms they wanted, but nothing that caused alarm. "Have you called Dot?" The café in town was central and there were plenty of places where the police could monitor comings and goings.

"Not yet," Amy said.

"Let's start with that." Darcy put his phone on speaker as he called the sergeant and they discussed options.

"I can't arrest them unless we get proof they're behind the incidents," Dot said. "Wanting to buy a property isn't a crime."

"I've got a recording device I can wear," Brandon said.

Both Faith and Darcy looked at him. "From where?" Darcy asked.

"Friend sent it up."

Dot sighed. "It won't be admissible in court but might give us a lead to follow."

"I'm going with you," Darcy said.

Brandon shook his head. "There's no need. If they

see you hanging around, they'll know it's a set up."

"I want to put a face to the son of a bitch who is threatening us."

"I've got the keys to the office space I'm leasing," Faith said. "It's opposite the café. You could park around the back and watch from there."

"You've leased an office?" Darcy said.

She winced. Way to break the news. "Yeah. I'll tell you about it afterwards."

"That would be perfect," Dot said. "Brandon, you could bring the keys in and drop them somewhere for me to pick up."

"I'll bring them," Darcy insisted.

Faith wouldn't try to change his mind. The Ridge was his lifeblood, and he needed to feel as if he was doing something.

Dot sighed. "Fine, but I want you in place an hour before the meeting."

"Will do."

They finished making plans and then hung up. "Do you think we'll get anything useful out of them?" Matt asked.

Brandon ran a hand over his hair. "I hope so. We can't keep going on like this."

Amy got up to put the kettle on and Darcy turned to Faith, his expression serious. "Can I have a word with you?" He nodded towards the door.

"Sure." Her heart beat a little fast as she followed him outside. She slipped her hand in his as they strolled away from the house. "What's up?"

"Are you staying in Retribution Bay?"

She couldn't read his tone. Perhaps he wasn't excited about the news. She braced herself. She'd decided to stay for herself first. "Yeah. With all that's been going on, I haven't got around to telling you. I'll practise law, part time initially because I'm not certain how much work there will be. I'll probably offer home visits to people who are isolated and look at nearby towns like Onslow and Tom Price to see if they need my services."

"I'm glad you're staying." His words were heartfelt.

All her nerves disappeared. "This place has captured my heart."

"I hope that's not all." Darcy turned to her. "Because you've captured mine."

Her pulse skipped a beat. This all-encompassing, overwhelming love was crazy. She pulled him close, caressed his cheek. "You're one reason I want to stay."

His kiss took her by surprise, drawing her in, bringing her passion and joy. When they finally separated, Darcy said, "I can't explain what it means to me that you want to stay."

She could guess. Happiness buoyed her and words fell from her lips. "I want to help the Ridge grow and thrive for more generations to come."

"I never thought I would find a woman who would want to stay here." He kissed her again and then sighed. "I love you, Faith."

Her whole being sang. She didn't care how fast this was happening. When something was right, you knew it. "I love you, too." She kissed him. "And I love Lara. I would protect her with my life."

He drew her into his arms and held her for a long moment. "You know, if you want, you can stay here as long as you like. You don't have to find a place in town."

The idea was far too appealing, but was she rushing things? "Let me think about it. Would Amy and Brandon mind?"

He shook his head. "No, but I have been thinking of building my own place, if we can get Stonefish off our case. I started before Sofia left, but there was no point continuing." He gestured to the frame before them.

"With Brandon and Amy getting married next month, I want them to have the main house to themselves."

"Is that what they want?"

He shrugged. "I haven't asked, but the oldest always inherits, which means they get the house."

Amy was pretty settled there, and Faith was almost certain she'd want to stay. If she sold her place in Perth, she could afford to build them their own house. The idea was thrilling and scary at the same time. "We'll work something out."

"I like the sound of that." Darcy tucked his arm around her and they started back to the house.

It felt like a new beginning.

Chapter 15

The next morning, Faith sat in the kitchen nursing a mug of coffee as she waited for Darcy, Matt and Brandon to return from their morning chores. It was still early, but her stomach churned in a mass of nerves about the upcoming meeting with Stonefish. She checked the time. If Darcy didn't get back soon, he wouldn't have enough time to get into position before the meeting. She heard the ute outside as Lara wandered into the kitchen. "Morning," she chirped, going straight to the pantry to get a box of cereal.

"Morning." Before Faith said anything else, Darcy strode in.

He kissed Faith. "I've got to get going. Can I have your keys?"

"Where are you going, Dad?"

Darcy froze, then slowly turned. "Morning, pumpkin, I didn't see you there. I have to go into town."

Faith handed him the office key. "It sticks a little."

He nodded.

"Can I come?" Lara asked.

"Aren't you going treasure hunting?" He leaned over

to kiss Faith.

"We can go later."

Darcy shook his head. "Not today." He gave Lara a hug and then he rushed out of the house.

Lara frowned. "What's going on?"

Nuts. They had hoped Darcy would be gone before she woke, and she'd assume he was working. "Your Dad has some things to do."

"What keys did you give him?"

Faith hesitated and Brandon walked in. "I need a shower before I go," he told Faith.

"Go where?" Lara asked.

He spotted Lara and winced. "Morning, La La. I've got a meeting in town."

She pursed her lips and her eyes narrowed. "Why didn't you go with Dad?"

"Don't know how long I'm going to be." He threw Faith an apologetic glance and continued out of the room towards the bathroom.

Great.

Lara carried her cereal over to the table. "What aren't you telling me?" Amy walked in. "Ames, why are Dad and Uncle Brandon going into town?"

"Brandon has a meeting," Amy said. "He didn't want Darcy to have to hang around until it finished."

"For what?"

"Business."

Lara's frown grew deeper. "Ridge business?"

"Yeah."

"Then shouldn't Dad be going as well?" she demanded. Her hand clenched her spoon in a death grip.

Faith didn't want to lie to her, but maybe she could distract her. "You'll have to ask him when he gets back," she said. "We should start our treasure hunt soon." The sky was clear of clouds.

Lara scowled. "I'll get changed." She flounced out of the room.

Faith let out a breath. She hated keeping secrets from the girl.

Brandon returned, kissed Amy and said, "I'll call as soon as I'm done."

"Be careful," Amy told him.

They would probably be fine, but someone had tried to run Faith over, so she couldn't help worrying.

"I'm going treasure hunting with Jay," Lara announced when she returned a few minutes later, both hands on her hips and her gaze one of pure defiance.

Faith suppressed a wince. What could she say to make Lara less angry? "I'll join you in a minute."

"No. You're not invited anymore." She stormed out of the house.

Faith exchanged a glance with Amy. "She's hurt." Perhaps they should tell her the truth. Her worrying for a few hours was better than her feeling left out.

"Maybe you can change her mind. I'll fill a backpack and you can take it over. Go get changed."

Faith hurried to dress in her riding gear, and Amy handed her the backpack when she returned. "It's got the radio, water and snacks in it."

"Thanks."

Outside, Lara and Jay saddled the horses. A dark bank of clouds hovered on the horizon, still some distance away. Perhaps they would get some rain today. "Hey. I brought you supplies for your expedition." She handed the backpack to Lara.

"Thanks." Lara barely looked at her.

"Can I come?"

"No. Dad and I never had secrets before you came." Hurt radiated from her. "You're supposed to be my friend too."

Faith felt as if she'd been whipped. She never

wanted to come between Lara and Darcy. Faith had to tell her the truth, but not in front of Jay. "Can I have a word to you in private, Lara?"

She shook her head and mounted. "We need to go before it rains."

Faith glanced at Jay. He shrugged apologetically, but didn't meet Faith's eyes. He was an experienced rider and had spent a lot of time on the Ridge. Amy had mentioned sometimes the two of them rode together when Darcy was still working. Jay would take care of her, and this defiance might make Lara feel as if she had some autonomy. She would explain everything when Lara returned. "All right, but make sure you're back before it rains."

"Absolutely," Jay agreed as he mounted. "I don't want to get wet."

Faith watched them ride off towards the ridge. The clouds moved closer so they wouldn't be gone long, and when they returned, Faith could explain. She joined Amy on the porch.

"You, OK?" Amy asked.

"They'll be fine, right?" Lara was her responsibility with Darcy gone.

"Jay will keep an eye on her and on the weather," Amy assured her. "How about we make some scones for when she returns? Then the three of us can do something in the craft room this afternoon to cheer her up."

"All right." Faith took one last look at the pair trotting down the path and entered the house.

***

Faith found it difficult to concentrate on her conversation with Amy, and the door continually drew her gaze to check if Lara had returned. After an hour, Faith couldn't sit still any longer and went outside to scan the surroundings. The dark clouds now hurtled towards the station and the temperature had dropped. Any minute it would start raining, but Lara was nowhere to be seen. She rubbed her arms. "They should be back by now."

Amy joined her. "Yeah, I agree."

Her confirmation made Faith nauseous. She'd hoped she was freaking out over nothing. "I'm going to search for them."

"Let's radio them first."

She'd forgotten about that. "Where is it?"

Amy showed her the two-way in the kitchen. "Calling Lara and Jay, over," Amy said.

No answer.

"Lara and Jay, do you read?"

Silence.

"The radio was in the backpack, would they hear it?" Faith asked. She hadn't told Jay it was in there.

"Maybe not."

"You keep trying and I'll saddle Fezzik."

Amy nodded and handed her one of the hand-held radios. "Take this with you."

Faith clipped it to her belt and ran across to the horses. As she finished saddling Fezzik, Matt drove into the yard and Faith hurried over to him. "Did you see Lara and Jay?"

Matt shook his head. "No. Amy radioed to say they weren't back yet, so I came straight here." He scanned the area, a furrow on his brow. "Lara knows better than to be out in this weather."

This was her fault. She should have told Lara the truth. "She was upset."

Matt swore. "Which way did she go?"

Big, fat drops of rain started falling, bouncing off the dry red dirt. "Towards the ridge."

Matt swore even more ripely than before. "It's

dangerous in this weather. Get your horse, I'll get Amy."

Faith's heart pounded in her chest as she led Fezzik out of the yard and across to the house. The rain fell slowly, but at any moment the heavens would open.

Amy trotted down the steps. "Still no word."

A shout in the distance made Faith scan the surroundings. Jay galloped towards them, waving one hand—alone.

Fear struck Faith's core. Where was Lara?

She mounted her horse as Jay barrelled into the yard. His horse had flecks of foam at its mouth and sidestepped. "Where's Lara?"

"Taken," Jay gasped. "A four-wheel drive appeared from nowhere." He panted. "I thought it was another guest, but when they got out, they dragged Lara off her horse and shoved her into the car before racing away. I was too far away to stop them."

Terror gripped her heart and squeezed the breath from her. Stonefish. It had to be. Brandon's ruse hadn't fooled them. Darcy was never going to forgive her. "Which way did they go?"

He pointed south.

"Why didn't you radio us?" Amy demanded.

"With what?"

"There's a radio in the backpack." Faith never should have let Lara out of her sight. "Could they still be on the property?" Her heart raced.

"Maybe," Matt said. "We need to find the tracks before the rain washes them away."

"And we need to call Darcy." Faith wanted to be sick. She'd said she would protect Lara. He would be frantic.

"Jay, come with me in the ute and show me where they took her," Matt ordered. "Faith, call Darcy and tell him what's going on. Ames, take your car and drive the main road around the property. Look for any cut fences or open gates. Take a radio with you."

Faith dismounted and phoned Darcy, her heart racing.

"Faith, everything OK?"

She squeezed her eyes closed. He would hate her. "No, Darcy. Lara's been kidnapped."

***

Darcy wasn't cut out for stakeouts. He'd been sitting at the back of the empty office with Dot for the past hour, and he was bored. Brandon had only just arrived at the café and sat at a table outside in plain view. At a table near him sat Nhiari, dressed in civilian clothing, reading a book. Darcy was impressed she barely looked up, but he knew she was monitoring the situation.

Fifteen minutes later and Brandon still sat alone. "Can't these people be punctual?" Darcy demanded.

"You wanted to be here," Dot told him. "Don't complain now."

He pressed his lips together. She was right, but that didn't make it any easier. His whole body itched to move, to do *something*.

Finally, a short man wearing a dark business suit and carrying a laptop bag approached Brandon. Although he wasn't many years off retirement, no greys appeared in his glossy, neatly combed, black hair. Something about him looked familiar, but he wasn't a local. Where had Darcy seen him before? Dot took a couple of photos as they shook hands and the man sat. The Stonefish man took paperwork out of his bag and passed it to Brandon.

Brandon glanced at it, then put it next to him.

Darcy wished the recording device Brandon wore had a receiver so he could hear the conversation. He paced the room.

"Be still, Darcy," Dot snapped. "You'll draw attention."

How could she be so calm? The bastard who had been threatening his family was less than fifty metres away.

A waitress brought out cake and coffee for the man, and he pointed at the paperwork. Brandon read, every now and then asking a question.

The man appeared unperturbed. What if Stonefish had people watching? What if Brandon was in danger sitting there out in the open?

Breathe.

The stress was making him paranoid.

He inhaled and exhaled, then flinched when his phone rang. Dot swore as he answered Faith's call. "Faith, everything OK?"

Across at the café, Brandon's gaze darted across to him. Had they heard his phone?

Her sharp intake of breath had every muscle in his body jumping to attention. "No, Darcy. Lara's been kidnapped."

He froze. "What?"

"She went riding with Jay this morning and Jay just arrived back saying a four-wheel drive stopped them and threw her into the car."

His brain short-circuited as he tried to process the news. Sofia wasn't still in town. She couldn't have taken Lara. "Dot, they've kidnapped Lara."

Dot whirled around. "Put it on speaker."

He did. "Tell me everything."

"Matt's driven Jay to where she was taken. He hopes he'll find tracks before the rain settles in. Amy's searching for where the four-wheel drive might have exited the Ridge. Jay said they were heading south."

Dot frowned. "Why would they continue further into the property rather than head for the nearest bitumen road?"

"I don't know," Faith said.

It didn't matter. One person could tell him where Lara was, and he sat across the courtyard at the café. Darcy charged out of the office, his gaze narrowed on the asshole in the black suit who was protected from the rain by a large umbrella. "Where is she?" Darcy demanded.

Both Brandon and the man glanced up at him in surprise. "Darcy, what are you doing here?"

He ignored his brother's question, focusing on the polished, smug bastard in front of him. "Where is my daughter?"

"I have no idea what you're talking about."

Rage overtook Darcy. He grabbed the man by his shirt front and hauled him to his feet. The man barely flinched. "One of your scumbag associates has kidnapped my daughter and I want her back *now*."

"If your brother signs the contract in front of him, she'll be home within the hour."

Darcy pulled back his fist to punch him and someone stopped him.

"Darcy don't." Dot turned to the suited man, pulling out hand cuffs. "You're under arrest for attempted blackmail and kidnapping."

The man's mouth dropped open. "Where did you come from?"

"I suggest you tell me exactly where the young girl is right now." Dot pulled the man's arms behind his back and handcuffed him.

"I don't know."

Darcy growled. "Tell me."

The bluster left the man. "Honestly! I don't know. I got a message to say she'd been taken."

"Who took her?"

The man shook his head. "I can't say."

"Dot, turn your back," Brandon stated. "We're going to help him remember."

"No! Truly. Look at my phone. It's in my pocket." The man's eyes widened and his voice shook.

Darcy had an awful feeling he was just another Stonefish lackey. He dug out the phone, flicked through the messages. The most recent one said, *We have her.*

The rain was a deluge now, soaking Darcy to the skin. This kind of rain would cause a flash flood. "Where have they taken her?"

The man shook, but whether it was from the cold or fear Darcy didn't care.

"This rain causes flooding," Darcy said. "If your people don't realise, they could be in real danger."

"All I know is the person who took her knows the Ridge. He's been staying there for months." He deflated before Darcy's glare, and Darcy remembered where he'd seen him. At the Ningaloo Café talking with Cheryl and Jay.

Fuck. "Jay." It had to be. Maybe he'd lied about the four-wheel drive. Darcy ran for his ute, Brandon on his heels. He peeled out of the car park, fishtailing on the slippery road. "Call Faith back," Darcy said. "Tell her Jay is behind it."

The streets were empty, and the rain already sat in puddles on the road. He had to get out of town before the road into town flooded. He pressed his foot closer to the floor. If Lara was still near the ridge in this weather, she'd be in real danger.

***

Faith paced the kitchen as the rain pelted the tin roof. Darcy had hung up on her and hadn't answered her return call. No news from Matt or Amy yet. She couldn't stay here waiting, but someone needed to be here in case Stonefish rang with demands.

Lee ran up on to the porch, shaking the water off himself. "Hey, Faith. Crappy weather today."

"Lee, I'm sorry. Now's not a good time."

His face fell. "What's wrong?"

"Lara's missing."

His mouth dropped open.

Her phone vibrated in her hand, startling her. Brandon. "Any news?"

"We think Jay took her," Brandon said. "The guy I met with said the kidnapper had been staying at the ridge for a while."

Her gaze darted to Lee. "I've got Lee right here." He'd been a regular guest since they opened as well.

"No, Jay would have recognised him. There was no four-wheel drive."

It made sense, but she kept her eye on Lee as she said, "Let me call Matt." She hung up and the next call went straight to message bank. Matt was out of range, but if she radioed him, Jay would hear. She had no other choice.

The knife block sat next to the radio on the kitchen bench. A weapon if she needed it. "Matt, do you copy?"

"Yeah, what have you got?"

She glanced at Lee. "We think the person who took Lara was staying on the station for quite some time."

Lee's eyebrows raised, and he shifted. Faith's fingers edged towards the knife, and Lee held up his hands. "It wasn't me." His gaze was steady, calm, with no fear or concern in them.

Odd, but she believed him. "Lee says it wasn't him."

A long pause and Faith held her breath. What if Jay attacked Matt? The heavy drops of rain on the roof created a racket, and she held the radio up to her ear. Finally Matt came back on. "Jay admitted to it. He left her tied up in the cave in the gully. I'm heading there now, but I'm pretty far to the south. The water's got to be rising." In the background Jay's panicked voice called, "I didn't know."

Horror filled her. Lara would drown. "I'm on my way."

She thrust her phone at Lee. "Call Brandon back. Tell him Lara was left in the cave in the gully. Darcy knows which one I mean. I'm going there now. I've got a radio if they need to contact me."

Lee nodded. "Be careful."

Faith ran outside and untied Fezzik from the post. She mounted him and kicked him into a gallop, riding hard towards the Ridge. The rain poured down in thick sheets of water, a kind of monsoonal rain she'd never imagined she would see here in this dry and dusty land. The trail she'd ridden down only a week before was the beginnings of a stream. She urged Fezzik faster.

If Darcy was in town, he wouldn't get there in time, Amy's car would get bogged, which left her and Matt. And she was the closest. The Ridge loomed in front of her and Fezzik slowed as he clambered up the side. At the top, Faith's heart stopped. The water ran in streams down the slopes, coalescing in the bottom of the gully which already streamed south like a river, but was still a metre from the cave entrance.

She urged Fezzik to descend the path she'd travelled with Darcy, and at the bottom he was ankle deep in the water. He baulked at going further. A movement on the opposite bank caught her attention. Starlight paced up and down as if wanting to cross but uncertain.

Faith snatched the radio from her belt and dismounted. "Matt, I'm near the cave. Starlight's here, and Fezzik won't go further. I'm going on foot. The river's ankle deep."

"Careful Faith, the torrent can get swift. Be as fast as you can."

She slapped Fezzik's hindquarters to send him home

before striding into the water and immediately felt the pull downstream. She headed for Starlight, who had spotted her and pawed at the ground. The horse should be heading to higher ground, the way Fezzik had already done behind her. By the time she'd reached the other side of the gully, the water reached her calves. She took Starlight's reins, murmuring to her and pulling her downstream towards the cave and the path up to the top of the ravine. When they reached the path, Starlight jerked her head, pulling the reins out of Faith's hands. Faith lunged towards her, but her hands slid right off the wet saddle and Starlight bolted up the slope to higher ground. Faith sighed. At least she'd be out of the flood.

Another movement further up the slope proved to be rock wallabies, sheltering amongst the rocks. If they weren't in the cave, did that mean it wasn't safe?

"Lara!" Faith stumbled on the uneven, rocky ground towards the cave entrance, reaching it as the rising water did. She blinked to adjust her eyes to the dim light. "Lara!"

The walls of the cave dimmed the noise of the rain, and a muffled yell came from the back. Wishing she'd brought her phone with her for light, she hurried forward. A rock jutted out, and behind it she found Lara sitting up, her wrists cable-tied together, ankles tied with rope which attached her to a rock. She desperately rubbed the rope against the rock, and it was already halfway frayed. Clever girl.

Relief filled Faith, and she pulled the gag out of Lara's mouth. "I've got you."

"Faith!" Lara sobbed. "I'm sorry I got mad and wouldn't let you come with us. Jay tied me up and left me here."

"I know. We need to get you out of here. Let me find a sharp rock to cut the ties."

"I've got Jay's knife in my pocket," Lara said. "He let me hold it on the ride, but I can't reach it."

Faith dug it out of Lara's pocket and flicked the knife into position. Quickly she cut through the cable ties. Lara groaned. "It hurts."

Faith rubbed her wrists. "You just need to get the circulation back into them. Rotate them while I cut the rope."

The rope took longer and she rubbed Lara's ankles before tucking the knife into her pocket. Something cold touched her foot, and she spun around. The water had already crept into the cave. Time to move. She held out a hand and pulled Lara to her feet. The girl hopped around, rubbing her wrists and arms.

"Come on. We need to get to higher ground." She kept her hand in Lara's as they waded into the water. The current wasn't strong in the cave, but they were already knee deep. Outside, the gully had become a frothing, debris-filled river. Faith moved as close as possible to the cave walls before stepping out into the current. It slammed into her, almost taking her feet out from under her. She let go of Lara's hand as she fought to stay standing.

"Faith!" Lara yelled.

"I'm all right." She shifted her body weight forward as she took stock. The ground outside the cave sloped and rocks hid under the surface of the rushing water. It was rising fast.

Her radio squawked.

"Faith, do you read?"

It sounded like Darcy. "Yes. I've got Lara. We're at the mouth of the cave, but the river's running pretty fast. I'm trying to figure out the best way out of here." As she spoke, she examined the outside of the cave. Lara might be able to climb onto her shoulders and on to the rock above the cave.

"We're about ten minutes away. Hold tight."

They didn't have ten minutes. With the water rising so rapidly, they'd be waist deep by then, and the pull of the river would be too much. "Matt, how far away are you?"

"The river's cut us off," Matt replied. "I've got to go the long way around."

They were on their own. She tucked the radio back on her belt and examined the cave again. "Lara, can you climb up there if I give you a leg up?"

Lara shivered, her face pale.

Faith wrapped her arms around the girl to share body heat. "La La, I need you to be brave. See that rock there?" She pointed and Lara nodded. "When I give you a boost, grab on to it and then haul yourself up as if you were mounting Starlight, OK?"

"What about you?"

"I'll climb up right after you," she lied. It was too far out of her reach, but hopefully Lara wouldn't realise. "Come on now." She cupped her hands in front of her. "On the count of three." Lara placed her foot in Faith's palms. "One, two, three." She used as much force as she could to lift Lara. The girl grasped the rock and swung her legs towards the overhang. She wouldn't make it. Faith pushed Lara, almost like pushing a barbell above her head, giving her support so she could scramble up.

Lara crouched, reaching a hand to Faith. "I'll pull you up."

Faith shook her head. "I'm too heavy for you. Climb the slope, out of the way so I can get up."

Lara shifted back away from the edge, up the hill where she would be safe from the river. Faith exhaled and called into the radio. "Lara's safe. She's above the cave, out of the water." The rain kept beating down, but Lara could stay out of the path of the rising river.

Faith replaced the radio on her belt, and something moved in her peripheral vision. A tree barrelled towards her, its branches a net. Fear pierced her and Faith shifted back, but her ankle turned on a rock and she stumbled. The water washed her off her feet and the tree branches dragged her under the cold, murky water.

Chapter 16

The terror which had Darcy's heart in its talons loosened as Faith's words came over the radio. Lara was safe. His baby would be all right, but he had to see her with his own eyes. He would have loved Faith for the rest of his life for saving Lara alone. Amy waited at the gate onto the property and she jumped into the tray of the ute as they drove past. He sped over the rough ground as he made a beeline towards the ridge. "Faith, are you out yet?"

No answer.

Chills ran down his arms. "Faith, do you copy?" Silence.

Don't panic. She might be climbing out and couldn't answer him.

The Ridge came into view and Starlight grazed at the top as if unconcerned by the torrential downpour she stood in. As he pulled up to the edge of the slope, Lara clambered towards him. She stopped, waving her arms and then pointing down towards the raging river below.

Where was Faith?

He shoved the car door open and half slid, half ran down the slope and swept Lara into his arms. "You're all right."

Lara struggled against him. "Faith," she sobbed. "A tree came down the river and hit her. She disappeared under the water and she hasn't come up."

His heart stopped. No. He placed Lara on the ground and turned her to face the river. "Where?"

She pointed to a tree right below them. It wasn't moving, so it must have caught on something in the cave. He prayed it wasn't caught on someone. Stones rattled behind him as Amy and Brandon joined them, Brandon had a coil of rope over one shoulder which he must have got from the ute tray. "Where's Faith?" Amy asked.

"She's still down there," Darcy said, amazed his voice sounded so calm. "Take Lara to the ute and check her for injuries. There's a first aid kit behind the driver's seat."

Lara shook her head. "I'm not leaving. Faith saved me."

He nodded. "Right now I need to focus on Faith and I can't do that if I'm worried about you falling back into the river, pumpkin. Go with Amy."

"But—"

"Now!"

She flinched, but Darcy didn't have time to argue. Amy shoved her handheld radio at Brandon, then put an arm around Lara and hustled her up the slope. Darcy started down.

"What have we got?" Brandon asked.

"That tree hit Faith. She went under and hasn't come up."

Brandon swore.

"That's the entrance to the cave," Darcy said. "Might be she's trapped inside, but still safe." It was the only option he would entertain.

"We need someone hunting downstream."

The pain in his chest made it difficult to breathe. "Radio Matt."

The slick, muddy ground and rocks meant he slid most of the way down. At the cave overhang, he lay on the ground, mindless of the water and the dirt, and peered into the cave. The water was halfway to the ceiling and the tree branches filled the remaining space.

"Matt's scouring the riverbanks." Brandon crouched down next to him. "See anything?"

"Just the fucking tree." He wiped the water from his face. Would the rain ever stop? He glanced up. Not a chance. "I have to get down there."

"Not without a rope."

Darcy shook his head. "It'll get caught on the branches."

"Don't be stupid, Darce. If she's safe inside, you need to be anchored by the rope to get her out. The minute the tree gets loose, it will wash down stream and you don't want to get washed with it." Brandon handed him one end of the rope.

"It's not long enough."

"You need to clear the tree first. It's plenty long enough for that." Brandon tied the other end to a rock jutting up above the cave and tugged it to make sure it was tight. "You got anything in the ute's toolbox which will help?"

"Might be an axe." He knotted the rope around his waist. Brandon was right. He couldn't be reckless. "There's a torch too."

He moved down the side of the cave and into the cold water. The river flowed around the tree trunk, pushing and shoving it, but something stopped it from carrying on down the river. It was too dark inside the cave. "Faith!" he yelled.

The roar of the water was all he could hear.

Above him, Brandon took the torch and axe from

Amy and carried them down to Darcy. He shone the torch into the cave. No Faith.

She had to be there somewhere.

Almost unwillingly, he directed the beam into the water. It didn't penetrate far enough to illuminate if a body lay underneath.

Another sweep with the torch showed why the tree wasn't moving. Two of the forked branches played off each other and prevented the tree from moving. If he chopped one branch, it should come free.

"Axe." He handed Brandon the torch and took the axe. He lowered himself into the water and was swept downstream into the branches. Pain shot through him as the wood poked and scratched him, but the rope kept him from being swept under them. He'd thank Brandon later.

Using the rope to pull himself to his feet, he moved into the cave. Right at the back, a light glowed, almost like a firefly, but they didn't get those here. "Faith," he yelled. The water hovered around his chest and soon he wouldn't be able to get the momentum to chop the branches.

"Darcy!"

His heart leapt as the light moved and Faith's head peered out from behind a rock. Alive! She was alive. "Are you hurt?"

"I'm stuck. I can't get past the branches."

"Hold on. I'll get you out."

He chopped at the nearest branches to get closer to the problem one. The water crept towards his neck, moving way too fast. The cave narrowed at the back and it wouldn't take long for the rest of the cave to fill. He worked faster, pounding the axe into the branches and ripping them away. Finally, he reached the offending branch. He tugged on it and it swayed, but otherwise didn't budge.

The water was at his shoulders now, making it difficult to swing the axe. He chopped as hard as he could, again and again, and finally he heard the crack. The branch sprang towards him, hitting him square in the chest as the river ripped it from the cave. His lungs emptied, and he was swept into the torrent, the branch scraping a line across his chest. Pain made him gasp in a mouthful of water, and he coughed.

"Darcy!" Faith yelled.

The rope jolted, holding him into place as he fought to stay above the waterline. Leaves and bushes brushed past him and still it rained. He grabbed the rope, and pulled himself slowly, hand over hand, back to the entrance. Brandon pulled the other end, helping him get out of the main flow of the water. "Faith's inside," he called.

Outside the cave, the water was too deep to stand. The cave was almost full. "Give me all the rope. I need to get her." She had to be afraid of being swept away. The rope slackened, and he took a deep breath, using the roof of the cave to pull himself towards the back where he'd last seen Faith. The rope pulled tight, and he tilted his head to the ceiling to take some more air. He yanked on the rope, but it had no more give. "Faith, you've got to come to me."

Her silhouette was about two metres away. "Hurry!" He gulped another breath of air as she lunged towards him. His hand grasped hers and he pulled her towards him. She wrapped her arms around his waist. The water covered them and he tugged twice on the rope, hoping Brandon would realise he needed to be pulled back. The rope moved. Darcy kept one arm around Faith and the other touching the top of the cave as together they swam towards the entrance. His lungs burned. The cave hadn't seemed this deep on the way in. But no, they couldn't have got turned around. He kicked harder and his hand encountered air. Frantically he grappled for the rock and pushed away from it, pulling Faith with him. They both breached the surface and sucked in lungfuls of air. Brandon reached for them, but the river pulled them away from the edge. Faith's body shifted away from him and she clutched his shirt.

She was slipping from his grasp. "Grab her!" Darcy yelled at Brandon.

Brandon gripped the rope in both hands, holding them close to the shore. Fuck. If he let go of the rope, they'd shoot back into the river. Above him, Amy scrambled down the slope towards them.

Faith slid further away.

"Hold on!" He shoved one arm under her shoulder and hefted her towards him. The water dragged him under and he struggled back to the surface. He found the rock face and pulled them both to the side.

Faith threw one arm over the ledge, panting. Darcy pushed her other arm over the rock. "Pull her up."

"You got a good grip?"

Darcy braced himself. "Yep."

Brandon dropped the rope and the violent pull of the water took Darcy by surprise. The river dragged him from the ledge and he crashed into Faith, taking her with him. She shrieked, reaching for him.

Their hands touched, clasped each other and then were ripped apart.

The rope around Darcy's waist jolted him to a stop, and he watched helplessly as Faith swept down the river.

***

Darcy's eyes, wide with horror, were the last thing Faith saw as the water dragged her under. The pull and violence of the surge was unbelievable as she fought to the surface. She gulped a mouthful of air, but with it came water and she choked, spluttering as the water tried to drag her under again. The distance between her and the others rapidly increased, but Darcy had hauled himself back to shore and was climbing out.

Relief calmed her. He was safe. She twisted to face the direction she was being swept. Her boots and jeans weighed her down, making it difficult to kick and stay afloat.

Again and again the water dragged her under, and she had to fight to reach the surface. Her arms grew heavy. No, she wouldn't give up. There had to be a way to the shore. Not wanting to put her head down in case she missed an obstacle coming towards her, she pulled herself through the water. A tree protruded from the surging river, its lowest branches less than a metre above the water. With every ounce of determination, she angled herself towards it and then lunged out of the water as she reached it. Her fingers scraped the bark, and she curled them around the branch, stopping her momentum.

The river tugged on her lower body and she dangled from the branch, her arms screaming in protest. She had to climb up somehow, but all her energy focused on simply holding on.

"I'm coming, Faith."

Darcy's shout gave her hope. She just had to hold on until he got there. Water dripped down her face and her muscles shook with the effort to cling to the branch. How far away was he?

She didn't dare twist around. The movement might tear her hands from the branch.

Her fingers scraped against the bark, slipping as debris in the river added to her weight. "Hurry." She meant to shout it, but it came out more like a whisper.

"Grab the rope."

What rope? She tilted her head. It was no use. All

she saw was the muddy water rushing by her. She inhaled deeply and yelled, "Where?"

"Below you on your right side."

She twisted her body slightly, and caught sight of the rope below her. The shift of her weight caused her fingers to slip on the smooth bark of the tree and she fell. She stretched and grabbed the rough rope as the river caught her body again. Her shoulders strained as she was pulled through the water, but she couldn't get her head above the surface. Her lungs screamed at her to let go so she could breathe.

Faith clenched her teeth shut and used one hand to swim up, while the other hand clutched the rope, her palm burning. Her face hit the air, and she sucked in a breath. Water blurred her vision, but there was a shape just there. Had to be Darcy. She reached out, brushed his hand, clasped it tight.

Thank God. Her feet scrambled to touch the ground, but the slope was too steep.

"Give me your other hand," Darcy called.

Faith blinked the water from her eyes. Brandon had hold of the rope again, and Darcy stretched his other hand for hers. All she had to do was let go of the rope and take hold of Darcy.

"Hurry!" The urgency in his tone scared her.

She lunged for his hand. Fingers touched.

Then something hit her in the side, and she was sucked under the water again.

***

Darcy swore as the log hit Faith and ripped her from his grasp. She disappeared under the water and he watched for her to resurface. "Give me the rope."

Brandon passed it to him and he moved, charging down river, slipping and sliding, as he curled the rope and tied a lasso at the end. Where was she?

Her head popped above the surface and she gasped.

There. The rope should be long enough. Swinging the lasso as he moved, he calculated when to throw. "Arms up, Faith."

She twisted, spotted him, eyes widened. Struggling, she threw her arms in the air. He let the lasso fly, and it landed over her head. She brought her arms down, locking it in place, and the rope jolted in Darcy's hands.

He had her. Not willing to celebrate yet, he pulled her in. Brandon reached him and together they dragged her to the shore. He hauled her out of the water and she collapsed into his arms.

Darcy lowered them both to the ground, his pulse hammering. Safe. Finally safe.

They clung to each other, the rain still beating down, but he didn't care. Faith was in his arms. "I've got you now."

"We need to keep moving," Brandon said. "The river's still rising and we're going to have to retrace our steps to get back up the slope."

Shit. He was right. Gently, he pushed Faith away. "Come on, Sweetheart. Let's get out of here."

She nodded, but when she stood, her legs buckled. "Sorry. Give me a minute."

They didn't have a minute. "Brace yourself." Without waiting for a response, he lifted Faith over his shoulders. "Move," he ordered Brandon. His brother would pick the best path to the top.

As they arrived on flat ground, the ute pulled up and Lara burst out of the passenger side, hurtling towards him. Carefully he placed Faith onto her feet and then opened his arms. Lara flung herself into them, sobbing. "I thought you were going to die!"

Using the last of his energy, he picked her up. "I'm fine, pumpkin, and so is Faith." He squeezed her and then put her on the ground. Faith leaned against

Brandon, and Lara dived into her arms.

"I'm so sorry, Faith. I'll never get mad again. I'm sorry, I'm sorry, I'm sorry."

He was missing part of the story, but it didn't matter. Both his girls were safe.

"There's nothing to apologise for, La La. This is all Jay's fault."

Darcy jerked. In all his panic, he'd forgotten about the bastard who'd left Lara there.

Brandon's radio squawked. "Any update?"

Poor Matt had no idea what was going on.

Amy leaned into the ute to respond. "Everyone's safe. We're coming home."

Tears blurred Darcy's vision. He liked the sound of that.

***

Lara sat on Faith's lap and they clung to each other as Darcy drove the ute home. They were all soaked, so he switched the heating to high, but it did little to help. Brandon was riding Starlight back, and Darcy dropped Amy at her car and waited until she shut the gate before continuing. She could get bogged in the mud.

Lara shivered and Darcy accelerated as he hit the bitumen.

Both Matt's ute and the police car were outside the house when they arrived, and Fezzik was back in the horse paddock. He must have returned home by himself. Lee stood on the porch waiting for them.

"We're home, pumpkin." He switched off the engine and then strode around to the passenger side to help both Lara and Faith out of the car. Both had their hair plastered to their head and were covered in mud splatter. The continuous downpour helped with the mud at least. The once dusty soil had turned into a shallow muddy lake as the soil struggled to keep up with the deluge.

He climbed the steps behind Lara and Faith and shook hands with Lee. "Thanks for your help."

Lee nodded. "Glad I could."

Lara had disappeared into the house but her shriek of fear slammed into Darcy. His skin tightened, and he stormed into the house, Faith right behind him. Dot, Nhiari and Matt sat at the table with a sombre Jay and his wife, Cheryl, sobbing, between them. Seeing the older man filled Darcy with rage. He strode over and hauled the man to his feet. "I ought to kill you."

"Put him down, Darcy," Dot demanded.

He ignored her. "Give me one reason why I shouldn't tie you up and throw you in that cave right now."

The man shook but stared Darcy in the eye. "Because my family was being threatened."

Darcy relaxed his hold a little. What was he talking about? Nhiari pushed him away. "Take it easy. There's a lot to get through." She looked at the others. "Do you need the ambulance?"

"We just need to warm up," Faith said.

"Right, well go for it. I'll put the kettle on."

Tension still hummed through Darcy's body, but when Lara slipped her hand into his, he turned his attention to her. Matt handed out towels and Darcy wrapped one around Lara's shoulders. "Are you hurt, pumpkin?"

She held out her wrists, which had red chafe marks. "Only where Jay tied me up."

He pushed down his anger. "Right, well let's get you showered and warm. I bet Dot makes a mean hot chocolate."

"I do," Dot assured her.

Lara held her hand out for Faith and the three of them went into the bathroom. Faith turned on the shower to heat while Darcy confirmed Lara hadn't been physically injured. While she showered, Faith fetched her warm clothes and then they accompanied her back into the kitchen. "Will you be all right with Matt and Nhiari while Faith and I have a shower?"

Lara shifted closer to him as she stared at Jay.

"I'm sorry, Lara," Jay said.

"I can take him outside," Dot offered.

"Can I wait in the lounge room with Matt?"

Matt stood before Darcy could answer and held out a hand to her. "Of course. Want a game of snap while we wait?"

She took his hand. "Maybe."

Darcy followed them down the corridor and heard Lara ask, "Will you tell me what's really going on, Uncle Matt?"

Darcy sighed. He would have to tell her everything. She deserved the truth after her ordeal. Faith waited for him in the bathroom. She'd prepared a pile of clothes for them both, but he ignored them and instead pulled her into his arms. She fit so perfectly.

"I'm OK, Darcy." She stroked his back, and he realised he was shaking. "We're all OK."

"I was terrified," he admitted. "First that Lara would die, and when I saw her I was so relieved until she told me you'd disappeared, and then the terror started all over again."

"I knew you'd come for me," Faith said.

He closed his eyes, rested his head against hers. He'd had three chances to save her, and he'd stuffed the first two.

"Come on. We both need to get warm." She stepped away and turned the shower on. Then she stripped off her wet clothes.

He hissed. A dark bruise covered her side and her chest. He brushed his fingers against it. "What happened?"

She looked down. "It must have been the tree that hit me and stuck me in the cave."

She would be sore for days. Faith stepped into the shower and he stripped and followed her in. The hot water hit his chest, and he flinched.

"What's this?" Faith said.

A red cut ran across his chest. "Same tree," he said. "Put up a fight when I cut it free."

He pulled her against him, and they stood under the hot spray warming up. She was alive, warm and safe in his arms. His eyes closed as the spray rained down on his back. She'd risked her life to save Lara's. The enormity of it was too much for him to comprehend right now, but one thing he could grasp. He didn't want her to ever leave. "Marry me."

Faith gasped and stepped back. "What?"

OK, he could have been smoother with the delivery. "Marry me," he repeated. "I love you, and I was as terrified of losing you as I was of losing Lara. That's how much you mean to me."

She closed her eyes and shook her head, and he froze. He'd rushed things, ruined them. Stupid. He shifted away from her and her eyes flew open. "Ask me again in a few days, when all of this mess is behind us and when we're both not full of relief that we're alive." She smiled at him. "Ask me after you've spoken with Lara and made sure she's happy with the idea. And then I'll say yes."

Happiness filled him to bursting. "I'll do that."

Chapter 17

Darcy couldn't keep the smile off his face. Faith wanted to marry him. He understood why she wanted to wait, but he didn't mind. He'd ask as many times as she wanted him to. It made the terrifying day easier to handle. Now he needed to hold his daughter and never let her go, and everything would be right with the world.

After they dressed, they walked hand in hand to the lounge room where Matt and Lara played a noisy game of snap. Lara jumped up when she saw them and ran over to hug them both. Having her arms around him filled Darcy with so much love and relief.

Matt tidied the cards and climbed to his feet. "Now you're both dry, do I get a hug too?"

Lara dragged him into their circle. "You came looking for me. Of course you can join in."

"We all have a story to tell," Darcy said. "Shall we join Dot and Nhiari in the kitchen?"

"Can I come too?" Lara asked, the hopeful expression tearing at his heart.

"Absolutely, pumpkin. It's time you knew what's going on." She might worry, but better she be alert and perhaps less trusting as well.

"Good."

They returned to the kitchen. Cheryl had stopped sobbing and now sat subdued next to Jay. Brandon and Amy had changed out of their wet gear and Lee hovered near the door as if uncertain whether he should stay or go. Darcy bet he had questions he wanted answered.

Amy poured the coffee, and Dot gave Lara a hot chocolate with marshmallows in it. The young girl sat at the table between Darcy and Faith and he kept his arm around her, to reassure himself she was really safe.

Dot flipped to a new page of her notebook and scanned the room. "Lee, I'll come and get your statement afterwards."

Lee hesitated and then nodded. "I'm glad Lara's back safely." He went out the kitchen door.

Probably for the best. They had thought Taylor was the only one at the Ridge working for Stonefish, but if Jay was, and Taylor hadn't known about it, it meant others staying at the campgrounds could also be involved. God, he hated the idea, but they couldn't afford to close the campgrounds.

Nhiari looked out the door and then nodded to Dot.

Before Dot said anything, Jay said, "I'm so sorry for hurting you, Lara."

Lara leaned into Darcy. "Why did you do it then?"

"Because they threatened my son."

"You'd better start at the beginning," Dot said.

Jay scanned everyone at the table with his gaze settling on Amy. "I told you about our son, Nathan. He's the only child we have left after our daughter died from a drug overdose."

Amy flinched, but nodded.

"Nathan was devastated when his sister died, but was determined to make the most of his life, doing everything his sister hadn't been able to do. He bought an expensive house, a fancy car, travelled on overseas holidays." Jay sipped his coffee. "He had a good job working fly-in, fly-out, so we figured he used the money he earned."

Darcy's instincts went on alert and across from him Brandon shifted, leaning forward.

"About twelve months ago we got a call from him. He'd been made redundant and was beside himself rambling about debt and danger, and it took time to get the entire story from him. Turns out he'd borrowed money from a private lender and now they wanted it back with interest. He owed them almost a million dollars and the bank wouldn't give him anything because he no longer had a job."

"Who was the private lender?" Dot asked.

"They call themselves Stonefish Enterprises. They're some kind of investment group."

Darcy exchanged a glance with Brandon. "So why did they give your son funds?"

"One of them befriended Nathan, and Nathan told him about his sister and how he was living for her. The man said they liked to help the Aussie battler achieve their dreams, and they'd like to help him with his." Jay shook his head. "I asked Nathan how he could be so stupid, but he said he'd known the guy for years and was a good friend."

"Were Stonefish threatening Nathan?" Faith asked.

"Yeah. They roughed him up and told him he had thirty days to pay them back."

Not much time.

"What happened next?" Dot asked.

"We took a loan on the farm," Jay said. "But Stonefish only took half of what they were owed. Said Nathan needed to work off the rest of his debt."

Brandon's eyes narrowed. "Doing what?"

Jay shrugged. "I honestly don't know. Nathan won't tell me, but it can't be anything good."

"Why didn't you go to the police?" Dot asked.

"Because they threatened our lives," Jay said. "Cheryl and I were as involved as Nathan by then. We knew enough to be a danger to them, so they showed us what they could do. They set fire to our haystack in the middle of summer, and if I hadn't caught it in time, it would have burned the whole farm down."

Nhiari shifted from where she still stood by the door. "Are you responsible for the haystack fire here?"

Jay glanced at Darcy and then down at the table. "Yes."

Darcy stiffened. He'd trusted the man. They'd worked together side by side. "Bastard."

"I ran to warn you as soon as I lit it, but Stonefish made me do it. If I didn't keep causing trouble for you, they would cause trouble for Nathan."

"They sent you here to the Ridge?" Dot asked.

He nodded. "We decided to retire early. Hoped if we only had the car and caravan, they wouldn't threaten us anymore. But the day before we left, we got a phone call to say Retribution Ridge was opening to camping and we should go there. Said for every day we stayed they would take a hundred dollars off Nathan's debt."

"Weren't you suspicious?" Matt asked.

"Of course, but when we arrived, we loved the place, and they rarely contacted us. Then your parents died, and we got a message to say that's what happened to people who crossed them."

Faith jolted. "Your parents were murdered?"

Darcy squeezed her hand. "We're not certain. Our ex-stockhand, Taylor cut the brake lines on the four-wheel drive. He only wanted to cause a nuisance, but Dad didn't notice until they hit the corner and by then they had no brakes." He cleared his throat. "But there were signs they were forced off the road as well."

Next to him, Lara started shaking. Faith slid her arm around the girl and shuffled closer. Lara leaned into her and Darcy fell in love all over again.

"When they contacted you, what did they want you to do?" Dot asked.

Jay focused on the mug in his hand. "Tell them about the station. It didn't seem like much. They wanted me to recommend a cattle company to Darcy."

Darcy straightened. "You told me about Livestock and Gear!" He swore. "I knew someone had. That bogus company has almost cost us the station." It made sense now.

"I'm sorry, Darcy." He met his eye. "Then we started getting requests to damage more of the property. At first, I refused, but then Nathan video called us, beaten black and blue and begged us to do what they said." Jay looked at Darcy. "He might be in his thirties, but he's still our baby boy."

Shit. He pressed a kiss against Lara's head. He gave a curt nod and some tension left his shoulders.

"What exactly did you do?" Dot asked.

Jay shrank lower in his seat. "Broke a couple of water trough valves, started the fire, left a few gates open in the hope the sheep would stray. I took those parts you ordered and hid them. I planned to leave them in the shed before I left." He hesitated. "I also told them where you moved the sheep to."

"Were you involved with the slaughter?" Darcy asked.

"No! Honestly. If I'd known they were going to do that…" He sighed. "I told them when they were moved, and they were getting ready to lamb."

Darcy stiffened again and Faith stroked his back.

"Did they tell you to kidnap me?" Lara's voice was quiet, but it commanded attention.

"I'm so sorry, La La. I never meant to hurt you."

"Don't call me that. You're not my friend."

Jay nodded, the sadness on his face clear.

"Tell us what happened," Dot suggested.

"I got a call on Friday. They asked me to make sure Lara was out of the house Saturday morning. Suggested I go riding with her."

"Who's they?"

"The guy calls himself Tan Lewis. I've never met him in person."

"Go on," Dot prompted.

"Saturday morning Tan calls back and says I need to kidnap Lara, leave her somewhere on the Ridge so they can pick her up and then lead the rest of you away from her." He glanced at Lara. "I said no, but they sent me a photo of Nathan with a gun held to his head. I couldn't risk it. I told Cheryl to pack the van. Lara would identify me as the one who kidnapped her, and I didn't want to be arrested."

"But you kidnapped her knowing Stonefish might hurt her." Darcy's voice was as cold as the terror that filled his body at the thought those monsters could have taken his daughter.

Jay stared him down. "It was her or Nathan."

"He apologised when he tied me up," Lara said. "He seemed sorry." She reached into her pocket and withdrew a utility knife, handing it to him. "This helped Faith free me."

Jay smiled. "Keep it. I hoped you'd use it."

"You gave it to me on purpose?"

"Yeah. I didn't want those bastards to get their hands on you."

"I couldn't reach it in my pocket."

"But it helped," Faith said.

"I never considered the cave would flood," Jay said. "When Matt mentioned it, I couldn't let Lara drown."

"What did they hope to accomplish by kidnapping Lara?" Matt asked.

"They wanted to force me to sign the contract selling the Ridge to them." Brandon turned to Dot. "What happened to the guy I was meeting with?"

"He's in gaol," Dot responded. "I read him his rights, locked him up and left Colin with him to get answers while Nhiari and I drove out here to arrest Jay."

"Is he talking?" Faith asked.

"He's terrified and worried about his wife. He owes them money too," Dot said. "Said when Brandon signed the contract, someone from the company would arrive to counter-sign."

"That means someone else must have been watching the meeting," Darcy said.

"Yeah," Dot said. "The shopping complex has three security cameras. We'll go through the footage and see what we can find."

With so many tourists around town, Stonefish might blend in. "Did the guy say anything to you when you had afternoon tea together?" Darcy asked Jay.

Jay frowned. "What guy?"

"Thursday afternoon you were at Ningaloo Café, sitting with the guy who showed Brandon the contract."

Jay exchanged glances with Cheryl. "Charmaine and Roger? I had no idea they worked for Stonefish. They came over and chatted to us."

"What about?"

"Retribution Bay. What we'd recommend they do in the area. I figured they were tourists."

How many people did Stonefish have working for them?

"I'll ask Roger about it." Dot tapped her pen. "Have you got anything else to add?"

231

"Only that Cheryl had nothing to do with this. I did everything."

Cheryl started crying again. "We didn't want to. They're going to kill our boy. I can't lose another child."

Lara stood and hugged Cheryl. "It's OK. Dot will find them and arrest them."

The confidence Lara had melted Darcy's heart.

Dot didn't look nearly as confident. "I'll do my best, La La. Do you want to tell your story now?"

His daughter nodded and sat. "I was mad because Dad and Brandon went into town without me and Faith wouldn't tell me why."

Darcy sighed. "I should have told you the truth, pumpkin. I didn't want to worry you."

"You should have," she said. "Faith wanted to come treasure hunting with us, but I said she couldn't." She glanced at Faith. "I'm so sorry."

Faith hugged her. "It's all right. You're allowed to be mad sometimes."

Lara spun her empty mug around. "Jay and I rode up to the ridge, but it was getting stormy and Dad said never to go into the gully when it's raining. I wanted to go back, but Jay said it wasn't far and we'd be quick. There weren't any wallabies near the cave, which means they know something we don't." She smiled at Matt. "Uncle Matt taught me that.

"When I got into the cave, Jay bumped into me and I fell to the ground. He tied me to a rock. I was so scared, especially when it started to rain, but I couldn't reach the knife in my pocket, so I had to saw the rope on the rock, and it took forever."

Jay hung his head. "If I'd known the gully would flood, I never would have done it."

"Then Faith arrived, and she freed me, but the river was running so fast already, and she almost slipped and was swept away. So she pushed me above the cave and then a tree hit her." Lara shivered, and both Faith and Darcy squeezed her. He smiled at Faith over Lara's head. They would protect her together.

"I ran up the slope, 'cos I heard a car coming. It was Dad."

"You were so brave, pumpkin. You helped rescue Faith because you told me what happened."

"I'm sorry you almost died because of me," Lara whispered.

"I would always choose to save you," Faith told her. "You have nothing to apologise for."

Lara threw her hands around Faith's waist and squeezed her. "Thank you."

"Anytime," Faith whispered. "I love you, Lara."

"I love you, too."

Darcy wanted to bundle them both up and keep them safe forever.

"Brandon, I need to get your statement about what Roger said to you during your meeting," Dot said.

"He didn't say a lot. Just went through the contract and asked me to sign. I asked him why they wanted the land so badly and he didn't know. Said it wasn't for him to question those higher up than him."

Which was next to useless to them.

Dot finished her questioning and then got to her feet. "Jay, you'll come with me."

"What will happen to him?" Lara asked.

"He's under arrest for kidnapping you and the property damage."

Lara glanced at her dad. "But they were going to hurt Nathan."

"He almost killed you, pumpkin."

She shook her head. "He didn't mean to. It was a mistake and you always say people are allowed to make mistakes."

Jay smiled at her. "It's OK, Lara. What I did requires punishment."

"Does it have to be gaol?" Lara asked. "Isn't that dangerous?"

Darcy sighed. "It's probably not safe for him out here if Stonefish keep threatening his son."

Nhiari held the door open for them.

"I'll be in touch," Dot said.

Perhaps Dot could help Jay and Cheryl in some way. Some kind of protective custody.

"Faith, do you want me to tell the others the riding session is cancelled?" Dot asked.

Darcy glanced outside. It still poured with rain, and he didn't want Faith driving into town. "I'll call everyone now," Faith said. "Thanks for reminding me."

"No problem."

Cheryl said a tearful goodbye to Jay, clinging to him for a moment, and then she ran through the rain to her caravan. It would be difficult for her, but Dot had told her to call the police if she was contacted by Stonefish again.

"Anyone hungry?" Amy asked.

"We need chocolate cake," Lara suggested.

Lara's answer to everything. Today she could have whatever she wanted. "Absolutely. Let's get the ingredients." He squeezed Faith's hand. "Why don't you make those phone calls and then join us?"

Faith nodded.

Darcy blew out a long breath as Matt and Brandon called out suggestions for what to have for lunch. Lara was safe, and the ordeal was over. Hopefully Jay's and Roger's evidence would provide enough to lead back to Stonefish and they would stop being harassed.

Maybe get their money back.

But either way, they would get through this.

***

By Sunday afternoon Darcy hadn't had a chance to sit down with Lara alone, and talk to her about Faith. He'd had to check the livestock and fix what the flood water had damaged. He arrived back at the house where green shoots already appeared all over the ground from the rain. It would be good for the sheep. The sky was blue and most of the signs of yesterday's downpour were gone. Lara and Faith gave Amy lessons in the horse yard.

His gaze shifted to Cheryl's caravan. The car was there, but Cheryl wasn't sitting under the awning like she had a habit of doing. Dot had called earlier to tell him she was waiting to hear from a couple of contacts in the city. Stonefish Enterprises fell under organised crime, which meant they were much bigger fish than Dot could catch on her own.

Darcy didn't want Cheryl on his property, but Lara had begged on her behalf. He wasn't as forgiving as Lara, though he tried to be for her sake. Yesterday could have gone far worse than it had. His muscles tightened. He could have lost both of the people he loved.

As he got out of the ute, Bennet jumped down from the tray. Darcy didn't want to break up the riding party, but Lara spotted him and ran over. "Dad!" She hugged him. "We're giving Amy lessons. Faith says I'm an excellent teacher."

She'd recovered fast. Perhaps allowing her to be there while Jay explained his motives had been a good thing. She had insisted on sleeping in Darcy's bed last night, which left Faith to sleep in Ed's old room, but neither of them minded. Which brought him to what he wanted to talk to Lara about.

"I'm going to check the wetland. Come with me?"

"Can Faith and Amy come too?"

He shook his head. "Actually, pumpkin, there's something I want to talk to you about in private."

"OK." She hopped into the passenger side of the ute.

"We'll be back shortly," he called to Faith.

She waved.

It took about ten minutes to reach the wetlands, and Lara chatted about what she'd done with Faith and Amy that day. Then she fell silent as the wetlands sparkled before them.

It was one of the wonders of the Ridge. The gully had channelled all the rainwater towards a small depression in the land and had turned it into a wetland teeming with birds and new growth. Life thriving in what was once a dust bowl.

It never ceased to amaze him, and it seemed like the perfect place to talk to Lara about what he hoped would be a similar change in their life.

"Awesome," Lara breathed.

"Yep. Let's go check it out."

They walked down to the edge and Lara squatted to splash the water. "How long will it last?"

"Depends on whether we get any more rain," Darcy said. "A couple of weeks, maybe."

"So cool."

She explored the banks, and he was content to follow where she led. Nerves bucked in his stomach. What if she wasn't ready for a step-mum? She was already dealing with her mother back in her life and a step-dad and brothers. Was it too much to put on a child all at once?

"What's wrong, Dad?"

Darcy blinked. She studied him with her head tilted. He hadn't realised she'd stopped exploring. "What makes you think something's wrong?"

"You're not exploring with me." Her face clouded. "Has something else bad happened?"

"No, nothing like that." He hugged her. "I want to ask you something and I'm worried about your reaction."

She rolled her eyes. "Well ask me, then you won't have to worry, because you'll know."

He chuckled. Great advice. "OK, so here's the thing." Where to start? Should he tell her how he felt about Faith, or should he ask her how she felt first?

"Da-ad, tell me already."

"I like Faith," he blurted. He shook his head. Smooth.

"Well, duh. I like her too."

He found a clear patch of grass and sat, pulling her down next to him. "I'm glad you like her because I wanted to ask her if she would like to be part of our family."

Lara's eyes widened. "You want to marry her?"

He couldn't tell how she felt about the idea. "Yeah, I do. It would mean she would move in with us…" They hadn't quite got to that part, but he was fairly sure she'd be OK with it. "And become your step-mum like Josh is your step-dad."

Lara nodded.

"So how do you feel about the idea?"

"Are you asking my permission to marry Faith?"

"Yeah."

"Yes!" She clapped her hands. "That would be awesome, 'cos I love her and she loves me and she can keep teaching me to ride and we'd be a new family and then you can have babies and I'd have little brothers and sisters."

Darcy laughed as relief coursed through him. "Slow down, pumpkin. There's been no discussion about babies yet."

"But there will be." She seemed confident.

He liked the idea, but there was no rush. "Well, I'm glad you agree. I'll ask her when we get back."

"Have you got a ring?"

"No."

The horror on his daughter's face was comical. "You can't ask her without a ring! You're supposed to go down on one knee and hold the ring box in both hands and stare into her eyes and ask her to spend the rest of her life with you because you love her."

She'd been watching too many Hollywood movies.

"Oh! We could ask her together, so she knows I want you to marry too," Lara continued. "We'd have to surprise her somewhere she's not expecting it. How about at pony club on Tuesday night? It will give you time to get a ring."

He appreciated her enthusiasm. "Lara there aren't any jewellers in Retribution Bay."

"Then we'll make one, so she knows we're serious." She pursed her lips. "What about with a keyring?" Her mouth dropped open. "I know! What about Granny's eternity ring that Georgie gave me?"

His breath stopped. "Pumpkin, that ring was your special item from Granny's jewellery." Gorgeous in its simplicity, a white gold band with diamonds in it, and would suit Faith perfectly.

"I know, but Granny would want her to have it. Besides, I'd still get to see it every day."

"It's a big decision, Lara. You need to consider it some more. It would mean you wouldn't have any of Granny's rings."

"But I have some of Granny's fancy necklaces and earrings," Lara said. She scrunched up her nose. "Will Faith think the ring is boring?"

"No, she won't."

"Then let's do it! Now we just need to figure out

how to make the proposal totally romantic. I won't let you mess this up."

He laughed. "I love you, pumpkin."

"I love you more."

Chapter 18

Faith was a little distracted as she took the pony club lesson on Tuesday afternoon. Right before it started, she'd received news she was desperate to share with Darcy, but he hadn't answered his phone and she'd been caught up talking to other parents when he arrived. Then he'd gone to get new tyres on his float.

Perhaps after she told him the news, she would propose. She was tired of waiting, and he'd had the opportunity to ask Lara how she felt when they'd gone to the wetlands on Sunday afternoon. She paused. Did that mean Lara didn't approve, or was he waiting the few days she suggested he wait?

So stupid to be worried about it. She'd simply ask him.

Sighing, she focused on the lesson, correcting Mischa's foot position and Natasha's posture. She'd picked up her parents from the airport that morning. They'd bought both a caravan and a new car, though it would be several months before they were ready. Her brothers and their families were well, and they had enjoyed their stay. Her father had put the business on the market and would put the house up for sale if she didn't want it.

She would definitely talk to Darcy about it tonight.

About fifteen minutes before the lesson ended, Darcy returned and parked at the far end of the stables, away from the cars and floats. Maybe he was avoiding Natasha's mum.

"Faith," Lara called. "I'm not feeling very well. Can I stop?"

Faith walked over. Lara looked a little flushed. "Of course. Why don't you join your dad?" She opened the gate to let her out and waited until Lara reached Darcy before she continued teaching.

The barrel racing took all her attention, and it was a relief when the class ended.

"All right!" she called. "Good job, everyone. Keep working on those things I pointed out and I'll see you all next week." The kids dismounted and led their horses to their floats.

"Faith!" Kristy called.

She winced at the imperious tone.

"I'll take Spirit, Faith." Lara appeared next to her and took the reins.

"How are you feeling?"

Lara grinned. "Much better. Dad gave me a headache tablet."

"OK, good. I'll join you in a minute." She went to see what Natasha's mother would demand this time.

By the time she'd spoken to all the parents, it was getting dark. Neither Lara nor Darcy had returned, but both horses had been loaded into the float.

Where were they?

Concern filled her. Had something happened? She scanned the stables, noticing a light shining from a stall behind the horse float. She strode forward, rounding the float, and frowned. Since when did the stalls have fairy lights?

The door of the end stall was open and light spilled out. "Darcy?"

"She's here!" Lara whispered loudly.

"In here," Darcy called.

A smile crept onto Faith's face. "What's going—" Her words caught in her throat. Darcy and Lara stood in the centre of a sparkling horse stall. Lara had changed out of her jodhpurs and into a dress covered in red flowers and instead of the red checked shirt he'd been wearing earlier, Darcy now wore a white buttoned shirt, black suit jacket and fitted jeans. Lara beamed at her, hopping from foot to foot, and Darcy wore a sexy smirk. Fairy lights hung all around the edges and in the middle stood a table with a white tablecloth and three covered plates on it.

Darcy stepped forward and held out his hand. "Lara and I have something we wanted to ask you."

She allowed him to pull her forward, her heart racing in her chest.

"Lara?" Darcy prompted.

She cleared her throat. "We both think you're pretty great and we'd like to cor... cordy... officially invite you to join our family."

Faith sniffed, and her eyes watered. Darcy got down on one knee and held up a beautiful ring. "Will you marry us?"

She stared down at his beautiful blue-grey eyes, and then across to Lara, who held both hands against her chest as if in prayer. She nodded, trying to find her voice. "Yes. Absolutely. I would love to marry you."

Lara shrieked, and Darcy swept her into his arms, and then his lips were on hers, and everything was right with the world.

Lara's laughter sank in and Faith pulled away. "Do I get my ring?" She held out her left hand and Darcy slid it on. "It's beautiful. Where did you get it?"

He couldn't possibly have had it sent up from Perth in time.

He smiled. "It was Mum's. Lara thought she'd want you to have it."

This time a single tear escaped. Beth had been a lovely woman. "Thank you." She opened her arms and Lara hugged her.

"It's an eternity ring, which means you're trapped with us for eternity now," Lara said.

Faith laughed. "There's no one else I'd want to be trapped for eternity with, pumpkin." She kissed Darcy.

He tugged her over to the table. "Let's eat before it gets too cold. Lara suggested the same meals as our first date." He uncovered the plates to reveal burgers and chips from the country-music themed restaurant in town.

"Perfect." Before she sat, she said, "I also have news to share."

Darcy looked up, interested. "Spill."

"Stonefish contacted me." At his frown, she hurried to continue. "They want to make a deal about the cattle."

His mouth dropped open. "We get our money back?"

She nodded. "At least some, but I'll push for all. The email made no reference to Lara's kidnapping, but with Roger talking, they probably want to distance themselves from the whole event." Faith hoped this would be the end of their troubles.

"Does this mean we won't lose the station?" Lara asked, eyes wide.

"It does," Darcy confirmed. He swept them both up in a hug and his cheer was full of triumph and relief.

Faith hugged them back, brimming with love and happiness. It was funny what a difference a couple of weeks could make. She no longer felt trapped in Retribution Bay.

It was home.

Thank you for reading!

I hope you enjoyed the book. It would be super awesome if you could leave a review wherever you bought it, because I love to hear what you thought of the story.

Acknowledgements

Retribution Bay is based on Exmouth, a town on the north-west peninsula of Western Australia. I got many of my ideas from a couple of trips I took there, one of which was possible thanks to a research grant I received from the Department of Local Government, Sport and Cultural Industries.

I interviewed a number of people while researching, so thank you also to Edwina Shallcross, Toni Roe, Lorraine Mauvais and Jimmy Small.

As always I'd like to thank my editors, Ann Harth and Teena Raffa-Mulligan and my cover designer, LJ from Mayhem Cover Creations.

Escape to Retribution Bay

Aussie Heroes: Retribution Bay

Ed's story is next. To be notified when it is up for pre-order, join my new release notification list. https://www.claireboston.com/new-release-signup/